MARY
NOT
BROKEN

DEBORAH L. KING

Mary Not Broken
Red Adept Publishing, LLC
104 Bugenfield Court
Garner, NC 27529
https://RedAdeptPublishing.com/

Dedicated to my biggest fans:

June Sevier Riley

Perry Riley

Deborah Davis

Richard Espy

In Loving Memory of

Christine Alexander

Chapter 1
March 1935
Flora, Mississippi

Hidden in the shadows of the front room hallway, fifteen-year-old Mary Johnson tugged at the front of her shirt and fanned the sweat that dripped down her chest. For early spring, between the sparse rains, the Mississippi heat was already oppressive. She watched through the screen door as her papa and the old preacher sat on the front porch, smoking their pipes. She listened to the two men talk about the weather and how bad the crops were looking this year. Her papa, Reverend Charles Johnson, complained about not having enough hay for the mules, and the old preacher, Will Bevers, talked about how Papa could give up the mules and get a real tractor or maybe one day get elevated to bishop and stop farming altogether.

This was Bevers's second time visiting the Johnsons, and today, her papa had told her that the preacher had come to court her. At first, Mary laughed and promised there was no way she'd entertain the wrinkly old man, but then her papa had threatened to get a switch, and it wasn't so funny anymore.

So Mary had sat on the front steps of her ramshackle wood-frame house, third step from the bottom, and the old preacher had stood in front of her, leaning on the rail and fanning himself with his hat. He talked about teaching at the college in Jackson and how different city life was from country life. He told her his house had a garden with food in the back and flowers in the front. Mary didn't know why he seemed disappointed that she wasn't impressed. He asked her a few questions about herself, but mainly, he talked about who he was, what he did, and what he had. Mary had sat quietly and mostly stared at the bugs in the dirt, wishing she had a stick to poke one or two. She hadn't hidden her relief when her mother announced that dinner was ready.

At the table in their wallpapered kitchen, Mary was seated next to Bevers, and she was careful not to glare at her parents over the seating arrangement. Dinner was Augusta Johnson's famous chicken and dumplings with homemade bread that earned her high praise from the old preacher. For dessert, Mary served an apple cobbler made with some apples she had helped put up last fall. During dinner, Bevers regaled the family with tales of life in the big city of Jackson. He bragged about his position in the college and talked about how smart you had to be to get in.

After dinner, while the men went outside to smoke, Mary had helped clean up and listened to her mother's lecture on being a godly woman and how blessed she was that a man like Will Bevers was interested in her.

"But, Mama, I don't want a man like him. He too old—"

"He ain't that old." Augusta stirred a pitcher of lemonade. "He just got some life behind him. All that mean is he know some stuff."

Mary carried a stack of dirty plates to the sink. "Please don't make me court that old man. He ugly too."

"Watch yo' mouth!" her mother snapped. "Shame on you! God don't make nobody ugly. You just ungrateful. You got a good man wantin' to court you, and you got nothin' but attitude. Like you too good for a godly man. But I bet you think that Carter boy is just fine, right?"

"But, Mama—"

"I see how you act when he come down the road. He ain't godly at all, and you just be smilin' and wavin' like one of them Jezebels. Tha's why yo' papa want you married soon. You'a pay a mighty price if you shame the family wit' that Carter boy." Augusta lowered herself into a kitchen chair and pointed at two glasses of lemonade. "Take those out front."

Mary sighed and picked up the glasses. Heading out onto the porch, she let the screen door slam behind her and placed the glasses on the small table between the two men. Her papa had grunted a response, but Will Bevers smiled and offered thanks.

So now, standing behind the screen door, Mary considered her options: be courted by an ugly old preacher and keep her family happy or spend time with Mason Carter and shame her family. It was an easy decision, really. She'd sit for the courtship on Sunday afternoons and then sneak and spend every other moment with Mason.

MARY ALWAYS KNEW PAPA wanted her to "marry up" when she turned eighteen—find a good husband with land or status—but now, at fifteen, after she took up with Mason Carter, Papa said she was too fast and might get big and shame the family, so on a warm March afternoon, he introduced her to Reverend William Bevers. The man had to be at least sixty if he was a day, and now every Sunday, Mary would hide when she saw the old preacher's fancy car coming up their dirt road.

At first, he just brought Mary flowers and candy. Then, he sometimes brought tobacco for Papa and flour or sugar for Mama or candy for her sisters. Soon, he started bringing Mary perfume, gloves, scarves, or books. Then, one day in May, he came with a bolt of white lace to make a wedding dress and offered to buy Papa a real tractor and help him get elevated to Elder in the church, maybe even get him into a fancy new church. He told Mary about his own big church and that her sisters could go to Jackson College and that his house was much better than the shack she lived in—*shack?*—and that she would have a maid. *Why would I want a maid?*

Reverend Johnson immediately agreed to the marriage, and a date was set for the third Sunday in July. Where her parents saw a bright future for all their daughters, Mary saw only an old man with beady eyes, wrinkled skin, and gnarled hands with thick knuckles. His mostly white hair stuck out from his hat, and he shaved his mustache into a thin little line. The thought of those old hands touching her or those old lips kissing her turned her stomach, and Mary smiled politely and prayed he would up and die before June.

But it was Mason's idea that if she got big, they could get married, so they went out to the barn, and Mary lay down and lifted her dress. She told herself it was okay because he was gonna be her husband, and when Ruthie caught 'em, Mary told her little sister that Papa would skin her alive and sell her to white folks if she told. Ruthie cried and accepted candy and some jacks and marbles for her silence.

When they weren't working on a baby, Mary and Mason sat under the willow tree and flipped through the *Chicagoan* and *New Yorker* magazines and dreamed of life outside Mississippi. Mason would play his horn in a club in the big city, and Mary would stay home with the baby, maybe finish high school and be a nurse or something. On the days he couldn't stay long, Mary would find letters under the loose boards in the hen house, and she would go to sleep dreaming of the high life with Mason.

"Mary, pretty soon yo' pappy'll hafta let us get married. Then we can go to Chicago."

Hidden behind the curtain of the old weeping willow tree, Mary leaned back against Mason's chest. She loved the way he smelled like earth and a hot spring day. She cradled his trumpet in her arms like a baby, stroking the bell with her thumb. "Well, we hafta hurry up. Papa wants me married next month."

Mason kissed his hand and laid it against Mary's belly. "You the finest girl in Mississippi, Mary, but why that old preacher want a young girl like you if he got a maid and all? His church prolly got plenty women his age. Why he cain't get none of them?"

"Cuz he old and ugly." Mary laughed. "Ain't nobody gon' look at him on Sunday and then every other day of the week too. Yuck!"

Mason wrapped his arms around Mary, squeezing her closer. "Well, we not gon' worry about him. We gon' get us a nice place in Chicago and live it up. I hear they got trains that run under the ground and up in the air. You gon' come hear me play and sit right up front, and I'mma play just for you."

Mary rocked the instrument she held. "We'll have a pretty little baby boy." She cooed at the trumpet. "He gon' look just like you, and you gon' teach him how to play, and y'all gon' make music together."

"Nah." Mason laughed. "It's gon' be a pretty little girl just like you, with yo' same pretty eyes and yo' same pretty smile, and I'mma hafta get a shotgun to keep boys away."

"Oh, you gon' protect her from boys like you?"

"Yup." He kissed Mary's cheek and then pressed his hands against her shoulders. "I need to go now. Yo' pappy be back soon and—"

"Yeah... we don't want him to get *his* shotgun." Mary stood up, still holding the trumpet like a baby. "A boy named Mason Carter Junior." She smiled down at Mason still sitting against the tree.

He stood up and brushed himself off then took his horn from Mary and kissed her cheek. "Go on... check if it's clear."

Mary quickly kissed his lips then ducked through the curtain of the willow tree and walked right into her younger sisters racing toward her. She held her arms out and caught the two girls, nearly tumbling the lot of them to the ground.

"Why y'all runnin' round like wild animals?" Mary fussed, she hoped, loudly enough for Mason to hear. "What you need under that tree?"

Martha, the youngest, spoke up. "Ruthie said you was under the tree kissing a boy!"

"I didn't say that!" Ruth snapped, reaching out to hit her little sister.

Martha ducked out of the way. "Yes you did!"

"Y'all are so silly." Mary herded her sisters back toward the house. "Didn't Mama have something for y'all to do?" Mary looked over her shoulder and caught a glimpse of Mason heading down the road, his trumpet gleaming in the afternoon sunlight.

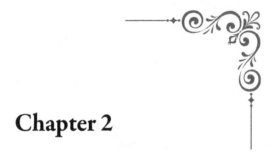

Chapter 2

"I didn't raise you to be nobody's maid nor mammy! Wit' that Carter boy, thas' all yu'a eva' be!"

"But Papa—!"

"Girl, tha's the end of it! That boy's got no schoolin'. His people got no land. Nothin'!"

Mary stamped her foot. "I won't marry that old man! I'll run away—"

She wasn't surprised by the slap. It was the second one in as many days. Her papa's rough palm scraped her cheek, and it stung, but she didn't move and wasn't about to cry.

"Girl, Bible say honor yo' mama and papa. You'a pay the price'a Job if you shame this family."

Mary matched her father's glare until he turned away.

"Gussie, talk to yo' daughter," he said as he walked out of the kitchen.

"Girl, why you need to have this fight every day?" her mother's tired voice asked Mary. "Yo' papa's mind is set, and you could do a lot worse than Reverend Bevers."

"Cuz I don't wanna be married to no old man, Mama!" Mary huffed. "I don't want him to look at me, I don't want him to talk to me, and I sho' don't want him to touch me!"

"Watch yo' tone, girl." Augusta Johnson rose from her seat at the kitchen table. Her back bent to balance her great belly, her fifth baby due any day now. "Quiet down. Ain't like you ain't been touched already. One man's touch just like any other."

"Mama, no, I haven't—"

"Ruthie, go cut me a switch fo' yo' lyin' sister." Augusta patted her second daughter's head. "Hurry now. Take Martha with you."

The nine- and five-year-old girls jumped up from their seats and took off out the back door without a word.

"Mama, would you at least listen—"

"To you lie some more? Why should I? Start gettin' them dishes to the sink."

Mary let out a long sigh and started stacking the dirty dinner plates while her mother waddled over to the sink.

"You a lie, and the truth ain't in you," Augusta chided. "Ruthie told me all about you and Mason layin' in the hay wit' yo' dress up an' yo' leg on his back."

The silverware Mary carried went crashing to the floor.

"Mmm-hmm," Augusta continued. "Surprised you ain't big as me." She turned and looked at Mary. "When yo' monthly?"

"It just passed," Mary mumbled, stooping to pick up the silverware. She stayed near the floor until she heard her mother's shuffling feet turn back to the sink.

"Good. Least you won't need cotton root today."

Mary left the silver on the table and threw her arms around her mother. "Please, Mama," she begged, pressing her cheek to her mother's back. "I don't wanna get married. I swear I'a quit Mason and neva' touch another boy. Mama, please. I promise I won't get big. Just don't make me marry that old man."

"Baby," her mother said with a heavy sigh. "I seen how you light up when that boy come down the road. You couldn't quit him if you wanted to. Yo' papa was gon' get the shotgun to him a couple of times. Preacher's daughter got no business with folks like them

Carters. We wanna give you the best life you can have, and tha's wit' Reverend Bevers in Jackson, not some dirt farmer here in Flora."

"Can I at least stay to help you with the baby? 'Til next spring? Please?"

"I'll talk to Papa about puttin' it off a few weeks, 'til after the baby, but you hafta stay away from that boy. Promise me!"

"Yes, ma'am! I promise."

As her little sisters ran in through the back door, sword fighting with braided willow switches, Mary lay against her mother's back and smiled. Her mother was right... about everything. She couldn't quit Mason if she wanted to, and her monthly was definitely late.

TWO WEEKS BEFORE HER wedding date, Mary actually cried tears of joy as her father relented and agreed that his wife needed their oldest daughter's help with the new baby, Elizabeth. The next day, however, Mary cried different tears as he raised welts on her legs and backside with a willow switch after he caught her kissing Mason behind the barn... and the wedding was back on again. A week before her wedding date, Mary told her mother her monthly was late, and her mother whipped her for probably lying but promised to bring her cotton root after the wedding just to make sure.

The night before her wedding day, Mary kissed her sleeping sisters and whispered blessings to them. Then she took the bag Ruth helped her pack, along with a sack of sweet-potato pie and wedding cake, and climbed out of their bedroom window. By the light of the full moon, she walked a mile to the crossroads, where Mason waited for her. They walked on in silence until Mary reminded him that he should be carrying her bags.

The gray sharecropper's cabin, where Mason lived with his mother and younger siblings, leaned slightly to the left and stood in a dirt yard littered with sleeping dogs that just sniffed the air when Mary and Mason approached. The carcass of a tractor lay beside a shiny car and a beat-up truck. In the distance, Mary could make out other such shacks dotting the field, shacks where Mason said his brothers lived with their families. Mary's papa said those were all slave cabins, but she kept that to herself.

Music and celebration could be heard coming from inside the cabin. Mary thought it sounded like the juke joints that always seemed extra loud on Sunday mornings, and when Mason opened the door, it looked exactly like she imagined a juke joint would look, except extra dingy. Lots of men who looked vaguely like Mason danced with women who were probably their wives. A table was piled high with food and jugs of something Mary knew she wouldn't touch, and an old phonograph in the corner cranked out worldly music that made her wanna dance too.

"So, this her?" A heavyset woman pulled Mary into a hug without waiting for an answer.

"Yes, ma'am." Mason placed a hand on Mary's back. "Mama, this is Mary. Finest girl in Mississippi. Mary, this is my mama, Miss Margaret."

"Pleased to meet you, Miss Margaret." Mary tried not to mumble as she struggled to breathe against the woman's giant bosom.

"I don't like that 'Miss Margaret' stuff unless you payin' me, baby." The woman released Mary but quickly pulled her into another hug. "I'm a Georgia girl, and folks call me Sweet. But in a few minutes, you gon' call me Mama Sweet just like all my boys' wives. Ain't that right, y'all?"

"Yes, Mama Sweet." A couple of women pulled at Mary's arm. "Now let her go so us can get her fixed up."

"Wait—!" Mary reached for Mason as the women pulled her toward the cabin's other room.

Mason took Mary's hand. "It's okay. I told you, we hafta get married tonight. Yo' pappy be here by sunup with his shotgun." He placed his hand against her belly. "I be dam' if somebody else gon' raise my kin. Once you my wife, ain't nothin' he can do about it, and we headin' north in the mornin.'"

Mary nodded and let herself be led off by her soon-to-be sisters-in-law.

The ceremony was so short that Mary wasn't sure it was a real wedding—no preaching or singing or anything, and the preacher from the next county had a drink in his hand the whole time! But in less than five minutes, fifteen-year-old Mary and eighteen-year-old Mason were Mr. and Mrs. Carter. Mary knew she wasn't far enough gone to feel her baby yet, so the pain in her stomach had to be guilt, and she prayed for forgiveness for shaming her family even as she celebrated her new freedom.

And then her papa walked in.

With his shotgun.

And the music stopped.

And all of Mason's brothers and uncles had pistols...

And so did the preacher...

And Mama Sweet.

But Reverend Charles Johnson only pointed his shotgun at Mary. "C'mon, girl. Time to go home."

"Beggin' yo' pardon, suh," one of Mason's uncles spoke up. "Y'all cain't come up in here pointin' no shotgun at our womens. How 'bout you put it down and join the celebration?"

"Papa." Mary held up her left hand. "Mason and me is married now." Even in the dim light of the cabin, she watched the vein throb on her father's forehead and the rage simmer in his eyes.

"Take off the ring and tear up the paper. I said it's time to go home."

Mason moved to stand behind Mary. "My wife ain't goin' nowhere, sir." He placed a hand on her shoulder. "She in the family way, and ain't nobody but me raisin' my kin."

Mary watched the rage in her father's eyes boil over and come out as a single tear when he lowered his gun with trembling hands. "Bible say honor yo' mama and papa. You gon' pay the price'a Job for shamin' yo' family, girl... the price—of—Job!"

"Tell me, *Reverend*." Mama Sweet stepped up, pressing her body against Reverend Johnson. "What kind of pappy cusses his girl-child like that? If you cain't celebrate these young'uns and they new family, I'mma need you to git outta my house."

"Mary," Reverend Johnson addressed his daughter over Mama Sweet's wide shoulder, "you can always come home." Then he turned and opened the door and left.

Surrounded by her new family whooping and hollerin', celebrating their victory and her father's shame, Mary stood rooted to the spot, feeling like a mule had just kicked her in the stomach. It wasn't until she found herself engulfed in Mama Sweet's arms that she felt herself break and let tears come.

"Hush now, baby," the older woman sang. "Yo' pappy still loves you. He'a come around soon enough. He just don't know we good people yet."

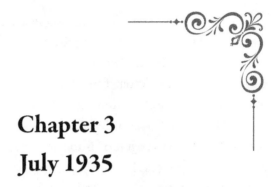

Chapter 3
July 1935

The newlyweds were in Chicago only three weeks before Mason announced that blues musicians were a dime a dozen and New York jazz was "where it's at." At the train station, Mary stood bravely as he kissed her goodbye, promising to send for her when he got settled, and then Mason climbed aboard the train headed to New York City. His aunt Liz and uncle Ike dried Mary's tears and assured her he'd be back. Mary felt in her heart this was the beginning of the *price of Job*.

Chicago heat was different from Mississippi heat. Instead of baking, you drowned in it, you suffocated in it, you died from it. Mary hated the heat, the noise, the smog, the stink. The rats were something out of her worst nightmares. And the Cordova building with its dark bricks and shaded courtyard—to Mary, the giant old tenement looked like a castle or a factory from a movie. But after Mason left, she shared a room with four of his cousins in a crowded three-bedroom apartment in that building.

During the day, to earn her keep, Mary took over housekeeping and minding Aunt Liz's two youngest daughters... and told herself she wasn't being a maid and a mammy. And at night, she'd go up on the roof, write postcards home, read letters from Mason, and look down at the city lights and up at the stars and wonder how she got there.

At first, Mary heard from Mason every week, sometimes twice a week; he was always lamenting the struggle to find steady work in the many jazz clubs in New York. When he finally found a gig in a club in Harlem, the letters came less frequently, but he sent pictures of himself with Dudley Emmons and the Uptown Jazz Marvels.

In March of 1936, on the table in Aunt Liz's kitchen, Mary welcomed Mason Carter Junior into the world. The tiny boy with the angry face looked just like her papa, and even as she fell in love with her newborn, Mary's heart ached a little whenever she looked at him.

It was a chilly day in April when Mason's band came to town for a four-week gig opening for Cab Calloway at the Regal Theater. After the first show, Mary vowed to never attend another one. She just didn't have the glamor of the women who followed the band. Mason promptly took a week's salary and bought Mary a sparkly black dress and a slinky gold dress and a red dress with fringes that wiggled when she walked. The next time she stepped backstage, the whole band whistled, and Cab Calloway himself kissed her hand.

While Aunt Liz watched the baby, Mary spent every night in the front row, and after the show, she'd go to a local club and sit on Mason's lap and watch the jam sessions. If somebody handed her a whiskey, she'd drink it. If somebody handed her a reefa, she'd smoke it, and if Mason wanted a kiss, she'd give him one right there in front of everybody. With Mason and his music, this was the high life he'd promised her, and when the Chicago gig was over, Mary was ready to hit New York.

"Now, Mary, Harlem ain't no place for a country girl like you!"

"But Mason, you promised!" Mary stamped her foot on the tar roof. "You promised and then you left me here for almost a whole year. My papa told me—!"

"Oh, here we go again! Well, my mama is a maid, and ain't no shame in that! As soon as I get enough money, I'mma get us a nice—!"

"No! I'm not waiting another minute! Either I'm goin' with you, or me and the babies is goin' back to Mississippi!"

"Aw, woman, stop talkin' crazy, you ain't... wait... what... *babies*?"

"Yes, Mason." Mary sighed. "I think I'm having another baby."

Mason ran his hands through his processed hair and paced the rooftop. He pulled out a pack of Lucky Strikes and offered one to Mary. She accepted and lit it off of his gold lighter.

"Are you sure?" Mason asked.

"Pretty sure."

"But when? I just got here...?"

"What the hell you tryin' to say, Mason Carter?" Mary snapped. "I been waiting for you for all this time, and you didn't just get here! You been here for over a month! I know why you don't want me to come! You probably the one two-timing... got some hussy up in Harlem while I'm here having yo' baby and you out with the reefa and the liquor—!"

Mary's rant was cut short by Mason's kiss, and her ire was further quelled when he wrapped his arms around her and held her until she forgot her anger.

"Please, Mason," Mary begged. "I don't wanna go back home. Take us with you."

Chapter 4

1941

Harlem, New York

Even though the heat seemed worse than Chicago, Mary loved almost everything about life in Harlem. On 115th Street off of Lenox Avenue, she kept their two-bedroom apartment spotless and hardly ever saw any roaches. With flowered curtains blowing in the hot summer breezes, she kept the windows open to let in the light and the street music. Some nights, Mary would go to the club and listen to the band. When she got too big to go to the club, Mason would bring the band home, and they would jam until the morning.

Baby Rose came in February, and in April, Mason stormed out of the apartment when Mary told him another baby was on the way. The couple named the twin boys Charles and Peter after their fathers.

At nineteen years old, with four small children, Mary grew a sharp tongue and a short temper. She was accustomed to handling small children and had helped with her younger sisters, but she'd never had to handle a brood, and she often felt like a mother hen trying to corral all her babies at once. Sometimes, the girl from downstairs came to help at bathtime, and she would babysit so Mary could have some peace and quiet and a nice long nap.

Mason Jr. had always been a babbling baby then a talkative toddler. He always had a question and an opinion on everything. He would keep his nose pressed to their apartment windows, yelling at the passersby, and he'd fuss when Mary tried to direct his attention elsewhere. Little Rosie was a clingy baby, and often, Mary couldn't walk for the girl child wrapped around her leg. She sometimes practiced leaving the little girl in her crib to scream herself to sleep, and Rosie would scream for a full hour or until Mary gave in and soothed her. Mary believed the twins knew she was tired, because they were quiet, still babies. When they *talked*, it was only to each other and with sounds only they could understand.

Mary would never say Mason abandoned her, because he provided well, but after he joined a new band that paid more, he travelled a lot, leaving her alone for weeks at a time. There were rumors of other women, and whenever Mary caught him at the club with a floozy, she cussed him out and told him to never come home. Of course, he brought gifts and tried to remind Mary they were still married. Sometimes, she'd let him stay, and other times, she'd send him packing, but in the end, they always made up, and Mary prayed for no more babies.

It was during one of these fights that Mason Jr. got the fever. Miz Cleo from upstairs said it was measles and would pass in a week or so. Sure enough, the four-year-old broke out in a brownish rash and lay shivering while Mary pressed cold towels to his head. When the coughing and wheezing started, the poor boy thrashed about so much that Mary had to lie beside him to keep him safe.

As the fever continued for a tenth day and the boy grew weaker, Mary cursed her husband and called on God, something she hadn't done since she left Mississippi. When her baby looked at her with unseeing eyes, she took to her knees, promising to never sin again. And when four-year-old Mason Carter Jr. wheezed his last breath, Mary climbed into bed beside her firstborn to keep him warm, and three-year-old Rosie told the old man next door that Mommy wouldn't talk and Mase wouldn't wake up.

Mason Sr. came home a day after the burial, and Mary slapped him. She slapped him and spit on him and kicked him and cussed him and damned him to hell for leaving her to bury their child alone. And her husband held her and loved her and promised her another son and showed her a tin with a needle, a spoon, and brown powder and told her it would make the hurt go away.

"Mason, I don't want no dope."

"Aw, girl, what you think reefa is?"

"Well, this all the dope I want then," Mary said, taking a deep drag on the tiny pungent cigarette. "I ain't puttin' no needles in me."

"I'll do it for you. It don't even hurt."

Mary looked into her husband's sleepy, bloodshot eyes. "I said 'no.'" She crushed out her reefa and kissed him before he could try harder to convince her. He would be leaving for a four-week gig in a few days, and Mary wasn't about to waste a minute of their time together.

A WEEK AFTER BURYING Mason Jr., Mary watched in horror as fevers and a brownish rash appeared on Rosie and two-year-old Charles and Peter. She stayed up around the clock, bathing all three children in cool water at once, keeping them beside her at all times, begging the club to find Mason... sending telegrams to her mother.

In the second week of the fever, Miz Cleo visited with candles, tea, and medicine. "This is Sulfa Elixir," Miz Cleo had said. "It's for fevers and sore throats and stuff. My daughter didn't need it, but maybe you might could use it. A little spoon every few hours, it says." Mary hugged the older woman and rested for an hour before Rosie's convulsions woke her.

Her vision blurred by tears, Mary gave all her children the medicine and screamed to the heavens. She ran to her closet and pulled out all of the shiny, sparkly dresses and stomped on them. In the kitchen, she poured all the liquor down the drain. She tore open a flour sack and tied it on as a dress and emptied the contents of every ashtray in the apartment on her own head. She tore out her hair and scratched herself until she bled, all the while begging God for mercy.

By sunrise, Rosie was cold. Mary never touched Charles or Peter.

MARY SAT ON THE COUCH, smoking a cigarette and watching her husband's face. She wished she could comfort him, but she'd nursed and buried four babies alone. He would hafta take the news like a man.

He opened his arms to her, his lips moving soundlessly.

Mary slowly shook her head.

He dropped to his knees, laying his head on her lap.

She pushed him away.

Mason got to his feet and staggered around the living room then down the hall. Mary heard him open the children's bedroom door and cry out.

She wished she could cry with him, but she was all out of tears.

Two hours later, Mary opened the children's bedroom door to find her husband's body on the floor beside a small bed—a needle still sticking out of his arm, a brown mosaic of dried blood pooled under his elbow.

She closed the door.

No tears left.

The price of Job had been paid.

It was time to go home.

Chapter 5

August 1941

Flora, Mississippi

"How come you don't look at me?" Mary glanced down and blew a puff of smoke at the dusty little girl playing in the dirt at the bottom of the front porch steps then went back to staring off into the distance. "I look at you every day, Ellie." She sat down on the top step and took another drag on her cigarette.

"No you don't," Ellie challenged. "Your face looks at me, but your eyes don't."

Mary shrugged and blew more smoke at her baby sister. "I look at you when you sleep."

"Oh, I know!" Ellie stood up and dusted herself off. "I make you sad because I look like—"

"Girl, go in the house and clean yourself up!" Mary snapped. "Mama is gonna cut a switch if she see you so dirty."

"But—"

"Get in the house, now!"

Mary kept her eyes on Ellie's dress as the six-year-old trudged up the five steps. The little girl was right. Mary never looked directly at her... couldn't look at her. Looking at Ellie, the spitting image of her lost Rosie, burned like looking into the sun.

Mary had been back home two days when she first felt a small child climb into bed behind her. In that space closer to sleep than awake, she knew it must be Mason Jr. because of his size. But as sleep slowly receded, Mary remembered her little big boy was gone, and she rolled over to look through half-asleep eyes into the chubby elfin face of Rosie. With her shimmering pecan complexion and matching hair and eyes, the little brown girl looked like she was born of the trees that grew in her grandmother's yard.

"Hi, Mary," the little girl had said.

"Baby, what are you doing in here?" Mary asked, pulling the child into her arms, surprised at how fast she was growing.

"You were having a bad dream. I came to sleep with you."

Her smell was different too. Earthier, not like the clean white soap Mary always used to bathe her children. Then the fog of sleep lifted, and the first rays of sunlight entered the small bedroom, and Mary's heart broke again like it did every morning. She held on to her baby sister and trembled.

"Don't worry, big sister," Ellie crooned. "I won't let nothin' get you."

SEATED ON THE TOP STEP on the front porch, Mary flicked the smoldering cigarette butt into the dirt at the bottom of the stairs. She hated cigarettes, but they were all she had. She'd tried Papa's pipe, but it was too much work. What she really wanted was reefa, but she ran out of that her first week back home, and she hadn't thought to keep the seeds. Sometimes, she thought about that tin of brown powder Mason had tried to share with her. Would it make her feel good now? No way to ever know.

Looking out over the landscape at the waves of heat coming up from the fields, Mary knew she was no longer a country girl. She hated the smell of dirt and the sound of crickets. She wanted more than anything to find a nightclub and hang off a barstool, listen to good music, toss back brown liquor, and laugh like ladies shouldn't laugh. All things that had brought the wrath of God down on her... things she knew a godly woman shouldn't do... all things she looked back for like Lot's wife.

Of course, there were juke joints, but she'd been to the Regal and the Savoy with Cab Calloway and Billie Holiday. There was no way she was going into a rundown shack full of dirt farmers. She'd heard there were places in Jackson—not a real big city but bigger than Flora. She could go there and live again. Her skin was bright enough; maybe she'd get a job as a waitress or dancing in a club. She'd already paid the price of Job for sinning and shaming her family. What more could God do to her?

She didn't look back at the sound of the screen door opening and closing, but the heavy footfall across the wooden porch and rich smell of tobacco told her it was Papa coming out. Reverend Charles Johnson took a seat on the top step beside his oldest daughter. "Hmph... another hot one." He puffed on his pipe as he lit it.

Mary just sighed.

"So, what's yo' plans for today?" Papa asked.

"Nothin.'" Mary stared down at the still-burning cigarette butt. "You need me to do something?"

"Yeah, matter of fact." The older man looked at his daughter. "I need you to understand that I didn't cuss you. It was prophecy."

"Mm-hm." Mary reached into her pocket for another cigarette and the gold lighter she took from Mason, the only thing of his she kept.

"See, baby, Lord put on my heart that you was gon' be tempted to sin and foolishness. Tha's why I tried to keep that boy offa you. Lord said you was gon' pay a mighty price, the price of Job, for yo' sin."

Mary silently smoked her cigarette.

"But even now, God is movin' to restore you and get on with his plan for you. All you hafta do is accept God's will. Honor yo' mama and papa. Do right by yo' sisters and be obedient to the Lord. Turn from wickedness, baby, and take what God has for you."

"Papa," Mary blew out a long puff of smoke, "God ain't got nothing for me. I'm a sinner. God took everything but my life."

"Now tha's where you wrong. Job lost everything and still praised the Lord, and you know what?"

"What?"

"God gave him back everything double. He got his children back and his animals and everything... and he got more!"

"So you think God is gon' gimme my life back?" Mary looked at her father. "My babies and my husband? You think God is gon' raise the dead and have 'em waiting for me in Harlem... or is he gon' make 'em be standin' right there in the yard?"

"Watch yo' mouth, girl." Reverend Johnson scowled at Mary. "You don't test God."

"Why not?" Mary took a puff on her cigarette. "God tested me." She laughed a little. "I guess I failed." She wiped a tear with her free hand. "I just want..."

"I know what you want. You gon' get everything back and more. God is gon' bless you with *eight* babies and a husband and a home and all yo' heart desires."

"I wish I could believe that, Papa."

"He has a plan f' you, Mary. You went yo' own way and God took yo' family... but *'lo, there's a ram in the bush!'* The true man of God that was sent for you is still waitin'. Will Bevers is a good man and still wants you, even though you already been married."

Mary shook her head and laughed a little. "So that's what this talk is about? Well, if God meant him for me—"

"You went up there to that sinful place, come back talkin' all hard, smokin' and drinkin' and ungodly. Lord knows what all you did up north, but he willin' to take you anyway. You been sittin' on this porch for two months now... time to start thinkin' bout yo' future."

Mary inhaled deeply, burning out half her cigarette. She sat there beside her papa, remembering the last time she saw Will Bevers. She looked out at the cotton fields. No, the old preacher wasn't her cup of tea, but what if her papa was right? What if this *ram-in-the-bush* was the beginning of her blessing?

"THE LORD TOLD ME YOU'D be back. It's good to see you, girl."

"Thanks." Mary blew out a puff of smoke and then tossed her cigarette into the dirt. In her simple brown church dress and brown shoes, she walked down the front porch steps, moving like the dress was sparkly red and the shoes shiny black. She stopped at the bottom of the steps and ground out the cigarette with her toe. "But I'm a grown woman. I ain't been a girl in a long time." She looked the man in the eye when she spoke. It had taken her father less than a week to get Reverend Bevers out to the house for Sunday dinner, and though she was still mostly repulsed by him, the old preacher was her ticket out of Flora and back to the city life she missed.

"Woman, you forgettin' yourself, ain't you?" the old preacher said, shifting his hat in his hands. "Grown women don't forget to call a man 'sir.'"

"Hmph. Then a man needs to call a grown woman by her name and not just 'woman.'"

"I see you got to learn some manners, *Miss Mary*."

"So do you, *sir*." Mary saw his flash of anger and wanted to laugh. Mason had gotten angry all the time, and all it took was a look to shut him down. This old man could get as mad as he wanted. Mary had no fear of men.

The screen door creaked open and then slammed shut behind Ruth. The scowling fourteen-year-old stomped across the porch and down three steps. "Here!" She held out two tall glasses.

"It's lemonade!" Ellie called from behind the screen door. "I helped make it!"

"Yeah," Ruth said. "Little loudmouth helped."

"Ruthie told me to spit in it, but I didn't!"

"*Shut up, you little*—!"

"Let's go for a walk." Mary ignored the lemonade and walked away from her bickering sisters, not looking back to see if the old preacher was following. She heard his footsteps behind her and slowed her pace some.

"Girl," the old preacher panted when he caught up to her, "you a lot more feisty now. Don't you know the man supposed to lead?"

Mary clasped her hands behind her back. "I'm used to leadin' myself now. Man that's goin' with me just gotta keep up."

"I see you got a smart mouth too. That ain't the way of a godly woman. Lord wants a woman to be in quiet submission to a—"

"And what if I'm not, *Reverend*?" Mary stopped walking and turned to face the old preacher standing there sweating in his light-gray suit and wide-brimmed hat. "What if I don't wanna be that way? What if God made me different?"

"Girl, that's crazy talk. God made all women from the same rib. You ain't made no different. You just got touched by worldly demons. A good, godly man'll get 'em outta you... get you back right with the Lord."

Mary turned away from him and continued walking. Was this a good idea? Was this the man God had planned for her? Was she really trying to get right with the Lord who'd killed her babies just to punish her?

"Listen, girl. I'm a patient man," the preacher said, "but I ain't gettin' any younger. Your daddy said I could marry you, but it's up to you this time. I still got the big house. Your sisters can still go to Jackson College. You sit up front on Sundays, and you serve coffee and tea when I have company. Cook the meals every day and make a good pound cake and peach cobbler sometimes. You be *the good wife*, and I'll take good care of you. But I'm the man, understand, girl?"

"You gon' call me by my name or you can go home right now." Mary felt around in her pocket and pulled out a cigarette.

"Woman, you gon' learn—"

"Goodbye." Mary turned and headed back to the house. If this was going to work, he needed to know some things up front.

"Miss Mary!"

Mary paused but didn't turn around. She pulled out Mason's lighter, lit her cigarette, took a long drag, and blew the smoke out in a thin stream.

"You cain't smoke like that in my house, Miss Mary! That's where I put my foot down!"

Mary took another puff and then dropped the cigarette and crushed it out. "As long as we understand each other, we'll get along just fine, *sir*."

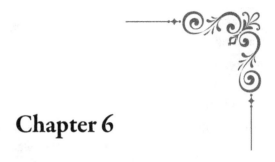

Chapter 6

When she started walking, Mary didn't know where her feet would take her; she just followed the gravel road, hummed to herself, and pitied the workers bent over in the cotton field. She was nearly at the gray sharecropper's shack before she realized her feet had followed music to the Carters'. After more than five years, the yard was still littered with sleeping dogs that merely sniffed the air when she walked through the gate. The tractor carcass was more rusted, and the once-shiny car was dented now and covered with a layer of dirt.

Mary doubted her knocking would be heard over the music and cackling laughter coming from inside the cabin, so she pressed the latch and opened the door. The main room was very different than she remembered. The walls had been whitewashed, and the windows were hung with the flowered curtains she'd insisted Mason send his mother for her birthday. A new doorway, where the wood stove used to be, led to what Mary assumed from the womanly laughter pouring out must be a newly added kitchen.

"Y'all quiet down now!" a familiar voice yelled in the kitchen. The laughter quickly died down. "Who dat what just come in? Bet' not be no kids; tol' y'all stay outside. Come in here where I can see you!"

Mary crossed the main room, passing a shelf with Mason's old trumpet and a collection of chipped knickknacks, all sent by her and Mason from New York and Chicago. She stood in the kitchen doorway and felt her eyes welling up at the sight of her mother-in-law standing at the head of the table, one hand reaching into her bosom, where Mary knew the woman kept a small pistol.

"Hey, Mama Sweet. It's me, Mary."

"Oh my Lawd!" Mama Sweet moved slowly around the table, her other daughters-in-law moving chairs and clearing a path for her.

In what seemed like only seconds, Mary was engulfed in Mama Sweet's arms and squeezed to her giant bosom.

And Mary cried for the first time in months, the first time since she buried her children and husband.

Through tears, seated in the sunny whitewashed kitchen at Mama Sweet's right hand, Mary told the Carter women of their late niece and nephews: of Rosie's pecan complexion, silky brown hair, and big brown eyes; Mason Junior, who took his job as occasional man of the house quite seriously; and Charles and Peter—not identical, yet each one the spitting image of their father. The women laughed and clapped at Mary's stories as they smoked cigarettes and drank liquor, and somebody would occasionally get up and stir the dinner pot. If any children did manage to get into the house, a woman would shoo them away like gnats.

Mary couldn't bring herself to describe her children's deaths, and she found she had only anger at Mason for killing himself. "Mama Sweet, why was he so weak?" Mary asked. "Why couldn't he... Why did he hafta..."

"God only made women that strong, baby," Mama Sweet said. "Only a woman can carry and bury a baby. Men ain't got it in 'em."

The other women in the kitchen tsked and hummed in agreement.

"And my son, bless his heart, I'm not surprised it was dope what got 'im. All he ever wanted was bright lights and high livin'." The older woman dabbed her eyes.

"Why you didn't kill yo'self too?" The petulant voice of a teenaged girl came out of a shadowed corner of the kitchen.

Chairs scraped the hardwood floor as women backed away from the table and Mama Sweet rose from her chair.

"Alice. You got something you wanna say." Mama Sweet's words were not a question but a dare.

Alice stood up straight. "Yes, Mama," she said. "I do." The girl's voice trembled only slightly, but she showed no fear of her mother. "Y'all talkin' 'bout my brother was weak and on dope. He love them kids, an' he wanted to be with them. Maybe she didn't love none of 'em—"

"Girl, tha's enough!" Mama Sweet snapped.

"Maybe she don't care 'bout nuttin' but herself—"

Two women slipped arms around Alice to lead her from the kitchen.

"My brother is dead! *Why you didn't kill yo'self too!*"

"Let her go," Mary said. "I got a answer." She stood up and walked over to the sobbing, trembling teenager, only a few years—yet it seemed a lifetime—younger than Mary herself.

"I didn't kill myself cuz I'm too stubborn, and God owes me." Mary reached out to touch Alice's face, but the girl shrank away. "God took my babies and my husband. If he wants my life... well... he's jus' gon' hafta strike me down and take me too—"

"Then I hope God strikes you real good." Alice shrugged off the women holding her and ran from the kitchen. A second later, the front door opened and slammed, shaking the whole cabin.

"She gone to climb that tree again," one of the women said. "Mason tol' her couldn't nobody see her if she was up there. Damn fool chile." They watched through the kitchen window as Alice pressed her forehead against the tree trunk, sobbing, and then began to climb.

THE SUN WAS STILL HIGH when the men came in from the field for their afternoon meal. They all stayed outside so as not to dirty up Mama Sweet's nice, clean house. The women carried their plates out to them and sat with the men to drink and smoke, and soon, nobody showed any inclination to get back to the field.

Mary leaned against the gray wooden house and lit a cigarette. She watched her *family*, sometimes talking to her sisters-in-law, sometimes just standing alone. When a passel of kids ran screaming by, Mary imagined her children playing with their cousins and felt a pang. Somebody turned up the music in the house, the same music from her wedding day, and she felt another bit of sadness. Looking at the couples laughing and eating together, Mary missed Mason more than ever.

"So, you was Mase's woman, huh?" A tall, lanky man with just-graying hair leaned over Mary, resting his hand against the wall above her head. "I'm his cousin Cecil. Pleased to meet you. What you say yo' name was?"

"I didn't tell you my name, Cecil." Mary blew smoke at the man. He reminded her of a younger, dirtier version of Will Bevers, the old preacher. The casual way he spoke and carried himself, Mary guessed he was probably lazy and might think too much of himself.

Cecil laughed. "Tha's okay. I know yo' name, Miss Mary." He took a swallow of his drink and then held it out to Mary, trying to press the tin cup to her lips.

She turned her head away. "You don't know me like that," Mary said.

"Well, I'mma get to know you." Cecil smiled, showing a gold tooth. "We gon' get to know each other. I think we be real good to-gether. We both feisty."

Mary didn't really like the cocky man, but an hour later, lying be-neath him in the barn hay loft, Mary let herself be transported back to the time when the feel of hay under her back was soft like a cloud.

The scent of livestock and fresh hay took her back to her youth... young and innocent... free and in love... five long years ago. Cecil's hands were rougher than Mason's had been, stronger and surer, but he smelled just like Mason had back when they made Mason Junior. She lay there remembering the feel of her late husband, his movements, his touches... his sounds, his sweat...

"See, I knew we be good together," Cecil said as he rolled off of her, still panting. "You might be the best woman I ever had."

Mary sat up and quickly wiped a tear. If Cecil saw, he didn't mention it.

"Listen, Mary." He propped himself up on an elbow. "I ain't got much, but I got me a house and a truck and a patch of land I work. Ain't got much schoolin', but I'm smart. I work hard, and I take care of what's mine. I need a good strong woman, and my four young'uns need a mama. I'm a good man. You be my woman, I won't shame you. I won't beat you; I eat whatever you cook."

"I gotta go." Mary stood up and adjusted her clothes.

Cecil quickly fixed his clothes and followed her back around to the front of the house. "Just think about it, Mary. I'a even go to yo' daddy's church!"

Mary didn't look back at him. Could this man, this Cecil, be the blessing God had waiting for her? She looked at the beat-up trucks and the sleeping dogs and the mud and manure. Suddenly, a stench hit her, and she realized it was the smell of this country man, this poor dirt farmer, this *Carter* on her skin... and Mary knew it was time to go. She slipped back into the house—the day's party still going strong—and hugged Mama Sweet and the other women. On her way out the door, she stopped and placed Mason's lighter on the shelf with his trumpet.

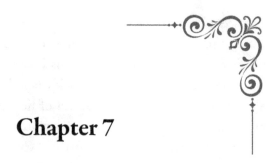

Chapter 7

"I should'a spit in his lemonade." Ellie pouted. "Why you hafta go with him?"

"Cuz Will is my husband now," Mary said to the little girl seated on the dresser in the wood-paneled room they shared. Perhaps things had moved fast, Mary conceded. It had been just over a week since her visit to the Carters, and here she was, just married to Will Bevers.

"Don't make no damn sense." Ruth lay back on the bed, not looking at her older sister. "Marrying that old-ass man. And now she gon' hafta lay—"

"Now, Ruthie, don't be such a sad sack!" Martha chimed in. The second-youngest sister had served as Mary's bridesmaid after Ruth refused. "This is a happy day for our big sister. She's rising like a phoenix from the ashes of her broken life and—"

"Shut up, Martha," Ruth snapped. "She need to be gettin' the hell outta here... again. She don't want him, and she know it."

"Ruthie," Mary said. "I'm right here. You got something to say to me, *little sister who don't know nothin' about life*?"

"I know you makin' a big mistake. You ran from him... now you act like you forgot why. You didn't just lose yo' family, you lost yo' damn mind."

Ellie jumped down from the dresser, and Martha jumped up from the bed. Both girls moved to stand between Mary and Ruth. In the two weeks leading up to the wedding day, the two eldest sisters fought constantly. It was usually over small things, but Ruth never hid her hostility for the old preacher or her opposition to the wedding. Martha and Ellie had quickly learned to get between the two young women, lest Mama come into the room wielding a switch, hitting anything and everybody.

"Can we please not fight?" Martha begged. "This is supposed to be a happy day."

"Ruthie, I *am* happy," Mary said over her sisters' shoulders. "I'm doin' wha's best for me. I need to get away from here—"

"You don't like us?" Ellie asked.

"Baby, I love y'all, and you know it." Mary went down on one knee and took her baby sister in her arms. "But I need more than this here."

"Mary, you said you didn't wanna be a preacher's wife. You said you wanted to go where the bright lights and the big city and the music..." Ruth's voice trailed off. "I was gonna come stay with you."

"Ruthie, you can still come stay with us." Mary let go of Ellie and took Ruthie's hand. "I'm movin' to a big house, and all y'all can come stay with us when it's time to go to college."

Ruthie snatched her hand away. "Jackson ain't no big city. Ain't no bright lights in Jackson."

"Well, it's a lot bigger and brighter than Flora." Martha took Ellie's hand while Mary stood up. "There's tall buildings and theaters and all sorts of sights."

"And I know it's a train goin' north there, too, right." Ruth huffed and sat down on a bed. "Well, I'm not stoppin' in Jackson. When it's time for college, I'm not even goin'. I'm headin' straight to freedom."

"Well, you do that." Mary picked up her gray suitcase. "I got a husband and a fancy big house with a inside toilet waitin' for me." She kissed each of her sisters on the forehead. "I'm not gonna be far away. It's only about a hour," she said to Ellie. She wiped the child's tears with her thumb. "You don't be playin' in that dirt so much, hear me?"

"Yes, Mary." Ellie pouted, folding her arms and flopping down on the bed.

"And you stay outta those trashy books, fillin' yo head with nonsense." Mary hugged Martha. "Mama knows they under the mattress," she whispered.

Even though Ruth remained stiff, Mary hugged her sister anyway. "I'mma always have a place for you, wherever I go. And when you get to the bright lights and big city, I'mma come stay with you, how 'bout that?"

"Yeah, whatever," Ruth said,

Mary looked around her childhood bedroom for the last time, again, and stepped out the door to her new husband and, she hoped, a new life in Jackson, Mississippi.

SEATED IN THE CAR BESIDE her new husband, Mary tried to guess what her new life would be like. A maid. What would she do with a maid? In Chicago, Mary had been the maid, and in Harlem, she'd done her own housekeeping. Maybe with a big fancy house, she'd need the help. And a new husband. Her mother had said that one man's touch was just like any other. So far, Mason and his cousin hadn't been that different, but this old preacher—what would he be like?

Riding into Jackson, the first things Mary noticed were the gravel roads turning into pavement and the sidewalks along the main streets. Riding through downtown, Mary smiled at the movie theater with its bright lights. As they got near the college, she saw some of the two- and three-story boardinghouses where the students lived. When the car stopped in front of a neat, white-painted one-story house, she was a little disappointed. This wasn't the big fancy house she imagined, but it was near the college and on a main street.

"Welcome home, Mrs. Bevers." The old preacher smiled at Mary. "This here's the place." The old man was beaming as he helped Mary from the car and held her hand, leading her up the path and then up three steps to the front porch. "I'm s'posed to carry you through the door—"

Before he could finish speaking, Mary opened the door and let herself in. "I can walk by myself." The tiny foyer was tight, and Mary set her suitcase down in the front room—Bevers called it *the parlor*. The room had two vases of fresh flowers and flowered wallpaper, and the couch—sofa, he called it—and chairs had floral printed fabric. She could see from the front room through the dining room to a room with a glass door and bookshelves that musta been Bevers's office.

"Looks like you got a woman's touch 'round here already," Mary said. She walked through the living room and ran her hand over the back of the couch. "It's real pretty in here."

"*You* real pretty in here." Bevers smiled. "My last wife really liked flowers. Only woman been here since she died is the maid, and she likes flowers too. You'a meet Mamie when she comes in tomorrow. She keeps the place real clean, real pretty, but she the only Negro woman in the South who cain't cook a lick. It's gon' be good to have a decent meal at home." He placed his hat on the hat rack and moved to take Mary's hand. "Lemme show you the rest of the house."

Mary had to admit the house was indeed bigger than her parents' house. Besides the parlor and dining room and office, there was a bathroom with a shiny clawfoot tub. The three bedrooms were all on the same side of the house, with one by the front room, one by the dining room, and one by the kitchen, each papered with sunny flowers. Mary promised herself to one day trade the paper for paint or something less busy.

In what he called the master bedroom, Mary submitted to her new husband's kisses. His lips were dry and rough, like he never licked them. She undressed down to her slip, and he offered to help with the clips on her stockings. When she lay beside him, she made a mental note to tell her mother that one man's touch was definitely *not* the same as any other's.

As the sun set, Mary found a plate of cold fried chicken and some potato salad in the electric icebox, and on the stove was a pot of collard greens. She had to call Bevers to help light the stove, and from the ingredients in the well-stocked pantry, she seasoned the chicken and greens and whipped up a pan of cornbread. After dinner, Mary washed and dried the dishes, wandered through all of the rooms, and looked in all the closets in her new home. Then she stood at the door of the old preacher's office and watched him fill and light his pipe.

"What's to do around here?" she asked her husband. "Where the people at?"

Bevers looked up from the book he was reading. "There's people all around, but it's not good a woman out at night. Ain't safe." He held his empty glass out to her. "Bring me some more tea. Why don't you listen to the radio or somethin'?"

Mary brought her husband his tea then went out to the front porch and took a seat on the top step. She reached into her apron pocket and pulled out a cigarette and her new silver Zippo lighter. She had barely taken a puff when she heard the screen door slam behind her.

"Miss Mary, what I say about smokin'?"

"You said not in yo' house. I'm outside," she said, inhaling deeply. "And ain't it *my* house now too?"

"Well, don't be doin' it out front where folks can see." Bevers look around. "Ain't seemly... preacher and professor's wife smokin' in public."

Mary crushed out her cigarette and stood up from the step. "So I gotta go out back in the yard?"

"If you wanna smoke, you gotta do it out back—"

"What about in the kitchen, with the window open. You smoke in the house."

"Fine, girl. You can smoke only in the kitchen by the window—"

"Old man, you know my name—"

The slap was fast, and it stung. Mary's hand went to her cheek as she glared at the old preacher. Mason had never raised a hand to her, and she'd only ever been slapped by her father.

"I don't know how you talked to that boy you was married to," Bevers said. "But I'm a man, and you not gon' disrespect me in my house, *girl*." He turned and walked into the house, letting the screen door slam behind him.

"Will Bevers, you ever hit me again," Mary whispered into the night, "you better sleep real light." She walked into the house and to the kitchen to have another cigarette.

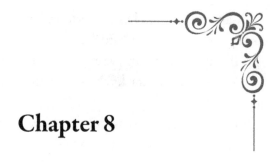

Chapter 8

Sunday morning, Mary rolled out of bed early. She found everything for a big Sunday breakfast and made grits, sausage patties, biscuits, and soft-scrambled eggs. While the sausage and grits were cooking, she squeezed fresh orange juice. She soon smelled her husband's pipe as his slippered feet scraped toward the bathroom, and then she tried not to listen to his morning ritual.

"So, what we doin' today?" Mary asked when she joined her new husband at the dining table. She dug into her plate of grits and mixed her eggs in a little. She looked over at Bevers and smiled. He was chopping furiously at his plate and shoveling food into his mouth like it was trying to escape. "Oh, I see you enjoying yo' breakfast. Maybe I shouldn't talk to you right now."

"Woman, this the best meal I had in a long time." He spoke around a mouthful of sausage and grits. "I cain't talk right now. Let me enjoy this." He picked up a warm buttered biscuit. "Lawd, these biscuits..."

Mary chose to accept the compliment and didn't correct him on her name. After breakfast, he kissed her cheek and helped clear the dishes.

"Don't take too long cleaning up. We gotta get to *church* soon," he said.

Mary quickly cleaned the kitchen, realizing that a maid might be a good thing after all. She chose a light-pink belted dress, a white hat, and white low-heeled shoes. She'd been waiting for an opportunity to wear the elegant outfit, but the dirt roads by her parents' house might have ruined it. Her husband complimented her outfit and beamed as they left the house.

Third Baptist Church was around the corner, a short walk from the Beverses' home. The white-painted brick building had narrow staircases on either side of the grand entry and a tall white cross on the steeple. Inside, the sanctuary had white walls and shiny dark-wood pews that smelled of fresh furniture polish. The tall windows along the walls had vases of fresh flowers on the sills, and the jewel-painted-glass squares cast rainbow hues around the great room.

Without introducing her to anybody, Bevers rushed Mary through the sanctuary and then through a side door marked Office. Inside, she inspected his vast book collection and planned to sit quietly and read until a knock at the door drew her attention. Bevers, seated at his large oak desk, didn't look up from the sermon he was preparing. "Come in!" he said.

"Good morning, Professor Bevers... I mean, *Reverend.*" The short, thin man in a dark suit placed a small stack of envelopes on the green desk blotter. "These were in your office Friday. One of them smells real pretty." The young man smiled and winked.

Bevers cleared his throat and didn't return the smile. "Mr. Floyd, this is Sister Mary."

The young man looked around, and when his eyes landed on Mary, his face lit up, and he smiled, showing the most crooked teeth Mary had ever seen. He straightened his tie and wiped invisible dust from his lapels. Then he stood up a full inch taller and approached Mary, his hand extended.

"Well, hello, Miss Mary." Floyd reached out and grabbed Mary's white-gloved hand in both of his. "It's a pleasure to meet a godly woman on such a beautiful day."

"It's good to meet you, too, Mr. Floyd."

"I guess you're new around here. I surely would've remembered someone like you. Are you staying nearby?"

Mary withdrew her hand and looked over the young man's shoulder at her husband, who was still studying and had yet to look up. "Actually, I'm staying with Reverend Bevers. We—"

"Mr. Floyd," Will Bevers interrupted. "Is there something else you need?"

The young man turned away from Mary and rushed back to his teacher's desk. "No, sir. I just wanted to deliver your mail and say good morning." He glanced back at Mary.

Mary smiled at him like she used to smile at the boys in the bands. Playful but not flirtatious. She wasn't attracted to him in the least, but she was flattered by his attempt at subtle advances.

"Good day, Mr. Floyd." Bevers still didn't look up. The young man practically bowed as he backed out of the room.

"You're a fine woman, Mary," Bevers said after Floyd left. "You're going to attract a lot of attention here."

"And what should I do about that?" Mary walked over and sat in one of the overstuffed chairs in front of his desk. "This what the Lord gimme." She crossed her legs and smoothed her dress over her lap.

The old preacher finally looked up. "Don't look at my students. Especially don't talk to them. Young Floyd is a good boy, but he's always sniffing around a pretty girl. All of 'em are. Got not a lick of sense."

"He seems nice enough," Mary said. "I'm sure he'll find a nice young girl one day. Why didn't you let me tell him we married?"

Bevers smiled as the swells of the pipe organ began. "I'm saving that for the sermon."

Leaving the office, Mary was greeted by two more students and understood what her husband meant. She would have sworn one of them literally sniffed her. She took a seat in the front pew as the deacons began praise and worship with an old Negro spiritual. She let the music get to her and soon swayed and moaned with the congregation. The church nurses in white uniforms passed out paper fans from the local funeral home, and a smartly dressed woman read the announcements in a clipped tone.

After the offering, Will Bevers approached the pulpit, and the congregation grew silent. "Giving honor to God, who is the head of my life," he began, "let us first bow our heads in a prayer of thanks, gratitude, and humility..."

Mary sat with her head bowed, surprised by her husband's prayer, not so much the words as the tone. His voice was no longer the voice of a country man but the formal tones of an educated professor. His voice was deeper, and he pronounced every word. Mary bit her bottom lip to keep from smiling. He sounded funny talking all proper.

"Let us begin in Genesis, chapter two, verse eighteen." He licked his finger and turned a page in the giant Bible in front of him as the congregation flipped pages in their own Bibles. "'And the Lord God said, It is not good that the man should be alone; I will make him an help meet for him.'" The congregation responded, "A-man," and he then turned to Proverbs and read more on the virtues of the good wife, then Ephesians to discuss wifely duties, and finally to 1 Timothy on a woman's place in the church.

Mary noticed the theme, and as men and women in the church clapped and stood in agreement, she kept her seat. She'd heard those verses her whole life and didn't necessarily agree with any of them.

"... and saints, God has blessed me recently... Sister Mary, would you stand up please?" Mary, three women, a little girl, and a nurse all stood up. Bevers laughed a little. "Forgive me. *Sister Mary Bevers*, would you please stand up?" Surprised murmurs spread throughout the congregation. "The Lord has seen that I was lonely and heard my prayers and provided me with *an* help meet..."

Mary would have sworn she felt a breeze when the whole room gasped.

"Brothers and sisters, this is my wife, Mrs. Mary Bevers."

A few people cheered and clapped. "A-man!"

Mary turned and bowed slightly toward the assembled group, and when she sat back down, a nice church mother beside her patted her hand. "Ooo-wee, baby. Some'a these womens gon' be mad at you." The old woman laughed.

After service, in the social hall for coffee and cake, Mary found herself snubbed by women her own age, and the women her husband's age just looked at her in disgust. The deacons shook her hand, and Reverend Bevers got pats on the back from nearly every man in the room. Mary took it all in stride and smiled back at anybody who smiled at her, even if it was mostly only the boys from the college.

ON THE WALK HOME, MARY took notice of the houses and carefully tended gardens while Bevers made sure to point out the homes of other prominent Negroes in the neighborhood. Many of the big houses were student boardinghouses, and one was rumored to be a brothel because of all the women there. Arriving at their front gate, Mary was surprised to see their front door open. In Chicago and New York, an unexpectedly open front door was a sure sign of break-in, but Bevers just opened the gate and led Mary up the path.

"Mamie is here. She probably cooked dinner." He sighed. "I told her you was coming today."

Entering the house, Mary smelled the telltale scent of roasted chicken and cornbread dressing and the sweet, spicy undertones of sweet-potato pie. "Yup... Mamie cooked." She looked up at her husband's wry smile. "Come on... it can't be that bad. Who don't like chicken?"

A harried-looking woman in a light-blue uniform and a stained white apron rushed into the front room. "Afternoon, Professor." She looked past Mary. "Where she at? This her daughter? Such a pretty girl." The old woman looked around.

Bevers cleared his throat. "Mamie, Miss Mary here is my wife."

Mamie tilted her head sideways. "Oh?"

"Yes, Mamie." He slipped an arm around Mary's shoulders. "The new lady of the house."

Mamie laughed out loud. "Professor, you be robbin' the hell outta that cradle, don't you! Ahahaha!" She fanned herself with a dish towel and headed back toward the kitchen. "Dinner be ready in a li'l while. I had to clean up 'fo' I could get started. It won't be long, though. I turned the oven all'a way up so everything cook faster." She looked back at Bevers and shook her head. "Professor, you a whole mess. Ahahaha!"

"Hmph," Bevers grunted. "Crazy old woman gon' burn up all the food," he mumbled.

"Well, I like her," Mary said, peeling off her white gloves. "I'll go change outta my church clothes and see if I can help, maybe keep her from burnin' everything."

"Naw, don't change." He laid a hand on Mary's shoulder. "Company comin' after dinner. Give Mamie the rest of the day off and see if you can make somethin' good. Maybe somethin' sweet... cake or cobbler or somethin'." He gave her shoulder a squeeze and retired to his den with his pipe.

Mary moved through the spotless front room and through the spotless dining room toward the spotless kitchen. All was exactly as she'd left it that morning, so she wondered what cleaning Mamie had been talking about. She tossed her gloves, purse, and Bible into their bedroom—ah, the bed had been freshly made—and walked into the kitchen. Mamie stood wiping the counter.

"Hi, Mamie. Where you keep yo' aprons?"

"In the pantry. What you want a apron for?" Mamie rinsed the dish towel in the sink. She squeezed it out and hung it on the metal drying rack. "You ain't tryin' to cook nothin' right now. Mess up yo' pretty pink dress."

"Yes, ma'am, I am. Will wants a cake or cobbler, so I'mma make one right quick. He say company is comin' after dinner." Mary went to the pantry and found the sugar, flour, some jars of peaches, and a deep iron skillet.

"Now, Miss Mary, I'mma hafta stop you right there. Professor said today was special, so I made a sweet-potato pie. It's in the oven with the chicken and dressin'." Mamie lifted the lid on a pot on the stove. "Got some okra boilin' wit' a little bacon, too. Cookin's my job. He want somethin' different, I'm the one to do it."

Mary watched the older woman fussing about. She'd never had a maid before, and she couldn't just disrespect an elder. "Oh, I almost forgot." Mary grabbed a big mixing bowl from the pantry too. "Professor said for you to take the rest of the day off. Go spend Sunday with your family. I'm sure your children would love to have you with them this beautiful day." She placed the mixing bowl on the counter with the skillet and other peach cobbler ingredients. "You got some nutmeg somewhere, right?" She opened a cabinet and found an old tin of nutmeg.

"The day off?" Mamie untied her apron. "Really? Naw, Miss Mary, I just couldn't." She lifted the neck strap over her head. "I got so much to do here, and you being new and all..." She scurried to the pantry and hung up the stained apron. "I just hate to leave you with all this mess." She took her hat and purse from a hook near the back door. "You sure, Miss Mary?" she said, pushing open the screen door. "I really shouldn't be leaving you like this—"

"I'm sure, Mamie," Mary said to the woman's back. "I'll be fine." The door slammed before Mary could finish her sentence. She laughed at the maid praising the Lord as she danced through the back gate.

"Wha's so funny?"

Mary jumped at the sound of her husband's voice. She hadn't heard him come into the kitchen. "Oh, nothing. Just Mamie takin' the day off." She opened the oven and pulled out the roasting pan of chicken and dressing. The small chicken's skin was crisp and stretched tight over the dried carcass. The dressing was a loose slurry. "That woman is a genius," Mary said, setting the pan on top of the stove. "Takes some talent to dry out a chicken and boil the dressin'."

Bevers looked at their ruined dinner. "Can you save it?"

Mary looked at the mess in front of her and then looked up at her husband. "Wanna watch me?" she challenged.

"Naw... I'll leave you alone with all this kitchen hoodoo." He puffed on his pipe. "Ain't a man's place anyway." He puffed his pipe as he left the kitchen.

She wanted to call after him that all the clubs in New York had men in the kitchen, but instead, Mary shook her head and got to work. She pulled the overcooked pie from the oven and set it on the kitchen table then whipped up an extra-buttery peach cobbler and slid it into the oven. Next, she tackled the roasted chicken. She almost laughed out loud as she realized the meal was indeed salvageable. It seemed Mamie had cooked the chicken upside down so that the dried-out part was only the back, wings, and thighs. The breasts and legs were safely submerged in the dressing mush—still tender and juicy. She took some of the dressing mush and fried it into cornbread dressing fritters; and then she grabbed some tomatoes and onions and fried them up in some bacon grease and added them to the okra with a bit of salt and pepper. Finally, she flipped the bird over and carved the breasts. In about forty minutes, she called her husband to the dining room for dinner.

"I was just playin' about that hoodoo," Will said as he dug into the meal. "But, woman, you sho' did some kinda magic." He took a long drink of sweet iced tea. "I'mma need some more of everything, and whatever you got still in that oven smell like heaven on earth." He looked up at Mary. "You might be the best wife I eva' had."

Mary couldn't help smiling. She was quite pleased with herself and wondered out loud how she would keep Mamie from cooking in the future.

"Easy." Bevers started in on his second plate of chicken and dressing fritters. "Just tell her you takin' over the kitchen. My last wife wouldn't let her cook, either. She got a bee in her bonnet, but she was fine after a while."

Mary sat back in her chair and sipped her iced tea. "So what happened to your last wife?" she asked. She watched her husband finish chewing his food and then take a sip of tea.

"She just dropped dead," he said simply. "She was a good woman, but one day, she just up and died." He took another swallow. "Doctor said it was a brain hemorrhage."

Mary watched him for some sign of emotion. There was none. "What about your first wife? What happened to her?"

His face darkened. "She left me. Went up north. I don't know nothin' else." He wiped his mouth and stood up from the table. He pulled out his watch and checked the time. "Company be here at six."

In the kitchen, Mary pulled the golden, bubbly cobbler from the oven and set it on the stovetop to cool while she cleaned up. Submerging her hands in the hot, soapy dishwater reminded her of the quiet times when her children were all asleep and she could clean in peace. She smiled a little. When a child would venture into the kitchen during her quiet time, she would boop them on the nose with a bit of suds, saying it was magic bubbles to make them sleepy. She forced back tears lest she be tempted to wipe her eyes with soapy hands. It was still hard to believe her babies had been gone three months.

WHEN THEIR GUESTS ARRIVED—DEACON Ledell and his wife, Lena—Mary served coffee and bowls of warm peach cobbler with sweet cream. She served exactly the way her mother always did when her papa had guests. The napkins were folded just so, and she used the best china she could find in the cabinets. Her cobbler earned high compliments from the Ledells and an appreciative nod from her husband.

"Sister Mary, this is the best peach cobbler I eva' had," the deacon said, wiping his hands and dabbing at his mustache. "If you had a little more back there, I wouldn't turn it down."

"Ignore this fool." Lena laughed. "Look at that belly. He don't need another bite!"

"I'd like some more too," Bevers said, nodding at Mary. "My wife is an excellent cook. She made a miracle with Mamie's chicken fiasco this afternoon." He laughed, and the Ledells laughed with him, apparently having experienced Mamie's cooking before.

"I guess this means you won't be joining us for dinner every Sunday anymore?" Lena asked.

"As long as this young lady keeps cooking like this," the deacon said, "why would he?"

Mary got up from the table as the conversation and laughter continued. She smiled to herself. Back in New York, she baked something almost every day Mason was home. She'd serve cobbler with brandy or maybe apple pie with whiskey. Mary shook off the memory and prepared two more bowls of cobbler. The men took their desserts to Bevers's den while the women cleared the table.

"So how you do it?" Lena asked.

"Oh, it's easy. Just some flour and sugar and stuff. The secret is you put the peaches on top."

"That's not what I'm talking about." Lena poured herself another cup of coffee from the pot on the stove. "How you catch the reverend? Women been after him for years. He was gonna get married a few years ago, but *she* apparently *died* right before the weddin'. He was mean as hell for a long time. Now, today, he suddenly show up with you." She took a seat at the kitchen table, pushing the abandoned sweet-potato pie out of her way.

"Well." Mary turned around and leaned against the sink. "I don't know nothin' about his old life. I just know I'm his wife now."

Lena opened her purse and pulled out a pack of cigarettes. She offered one to Mary. Mary accepted it, pulling her lighter from her pocket and lighting the older woman's cigarette before lighting her own.

"You want babies?" Lena asked, taking a long drag on her cigarette, closing one eye as the smoke rose in her face.

Mary shook her head. "I don't really care—"

"Well, you prolly don't hafta worry about that. Man that age, that many wives, never made no babies, ain't likely you gon' get anything outta him." Lena took another puff. "And old as he is, you gon' be a widow soon enough. You got plenty time to have babies."

"Woman, you in here gossipin' again?" Deacon Ledell asked as he headed to the bathroom. "Got no manners at all."

"Hmph." Lena crushed out her cigarette in a pretty blue ashtray. "After twenty-two years, that man still always in women's business." She reached across the table and turned on the shiny brown Philco radio. She turned the knobs until the jumping sounds of Cab Calloway filled the kitchen, and she lit another cigarette but this time didn't offer one to Mary.

Mary smiled and blew out a long, thin puff of smoke. That music took her back to a happy, fun time. She closed her eyes and moved and hummed to the music, and when he got to the "hi-de-hi-de-hi" part, it was all she could do not to sing along. She opened her eyes at the sound of Lena's laughter.

"Ooo chile!" Lena laughed. "That ol' preacher ain't gon' keep up with you. I see you like to dance, and that ain't the Holy Ghost you got happenin'."

Mary smoothed her dress and flicked her cigarette into the sink. "Aw, I'm just havin' a li'l fun. Sometime, the music gets so good, you just hafta move." She did a little shimmy, and Lena laughed even louder. "Sometimes a girl needs to cut loose."

"Well, cuttin' loose ain't the way of godly women."

The two women jumped at the sound of Bevers's voice. He walked into the kitchen and very carefully deposited dishes into the sink. "Need to forget about all that ungodly mess. Women pay high prices for sin and shame." He looked at the deacon's wife. "Isn't that right, Sister Lena?"

Mrs. Ledell slowly crushed out her cigarette and stood up. She was nearly as tall as the older man, and she kept her head up and looked him in the eye. "Yes, sir, Reverend. But I'm sure Sister Mary is a upright and godly woman."

"Yes. Yes, she is," Bevers said, looking at his wife.

Mary didn't look him in the eye. She wasn't godly, and she wasn't planning to be.

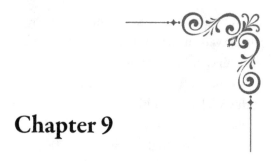

Chapter 9

After the chicken fiasco, Mary decided that her best bet would be to teach Mamie how to cook. Improving Mamie's cooking was often as simple as adding seasoning and controlling the oven temperatures. At first, Mamie resisted Mary's interference, but when Bevers started complimenting the meals, she slowly accepted Mary's help.

"Taste this, Miss Mary." Mamie carried a bit of tomato sauce on a wooden spoon over to the kitchen table.

Mary used her finger to taste the sauce. Besides sweet garden tomatoes, Mary tasted onions and garlic. "It needs some salt and some herbs... maybe some basil and oregano?"

Mamie brought the spoon to her lips and tasted it. "I see what you mean about the salt, but you be puttin' that green stuff in everything."

"Well, the professor likes it better that way." Mary tapped her cigarette on the ashtray. "You should try it sometimes."

"Hmph... I like the taste of plain ol' tomatoes, but I'll go next door and see do she got some of that stuff... what was it now?"

"Basil and oregano." Mary stood up from the table and folded the newspaper closed. She made a mental note to make sure Mamie added the herbs to the tomato sauce.

The two women went out the back door, and Mary watched Mamie head to the neighbor's back gate. She knew Mamie would be gone for a while, so she took the opportunity to explore the garden.

She had to admit the garden was spectacular. The collards were already bigger than any she'd ever seen, and even the melons on the vines looked plump and juicy. The tomatoes were various shades of red and green, and the three different peppers bent their stalks nearly to the ground. The only herb she found was a low sage plant. She squeezed a fuzzy leaf between her fingers and sniffed them. The fresh smell reminded her of the herbs growing outside the back door at her parents' house. She wiped her fingers on her dress. When she went home to visit in the next week or so, she would be sure to get cuttings to start her own herb garden.

It was nearly noon, and Mary was bored. After two weeks in Jackson, she was going stir-crazy. At least back in Flora, there were chores to keep her busy. She'd browsed her husband's library and found nothing worth reading. All he had were schoolbooks and Bibles. There was very little interesting on the radio. Besides the news, the few stories she listened to were silly dramas, and all the music was usually boring Bing Crosby or equally boring so-called gospel.

Mary looked closely at an okra plant. A fuzzy caterpillar inched its way up the stem. "What kinda butterfly you gon' be, li'l fella? You know, I useta be a butterfly, but I turned back into this here worm. But I'm gonna be a butterfly again real soon." She blew on the tiny creature. The plant swayed a bit. She blew harder. The caterpillar stopped moving. Mary blew again as hard as she could, but the caterpillar held fast. "Tha's right, li'l fella. Hold on. You gon' be able to fly away real soon."

IT WAS JUST AFTER NOON when Bevers walked in the front door. He was hours early, and Mary thanked the heavens that she had just come in from having a cigarette on the front porch swing.

"Somethin' smells good." He hung his hat on the hook in the foyer and nodded at Mary seated in the fancy armchair near the big radio. "You cooking dinner now?"

"Naw. Mamie is just puttin' up some tomatoes. Seems we got too many too early. She say the neighbors don't want no more." Mary laughed a little. "You home early. You hungry? I saw you left your lunch pail." Mary put aside the newspaper and stood up. "I put your lunch in the icebox."

"Yeah, I could eat somethin'. I'm goin' back soon, though. Got a class at one."

While her husband took a seat at the dining table, Mary placed the contents of his lunch pail on a plate—a ham sandwich, potato salad, a slice of pound cake, and a peach. She poured two glasses of iced tea and carried the tray to the dining room. After serving Bevers his lunch, she sat down across from him with her own glass of iced tea.

"I'm bored. What they got at the college?"

"Nothin' you'd be interested in. Ain't the place for a woman like you."

"A woman like me?" Mary put down her drink. "What you mean by that? A woman like me—"

"Did you finish high school?" Bevers talked around a bite of sandwich.

"What that got to do with anything?" Mary asked. "I'm smart enough for college."

"Girl, no, you ain't. You gotta finish high school before you go to college. They don't let just anybody in—"

"Oh, so you tellin' me a professor's wife cain't go to college, but my sisters can?"

The old preacher took another bite of his sandwich. "When they finish high school, that means they smart enough. They can go to college."

Mary glared at her husband. "What ah'm supposed to do around here all day?"

He took a swallow of iced tea and smacked his lips. "I got that whole library in there. You read all them books, you have more knowledge than most of these educated fools." He pushed his empty plate toward Mary. "Gimme some more potato salad."

Mary got up from the table, took his plate to the kitchen, and filled it with the last of the potato salad while preparing her next argument. Maybe there was a library at the school where she could find books.

"Do the college have a library?" Mary set the plate in front of her husband. "I'm sick of being stuck in this house."

"You stay away from the college. Yo' place is at church and here at home."

"Well—"

Bevers slapped his hand on the table, rattling his plate and fork. "Tha's the end of it. You not goin' near that college, understand? Ain't talkin' 'bout it no more!"

Mary rolled her eyes at her husband and shook her head. "Ain't nothin' to do here. Mamie keep the house clean, and I'm tryin' to teach her how to cook—she ain't tryin' to learn, though—but ain't nothin' for me to do. Wha's to do at the church?"

Bevers spooned potato salad into his mouth. "Plenty to do there. Ladies' Auxiliary, all kinda stuff. Women's Bible study this afternoon at three. You should go. Maybe get to know some of the other ladies. They got a sewin' circle, I think. I guess you too young for the Mothers' Board, but I'm sure the Usher Board could use you. Maybe the Altar Guild. Take care of the plants and flowers."

He stood up from the table. "Gon' 'round to the church. I be there later on after class."

Feeling summarily dismissed, Mary watched her husband leave the house without so much as a good-bye. She already knew about the Bible study; Lena Ledell had invited her. She had no intention of going. Spending Sundays with *God* was enough church for her.

IN THE KITCHEN, MAMIE hadn't returned yet, so Mary turned off the simmering tomatoes and hung up her apron. She found a hat to match her yellow shirtdress and stepped out onto the front porch. Outside, the sun still burned, and a car or two cruised up the busy street. Mary's first stop was at a corner store for a Coca-Cola, and she drank her cool, sweet treat on her way to her final destination, the brand-new Ray theater. After purchasing her ticket and a bag of popcorn, she followed the arrows that said COLORED and made her way up to the practically empty balcony. She'd always felt that balcony railings were dangerously low, so Mary took a seat near the center in the back. The movie was about to start, and she found herself somewhat enjoying the newsreel and the Mickey Mouse cartoon. When *The Reluctant Dragon* started, Mary sighed. She would have loved to have taken her children to see it.

After the movie ended, the sun still shone brightly outside, and traffic on the streets and sidewalks had picked up. Mary moved at a brisk pace, acknowledging the hat tips from the gentlemen as she walked by. Her walk took her in the direction of the church, and she considered visiting the Bible study, but at the last minute, she changed her mind. Instead, she headed for the college... just to take a look around.

She knew the general direction, but she wasn't exactly sure of the location, so she followed a group of girls talking and carrying books. Sure enough, after a few minutes, Mary stood looking up at a three-story, white-painted brick building. She pressed the latch on the heavy wood door and followed the girls inside.

She first noticed the smell... like fresh paint and fresh sawdust and fresh lemon oil and fresh air. The building smelled new. Mary then noticed the dark-wood doors lining the hallway where she stood. Most were closed, but a few stood open onto empty rooms with chalkboards and more desks than she'd ever seen. She walked slowly past the open doors of occupied classrooms. The lessons didn't sound so hard... perhaps she might learn something if she listened. She moved through the halls of Jackson College, exploring the upper floors and even the basement. The building had everything, including a chapel, and on the top floor, she found the library.

A young man was leaving and held the door for Mary to enter. Of course, it wasn't as spectacular as the libraries in Chicago and New York, but Mary was impressed nonetheless. Dark mahogany shelves nearly to the ceiling lined the walls between the tall windows. Polished bookcases filled one side of the room, and a bank of cabinets with tiny drawers stood beside what Mary guessed was the circulation desk.

Trying to move around and not stare too much, she walked up and down the aisles, hoping to blend in with the other students. She saw the girls she'd followed huddled at a table, whispering over their open books. She noticed boys studying and scribbling furiously on notepaper. In an aisle near the front, a young man squeezed past her, touching her arm and begging her pardon. Mary nodded and tried not to smile too hard. Here she was, a common not-so-country girl, rubbing elbows with college students. When the librarian ventured down her aisle, Mary grabbed the first book she could reach and made her way over to a table near a window.

Mary had never had much interest in books or reading after she had left school, so she was a little intimidated by the book she'd accidentally chosen—*The Encyclopedia Britannica World Atlas*. She opened the big book and looked over the title page, running her fingers over the thin fancy paper. She flipped a few pages and saw charts with columns of numbers and tiny words. Finally, she turned several pages at once and suddenly stared at a beautiful map of the world. *Ah, world atlas... a book of maps.* Mary slowly leafed through the thick pages, each colorful map protected by a thin sheet of paper. She looked at the maps of the United States, each set of state maps showing mountains and flatlands, some green, some brown. When she landed on the map of Mississippi, of course, Flora wasn't there, but Jackson and Biloxi were clearly marked.

"Well, hello, Sista Mary. I didn't know you were a student too. Or are you one of the new teachers this term?"

Mary looked up into a smiling face. Annoyed at first, she frowned, but then she recognized him as Mr. Floyd, the young man from church. She smiled as he took the seat across from her. The librarian shushed at them, and Floyd dipped his head and leaned in close to Mary. "Sorry 'bout being so loud. It's good to see you, Mrs. Bevers."

"It's good to see you, too, Mr. Floyd."

"So, Miss Mary," he whispered, "which is it, student or teacher?"

"I'm just visiting." Mary closed the big book. "But I really need to be getting back home."

"Oh, please don't run off on my account. I'm just surprised to see you here, that's all. Didn't mean to bother you."

Mary stood up from the table. "I'm not leaving cuz of you." She smiled at the short young man. "I just got a few things to do. I'm late as it is." She moved around the table and headed for the door. "Nice to see you again, Mr. Floyd."

"Well, at least let me see you home." He scurried after her, catching up and holding the door open. "Professor would have my hide if I let you walk home alone. Ain't safe for a lady to be out and about these days."

Mary didn't acknowledge the gesture, but she did slow her pace to allow the man to accompany her. From the way he spoke and moved, she imagined he was from a comfortable family. He didn't have the drawl of the country boys. She guessed he was probably local or from one of the nearby cities. His clothes were neat and his shoes shiny. Mary wouldn't have been surprised if he had a car or at least a bicycle somewhere nearby.

"Ooo-wee, it's a hot one, ain't it, Miss Mary?" The young man pulled out a handkerchief and wiped his brow. "Too hot. Can I stop and buy you a coke?"

"No, thank you, Mr. Floyd." Mary picked up her pace a little. It must have been nearing evening, because the sun hung lower in the sky. She thought about what might be left over in the icebox that she could turn into a proper supper while the young man beside her prattled on and on about his prestigious membership in the exclusive Phi Beta Sigma fraternity.

"So what's your first name, Mr. Floyd?" Mary interrupted his nonstop monologue, startling him.

"Oh... I'm so sorry, Miss Mary. I should'a properly introduced myself." He quickly stepped in front of Mary, turning to face her and causing her to nearly stumble. "I'm Joshua Floyd." He vigorously shook her gloved hand. "Joshua Floyd, born and raised right here in Jackson."

Mary withdrew her hand. "Nice to meet you, Joshua Floyd." She stepped a little to the side and continued her walk. "Wha's fun to do in Jackson? I been here two weeks and ain't seen nothin' but church. Where's the people at?"

Floyd chuckled. "You talk like them big-city girls down from Memphis. What kinda fun you lookin' for, Miss Mary?"

"Oh, anything, really... nice music, maybe some dancing, you know, fun."

"Well, you want the Tip Top Club." He danced a little jig. "Not too fancy, but good music. Good liquor, if you were the type to imbibe, that is."

Mary ignored his wink and continued walking. "Where's that? I didn't see it downtown."

"It's not too far. You should let me take you some time."

"Say what?"

"Oh no! Oh, my Lord! I'm so sorry, Sista Mary... I mean Mrs. Bevers." He pulled out his handkerchief and began wiping his brow again. "I didn't mean nothin' bad. I meant maybe if you and some other ladies or even the professor needed a ride..."

Mary laughed out loud. "Calm down, Joshua. No need to fret." She laid a hand on his arm. "I'd love to see the Tip Top Club. I don't think your professor wanna come, but I know I could use some fun." She stopped walking. "This here's my house."

"You got a real nice house, Miss Mary." Floyd didn't look at the house. "Thank you for letting me see you home." He reached for her hand and then pulled away. "If you like the library or you wanna have a little fun, just say the word, and I'm your guy." He smiled and opened the gate for her.

Mary took a few steps through the gate and then paused and looked back. "Mr. Floyd, we don't need to tell your professor we was at the college library, okay?"

Joshua Floyd looked a little confused, but then a slow smile spread across his face. "Yes, ma'am. I mean, no, ma'am, Mrs. Bevers. We don't need to tell him a thing."

MARY CONTINUED HER surreptitious trips to the college. She usually went right after lunch and made sure to return home in time to prepare or *repair* dinner. She only went two or three days a week, and if she saw a book she really wanted to read, she'd ask the librarian to hold it for Joshua Floyd, and the nice young man would check it out for her. This scheme worked perfectly... for about three weeks.

"Didn't I tell you to stay away from the college?"

Mary took a puff of her cigarette, rolled her eyes at her husband, and went back to staring out of the kitchen window. "I don't know what you talkin' 'bout."

"You was at the college today—"

"I said I don't know what you talkin' 'bout, you—"

The slap caused her to drop the cigarette on the windowsill, burning a bit of the flowered curtain. Mary stepped back, bumping into the stove. Bevers slapped her again.

"What I say about staying away from the college, huh?"

Mary grabbed a small skillet from the counter and turned to face her husband. "If you wanna fight, we can, but Mamie gon' find you knocked out on the floor!"

Bevers snatched the skillet from Mary's hands and slapped her a third time.

Mary's hand went to her face, and she glared at him. "Old man, you crazy—" The slaps didn't really hurt, but Mary wasn't going to let them go unanswered.

"Nah." He placed the skillet on the kitchen table. "I ain't crazy. You crazy if you think you gon' disobey me or pull the wool over my eyes." He pushed a pair of gloves in her face. "You left these in the library. One of them boys that seen you in church brought 'em to me."

Mary took the gloves from him—light blue with pearl buttons, matching the dress she had on. She stuffed them in her apron pocket and picked up the cigarette still burning on the windowsill. She stepped away out of his reach and took a long puff.

Bevers folded his arms. "I see you one of them hard-headed women. Why you cain't listen?"

"I can hear you." Mary said. She took one last drag on her cigarette and flicked it in the sink. "And I listen if you say somethin' that make sense."

"What don't make sense? Ain't nothin' fo' you at the college. Why you cain't just spend time at the church like a good Christian woman?"

"I spend every Sunday at church, all damn day." Mary pulled her lighter and another cigarette out of her pocket. "An' when you have church stuff here at the house, I be here too. Why I cain't go to the college library? You ain't got nothin' but Bibles and schoolbooks—"

"What else you need? Ain't nothin' good for you in all them other books." He turned and opened the icebox. He took out a pitcher of iced tea and placed it on the counter. "A godly woman obeys her husband and studies on the Lord." He poured himself a glass and drank it down then poured another one and took a seat at the kitchen table.

"So you sayin' the college girls ain't godly?"

"They out all the time wit' the drinkin' and smokin'. Two girls had to leave school cuz they got in trouble. They ain't godly at all. It's all that wild livin' and book learnin'. Women don't need that."

"Will Bevers, why you marry me?" Mary lit her cigarette. "Why you think I was a godly woman?" She leaned back against the sink and took a long puff.

"Well, Miss Mary." He took a sip. "When I first met you, you was nice and quiet. A good, polite, obedient girl. A man needs a wife, and you'd'a made a perfect wife for a preacher."

"Hmph... yeah, you *thought* I was godly back then. But that was a long time ago. I grew up." Mary blew out smoke, and her anger lessened. She wished she could smoke two cigarettes at the same time and relax even more. She almost smiled at the image.

"I know that now, but honestly, Mary, you still the finest woman in Mississippi. Any man be blessed to have you on his arm. An' every Sunday when we walk up in that church... ooo-wee!" He took another long swallow and wiped his top lip with the back of his hand. "And yo' cookin'? Ain't a man alive wouldn't want a woman like you."

Mary just stared at her husband. He was actually serious. "So, you want me dumb and pretty and in the kitchen?"

Bevers shook his head and laughed a little. "Woman, tha's what every man wants... an' maybe a li'l mo'." He drained his glass and stood up from the table. He walked past Mary and then paused in the kitchen doorway. "Okay, fine. You can go to the library, but don't get no ideas 'bout goin' to classes. Tha's where I put my foot down. I'm the man and what I say—"

The blow to the back of his head didn't knock him out, but it definitely interrupted his train of thought. He leaned against the door jam and slowly turned around.

Mary held a cigarette in one hand and the skillet in the other. "If you gon' hit me, you better learn to not turn yo' back."

Bevers shook his head and took a step backward. "Woman, you crazy."

"As long as we understand each other."

The old preacher staggered away from the kitchen, and Mary took a long drag on her cigarette and then crushed it out in the pretty blue ashtray.

Chapter 10

Every day, Mary exercised her new freedom to visit the college library. She made friends with Pearl, the librarian, and checked out books on anything that caught her eye. Joshua Floyd continued to visit and walk her home almost daily. She could tell that the young man was more than interested in her, and she didn't outright discourage him, but she was careful to offer no encouragement, either.

"Joshua, don't you have a girlfriend somewhere, some nice girl you should be walkin' with? Why you all'a time be following me around? You just tryin' to get in good with my husband, ain't you?"

"Well, Mary. I told you already. It ain't always safe for a lady out here." The short, skinny young man carrying Mary's books wore a brown suit today, his lapel adorned with his ever-present Phi Beta Sigma pin. "Now, I admit, if you was to tell the professor that I walked you home, he might think a little higher of me and might go a little easier on me... but I'm not tellin' him—"

"... and I'm not tellin' him, either. Anyway, it's just two people walking from the library." Mary stopped at her front gate and turned to face him. "Joshua, would you like to come 'round back for a glass of cold lemonade before you go back to the school?"

Joshua smiled but then shook his head. "Miss Mary, I'd love to have a lemonade with you, but you a married woman. Me sneakin' 'round yo' back door ain't proper. Now, if you wanted to join me where I live back at the Sigma house, we could go inside—"

Mary laughed and squeezed his arm. "Now who's talkin' 'bout sneakin'?" She walked through the gate, took her books from Joshua, and headed up the front walk. "Good-bye, Mr. Floyd," she said.

"Goodbye, Mrs. Bevers. See you soon." Joshua put his hands in his pockets and turned around, heading back to the school.

Mary walked into her house and was surprised to see the door to her husband's office closed, but she could hear Bevers's voice and loud laughter from his guests. Not only was he home extra early, but he was also in a good mood. She placed her library books on an end table and moved quickly to their bedroom to put away her hat and gloves. If there were guests, her husband would likely want her to make something sweet. She found Mamie in the kitchen, dancing and stirring a pot.

"Oh, Miss Mary, I'm glad you home!" Mamie smiled. "I did these crowder peas just like you say. I fried the bacon first and then added the peas and water. Then I put in some of them herbs and stuff you like." Mamie grabbed a spoon from the nearby drawer, dipped it into the pot, and passed it to Mary.

Mary was sure the concoction would be terrible, but aside from the peas not being tender yet, the dish was actually good. "Mamie, I declare, this is real good. When the peas get done, they gon' be perfect." She looked around the kitchen. "What else you got?"

"Aw, this is it. Been shellin' peas all mornin'. Didn't have time to cook no meat. Pork chops in the icebox, though. And I left the cornbread for you to do."

Mary shook her head. She went to the pantry and tied on a clean apron. "Thanks, Mamie. I'll do the pork chops right quick. You gon' home and—"

"Now, Miss Mary, Professor got company and say more folks coming after dinner. You the lady of the house and all, but I'm the maid. I'm supposed to serve e'rybody and clean up. I know you like cookin' and whatnot, so I'll stay outta yo' way, but..."

"Okay, Mamie," Mary said when Mamie finally paused. "Did he say how many?"

"Yes, ma'am. He got two in his office right now, and some boys from school is comin' later. He got the deacon and Reverend Johns in there. Reverend Johns come every year to talk at the college. He always stay here at the house in the spare bedroom. Real nice, and smaaart... ooo-wee. They say he a doctor, but he not the regular kinda doctor. He a teacher and a preacher, just like the professor."

As she laid the package of pork chops in the sink and unwrapped them, Mary listened politely to Mamie's ramblings. After nearly two months, it turned out Mamie was a reasonably competent cooking student, and Mary found herself getting used to having the older woman cleaning the house and adding bleach to everything.

After she seasoned the pork chops, she glanced at the kitchen wall clock. Four o'clock—plenty of time to make a decent dessert and finish the cornbread and pork chops.

"Yoo-hoo!" Lena Ledell pulled open the back screen door. "I came 'round this way cuz I knew you'd be in the kitchen," Lena announced. "I just came to rescue you from this... whatever a hen party for men is called." Lena took a seat at the kitchen table, turned down the radio, and lit a cigarette. "So, what's for dinner?"

In the short time Mary had been in Jackson, Lena Ledell had become the closest thing to a girlfriend she had ever had. In Chicago and Harlem, Mary was always too busy with babies to have time to make friends. And now, here in Jackson, there were plenty of women at the church, but she felt too old for the women her own age and too young for everybody else.

"We havin' pork chops, crowder peas, and a cobbler. So how you gon' rescue me?" Mary asked Lena. "I gotta serve dinner."

Mamie cleared her throat loudly but didn't say anything.

"I mean, I hafta be here when dinner is served. Is that better, Mamie?"

"Mm-hmm," the maid responded but still didn't speak.

"Okay, then." Lena blew out a puff of smoke. "After dinner, we'll go to the Tip Top Club. It ain't far, and you can do yo' li'l shimmy-shimmy dance for a while." She took another long drag on her cigarette. "We won't stay too long."

"I don't know, Lena. Don't the students from the college like to go there? I know a lot of 'em. What if they see me?"

"So what? Just cuz you married to they teacher, you cain't have a li'l fun?"

The women laughed and continued their conversation, with Lena talking about all the fun to be had at the club and Mary vacillating between going and not going. After she seasoned the pork chops, Mary whipped up a cobbler and a pan of cornbread. By quarter to five, she was frying the pork chops. With the hot grease and the oven on, the heat in the kitchen was nearly unbearable. Mary vowed this was the last baked dessert until the weather got cooler.

Just as the Beverses and their guests finished dessert, the group of students, including Joshua Floyd, arrived, and Mary and Lena said their goodbyes and left to "get out of the menfolk's business." Mary ignored her husband's glare as she headed out.

"So where is this place you takin' me?" Mary patted her hair and adjusted her hat.

"Not too far." The two women walked a short distance to the Ledells' house. "It's over by Farish Street."

"Lena, I'm not about to walk all the way over there in these shoes—"

"Don't be silly, girl." The older woman laughed. "I'm gon' drive us."

"What? In a car?"

"No, I'm driving a mule."

Mary heard herself and shook her head. In Harlem, she had seen plenty of women drive. "I mean, I'm just surprised, that's all. I never seen a woman driving since I been here."

"Well, I know this ain't the big city, but we not *that* backwards." Lena stopped next to a light-painted Chrysler and opened the driver's door. "Get in," she said. "Ain't no man to open doors for us tonight."

Though Mary would never admit it to Lena, of all the time she'd ridden in cars, she'd never ridden with a woman driver, and all the men drivers constantly complained about women driving crazy and causing accidents. After riding with Lena and wishing to God there was something to hold on to, Mary found herself agreeing that women had no place behind the wheel and seriously considering walking all the way back home from Farish Street.

Riding up the busy street, Mary watched the scenery—glowing neon and flickering light bulbs, Coca-Cola and Pepsi signs, and a few shops still open as the sun was setting. They took Farish Street to the edge of town and then turned on a poorly lit side street. In the dim light, all Mary could see nearby was a row of warehouses, one with several cars parked haphazardly around it. When Lena found a clear space and cut the engine, Mary's hopes for a real night club faded.

"Is this it?" she asked, staring at the gray wooden building with curtained windows on the front. From the loud music, of course, she knew that it was, but she was hoping against hope that this giant juke-joint-looking building was not the storied Tip Top Club.

"Yup... Don't let the outside fool you... it's real swanky inside."

The women walked through the parking area, passing smoke-filled cars and laughing young people. The door opened as they approached, and entering the building, Mary was indeed impressed. No, it wasn't nearly as nice as the places she'd frequented, but it was definitely far from a dirt-floor juke joint.

The first thing Mary looked for was the exits. After the fire in Natchez last year, Mary didn't like going into places she couldn't see a way out of. The music was loud, and the band was pretty good. The dance floor was full, and the tight scattering of tables and chairs were mostly occupied with students and what Mary assumed were locals. Locals. She was a local, a *townie*, the students called them. In the dim light, she could barely see the poster-covered walls, and string lights hung from the rafters.

The two women found a table that had tipped-over glasses. The occupants were probably out back or on the dance floor, but Lena pulled out a chair and took a seat. "Sit down," Lena said. She opened her purse and pulled out a silver flask. She opened it and took a swallow then held the flask out to Mary.

"So, they don't have a real bar, huh?" Mary accepted the metal container, surprised at how heavy it was. "What's in it?"

"Just a li'l whiskey. Gotta bring your own in here. Jackson is still dry." Lena lit a cigarette. "Backwards-ass state."

Mary tried not to stare at the deacon's wife sitting with her in a nightclub, cussing and drinking and smoking. Of course, she wasn't shocked by the woman's actions, but Lena's behavior was hardly becoming of a church lady. Mary sniffed the flask. It was whiskey, and by the smell of it, not very good whiskey.

"You gon' sit there snortin' it like dope?" Lena blew smoke across the table at Mary.

"I just wanted to see what it was." Mary took a swallow. It tasted like bad whiskey and burned going down, but when she inhaled through her mouth, she closed her eyes and let the aroma and aftertaste take her back to the low-end clubs in Chicago. She took another swallow and swayed a little to the music. The scraping of a chair close by made her open her eyes just as a big man in a gray jacket took a seat at their table.

"How y'all just gon' come in and snatch my table?" The man reached up and waved the cigarette girl over. "I'mma hafta turn both of y'all over my knee!"

"Ha!" Lena laughed. "You been promisin' that for years, Slim. You full'a shit." Lena threw her head back and laughed out loud.

"See, this woman ain't got no manners." He turned to Mary. "Hi." He offered his hand. "I'm Slim, one of the proprietors of this establishment."

His deep voice was like rumbling thunder. Mary liked the way he said the big words. She put down the flask and moved to shake his hand. He turned their hands and kissed the back of Mary's.

"She's married, Slim." Lena blew smoke at the man.

"You are, too, ain't you." He spoke without looking at Lena. "But you in here every week."

"She married, and she tryin' to drink all my liquor." Lena reached across and took her flask from Mary.

"Hi, Slim. I'm Mary." Mary turned to Lena and reached for the flask again. "Why every man think they somethin' wanna call hisself *Slim*?" She rolled her eyes at the giant of a man. "What you got good around here, *Mr. Proprietor*?"

Slim leaned in close to Mary and smiled. "I don't guess you wantin' a Coca-Cola, huh?"

Mary turned up the flask one more time. "Do I look like I want a Coca-Cola?"

The big man took Mary's hand again. "Baby, I got whatever you want. You name it, I got it."

Lena kicked Mary under the table. Mary ignored her and squeezed the man's hand. "Okay, Slim. Show me what you got."

MARY TOOK A DEEP, HEAVY drag, filling her lungs with the pungent smoke. She had no idea what kind it was, but she knew it was the best reefa she'd ever had. She passed the cigarette back to Slim and leaned back against the car. She was mildly impressed when he pinched out the lit end with his fingers. Looking up at the moonless star field above her, Mary had to hold on to the car because it felt like the whole sky moved when she turned her head. She held her breath as long as she could and then exhaled slowly, letting the floaty feeling lift her. She laughed.

"You got to be the silliest woman I ever met." Slim wiped his hand on his pants. "You always laugh out loud when you smoke?"

"Man, I ain't had a drink or a smoke in months." Mary chuckled again. "I guess I laugh when I feel good. Ain't felt this good in a long time."

Slim reached over, grabbed her hand, and pulled Mary to him. "So, you gon' come back and see me again next week?"

Mary took a step back and looked up at him. In the dark, she could hardly see his face, but he had an attractive scent, manly with liquor and reefa. He reminded her of a drummer in one of Mason's bands—big and threatening but really a teddy bear. "Maybe I'll come back with Lena. Woman like me cain't be coming to a club to see a man." She staggered a bit and reached out to steady herself. "I been out here too long as it is. Need to go back in. Lena gon' think we run off together." Mary laughed again.

"Yeah, come on." Mary's hand was dwarfed in Slim's, but she remembered to let go of his hand before they reentered the building. The woman on stage was growling out "St. Louis Blues" to applause and cheers from the crowd. Lena stood off near the makeshift bar, slow dancing definitely not like a *godly* woman should dance. Young people—actually people Mary's age—sat at tables, playing cards and passing bottles and flasks. In the smoky, dim light, she didn't see anybody she recognized, but she wouldn't have been surprised if some of the eyes she imagined staring at her were her husband's students.

The tables were all full, so Mary tapped Lena on the shoulder and then took a seat at the bar. While she swayed with the music, enjoying her buzz, Slim walked around behind the bar and poured her a whiskey. "So, why yo' man let you out at night like this? Ain't you got no babies at home waitin'?"

"Nope, no babies," Mary took a sip of whiskey and wondered how they washed the glasses. "And I'm a grown woman. I can be out when I feel like it."

"Well, no woman of mine be up in here like that one over there." He nodded in Lena's direction. "She fine an' all, but she a li'l too wild and free fo' me."

Mary watched Lena's dancing and agreed with Slim. The woman was too wild and free. She wondered what the good deacon thought of such behavior or if he even knew about it. Did the Ledells ever go out together? Back in Chicago and Harlem, Mary had never gone out without Mason, and she'd only ever danced or drunk or smoked with him. With Bevers, they'd been married almost two months and hadn't been anywhere but church, but she didn't actually want to go out with the grumpy old man anyway. Then she looked up at Slim. By the light of the bar, she could see his dark skin had a scar from the corner of his mouth down to his chin. One eye drooped a little, but his smile... perfectly straight white teeth, luscious full lips, and dimples...

Mary shook her head. That reefa was stronger than she thought. Here she was, having lustful thoughts about a man easily twice her age. Then she laughed a little. Her husband was three times her age, but she didn't have lustful thoughts about him. This struck Mary as really funny, and she laughed out loud.

"Woman, you still bein' silly?" Slim topped off Mary's drink and hid the bottle under the counter.

Mary giggled again. "Yup. Don't know what you gave me, but it sho' was good." Mary laughed some more. "It's like everything funny now." She looked at the man smiling down at her. Slim was nothing like her husband and nothing like Mason. "Slim, where's yo' woman? Ain't *you* got babies at home waitin?"

"Nah. My babies all grown. Woman is gone north to her mama. Don't know when or if she comin' back. We don't get along so good."

"So you sayin' ain't no woman in here lay claim to you?" Mary motioned around the room.

"You see all these li'l gals? I ain't got time fo' nobody same age as my kids."

Mary laughed. "Well, you had time fo' me. I'm same age as these *li'l gals*." She laughed again.

"Well... you don't act like it. You act like you got some life behind you. I bet you done seen some stuff."

Mary sighed. "Yeah, I have. Ooo-wee, I seen some stuff—"

"So, what y'all talkin' bout?" Lena walked up and draped an arm over Mary's shoulders. "Why you ain't dancin' with nobody? I thought you wanted to do yo' shimmy-shimmy dance." Lena wiggled her shoulders and her hips, imitating Mary's dance. "Whew, girl, I'm tired." She leaned against Mary.

"Woman, cain't you see grown folks talkin?" Slim set a glass in front of Lena. "Ain't it yo bedtime or somethin'?"

"Is that a invitation?" Lena blew a kiss at Slim, tossed back her drink, and headed back to the dance floor.

Mary watched her friend dance away. She knew Lena was in her forties, but the woman could easily pass for late twenties. Mary watched her dance and flirt with the young men. She even kissed one, sending the startled young man staggering away from the dance floor. Mary pushed away thoughts of being wild and free like Lena. She didn't want a wild life. She wanted a fun, luxurious life. She sat at the bar, swapping stories and smiles with Slim, floating on her buzz, wondering when Lena would decide it was time to go home.

MARY TRIED TO MOVE as little as possible carrying her husband's breakfast plate to the table, but the more she moved, the more her head pounded.

"Tha's what you get. I hope it hurt so bad, yo' head fall off!" He slapped the table, causing Mary to shudder.

Her head ached, her stomach roiled, and she promised herself she'd spend the rest of the day in bed. She also promised herself never to drink cheap whiskey again... but when she thought about Slim and that good reefa, she couldn't help but smile a little.

"Listen, *Miss Mary*." Bevers said his wife's name, so Mary tried to listen to him. "Don't know what you did or where you went last night, but you ain't goin' out with that woman no mo'. She ain't nuttin' but trouble, and she'a lead you straight to hell." He shoveled grits into his mouth. "She just a snake, waitin' to turn you to sin."

"We went out to a club and had a little fun, tha's all—"

"And came in smellin' like liquor and reefa and sin and shame—"

"An' you cain't tell me who I can be friends with. I'm a grown woman and—"

Bevers slapped the table again. "And you my wife, so you gon' do what I say! You stay away from that woman. She ain't right, and you know it!"

Mary covered her ears to block out her husband's yelling. She had come home just before sunrise, and she did, indeed, smell like liquor and reefa and maybe a little sin, but no shame. She'd climbed into bed, still floating, careful not to wake her sleeping husband. She hadn't heard the alarm, and when Bevers shook her awake, she nearly threw up on him.

"You comin' in all hours of the night. Yeah, I know what time you came home. Only whores let the sunrise catch 'em. How it look you goin' in there, stayin' out all night? That place ought to be shut down. Drinkin', gamblin', dope! Everything!"

"Now, you listen." Mary's own voice grated on her ears. "You don't take me nowhere but church. I'm bored. I could'a stayed out in the country to sit around an' do nothin' every night. Well, if you ain't gon' take me out, I'm goin' out anyway."

Bevers stood up from the table and glowered down at his wife. "Woman, ain't gon' be no discussion. I'm not tellin' you again. You keep away from that hussy. I mean it!"

Mary bit her tongue. She didn't feel like fighting this morning, and she knew there was really no way he could keep her out of the club if she really wanted to go.

BY MIDDAY, MARY'S HEADACHE was almost gone. She'd managed to bathe and dress and enjoy her morning out on the porch swing. Still feeling queasy, she left dinner preparation to Mamie and took herself out for a walk. The heat was as oppressive as always, and when she turned onto the Ledells' flower-lined walkway, she was anxious for a glass of water with maybe a little baking soda.

"Well," Mary said when Lena came to the door. "Old man say we cain't go out together no more."

"An' what did you say?" Lena motioned for Mary to follow her to the bright-yellow kitchen. She sat at the table and lit a cigarette. "Have a seat. Did you tell him off?"

"Well, not exactly." Mary pulled out her own cigarettes and lit one. The deep breaths calmed her stomach somewhat. "But I did tell him I'm a grown woman, and he cain't tell me who to go out with."

Lena sat back in her chair and crossed her legs. She took a long puff on her cigarette and blew it out. "So... you gonna get with Slim? He likes you, ya know. He don't set out his stuff for just anybody."

"Hmph," Mary snorted. "You forget I got a husband? An besides, I ain't got time f' messin around with no hoodlum."

"Well, if it was me he was lookin' at, I'd be on him *lickety-split*. Ahhahaha!"

"Lena, you crazy! Gimme some water with a li'l baking soda. My stomach still messed up from last night."

The two women sat and talked and smoked for a couple of hours, working out a scheme to get Mary back to the Tip Top Club as often as she wanted.

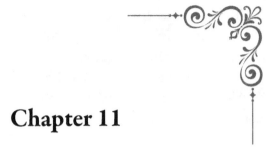

Chapter 11

"What you say, *Miss Mary*?"

"I said, *Sir*, you gon' be a papa." Mary tried to keep her tone serious, but she couldn't keep the smile out of her voice. Looking across the Saturday-morning breakfast table at her husband, whose touch she still barely tolerated, she hoped that whatever the child was, it looked nothing like him.

"Get rid of it," the old man said without looking up from his morning newspaper.

"What?!"

"You heard me. Get rid of it. It ain't mine, so get rid of it."

Mary stood up from the table, nearly taking the tablecloth and all the dishes with it. "It ain't yours? What the hell you mean, it ain't yours?"

"Woman, you really must think I'm stupid. We ain't been married but two months and you in the family way? Cain't be mine. You was probably out there whorin' around. Tha's why you was so quick to marry me." He pounded his fist on the table, making the dishes rattle. "Well, I'm not raisin' another man's bastard, so get rid of it, like I said!"

"Old man, you crazy." Mary scoffed at her husband. "Hard as you been workin', it might be twins." She moved around the table clearing the breakfast dishes.

The old preacher got up and followed Mary around the table. "You a schemin', connivin' hussy! That's what you are. But you *my* wife, and you gon' do what *I* say."

Mary turned to face him. "No, I'm not."

She didn't see the backhand coming. It wasn't a slap—it was a closed fist that landed against her cheekbone and nearly knocked her off her feet.

"Don't sass me, *woman*. I'm the man in this house!"

Mary's primal snarl seemed to startle the old man, and when she lashed out, her fingernails dug trenches through the dry skin on his face. "Nobody is takin' this baby from me! Nobody!" She moved like a predatory animal—arms swinging, claws extended—taking down prey larger than itself.

But the first blow to her stomach knocked the wind out of her. The second one made her drop to her knees. Mary felt his hand roughly gripping her hair, pulling her to her feet. She reached up and clawed at his fingers. "You sonofabitch!" she panted. "Let me go!"

She felt another blow to her face and tasted blood. She spat it on the old man's light-gray suit, earning herself another blow to her midsection.

"Woman, either you gon' get rid of it, or I will! I know just what'a change yo' mind. Yo' papa losin' his church, and yo' sisters missin' out on college, all because you out whorin, tryin' to make me raise yo' li'l bastard."

Mary paused her struggle for a moment, trying to catch her breath. She clawed at the gnarled knuckles twisted in her hair.

"None of my women ever had no babies. My seed don't grow!" Bevers gripped her hair tighter, shaking her head as he spoke. "Any baby you havin' cain't be mine, ya hear me! Not my wife, not my girl-friends, nobody. So you been out whorin', probably right before you married me!"

Mary felt her lips tingling and her face swelling. Her belly and sides ached as she dry heaved. She'd almost forgotten about Cecil. Could the baby actually be his? Just that one time? "No," she managed to gasp out loud. "Maybe they was all barren." Her breathing grew labored. "Or it wasn't the right time—" She felt the pressure of another slap, but her face was going numb, and darkness clouded the edges of her vision.

Mary awoke on her bed with a wet cloth on her forehead. She watched Mamie enter the room carrying a teacup. "Good, you woke. Professor say you got female trouble... but I see you got a little sass in you too," the older woman said. "Man don't whip you like that for no reason." She set the cup down on the bedside table. "I made you some tea. It'll make you feel better. Get you cleaned right out."

Mary sat up and swung her feet to the floor. She tried to stretch, but her body ached all over. She picked up a hand mirror from the bedside table. Her left eye was bloodshot and swollen nearly shut, and there was a cut on her lip. "Where he at?" She looked around the room. "He still here?" Putting down the mirror, she stood up and went to the closet. She tried to reach her gray suitcase on the shelf above the rack. "Help me get this down," she said to the maid.

"You tryin' to leave, Miss Mary? Where you goin'?" The maid remained where she was.

"What it look like I'm doin'?" Mary reached up and bounced on her toes until she snagged her target. She pulled the suitcase down from the shelf, barely missing her own head. Laying the suitcase open on the bed, she started pulling her clothes from the closet. "I'm not stayin' here, fightin' no man, cuz he crazy," Mary fussed, mostly to herself. She only noticed Mamie had left the room when she heard the door click shut and a key jiggle in the lock.

"You crazy old witch!" Mary ran to the door and couldn't open it. "Dammit, Mamie, you open this door right now!" She turned the knob and pulled, but the door was locked tight. "You open this

damn door, or I'a break every damn window in this damn room!"
She took a step back when she heard a key turning in the lock.

The door opened slowly.

"Yeah, you *better* let me outta here!" Mary yelled.

"Woman, why you makin' all this noise?" Will Bevers stood in
the doorway, a slightly amused smirk on his face. "Where you tryin'
to go?"

"I'm goin' back to my family, that's where I'm goin'." Mary
snapped as she closed her suitcase and pressed on the top to buckle
it. "I'm gettin' the hell outta here, cuz you crazy."

"I see." The old preacher puffed on his pipe. "So you gon' shame
yo' family again, huh?" He took a step into the room, clearing Mary's
path to the door. "Go right ahead. You promised to be the good wife,
but whorin' caught up with you. What's yo' papa gon' say when I tell
him you carryin' a bastard child, tryin' to blame it on me? What's he
gon' say when he find out you bringin' shame on yo' family again?"

"I'm not shamin' my family!" Mary snapped. "You a preacher!
Don't yo' God make miracles? Why cain't this baby be yo' miracle?"

"Girl, don't try to tell me about God. I'm a preacher *and* a professor. I know God. You just hard-headed—"

"I'm gettin' outta here." Mary picked up her suitcase and headed
for the bedroom door.

"Didn't God punish you for sin once already?" He puffed on his
pipe again. "No, wait... he punished you four, five times. You asking for it again, huh? You cain't swear to God that baby is mine, can
you?"

Mary paused in the doorway.

"Swear on yo' babies' graves. Gon', do it!"

Again, Mary thought of her husband's cousin Cecil. She laid
with him just before her wedding to Bevers. She could not swear that
this baby wasn't Cecil's. "I don't believe in God no more," Mary said.

"And I don't swear on' nothin', and don't you ever mention my babies again."

"You walk out that door, how yo' sisters gon' go to college? How they gon' be anything but maids? Folks find out you left cuz you a whore, ain't nobody gon' want no Johnson girls. Then what? And what about yo' papa? Losin' that tractor... limpin' along behind them mules again... and how he gon' preach the gospel with you and yo' bastard in his house? He sho' won't ever be more than a lowly country preacher, that's fo' sho'!"

Mary put down her suitcase and pressed her hands over her ears. There was no way Ruthie would be anybody's maid. And Martha, she would find the love and romance she dreamed of. But Ellie... the little girl was feisty and smart. She needed to go to college. And Papa needed that tractor.

"You shamed yo' family once and paid a mighty price. What's gon' be the price fo' yo' selfishness this time?" The old preacher walked over to Mary, picked up her suitcase, and held it out to her. "Don't know when the next bus leaves, but if you goin' somewhere, you might wanna get moving. If you gon' stay here, you gon' do what I say. I'm sure Mamie know how to get you taken care of. If God made a miracle, he'a make another one." He nodded toward the bedside table. "Mamie say a few cups of that tea'll fix you up." He put down the suitcase and laid a hand on Mary's shoulder. "You know the right thing to do."

Mary shrugged him off as he walked away leaving a cloud of smoke behind him. She stared at the cup on the bedside table. Cotton root. That was probably what it was. She knew of it and had tasted it when she was thirteen and had cramps for the first time. Sure enough, after a few days of drinking the vile brew, her first monthly came and scared the devil out of her.

Her midsection still aching from the beating, Mary placed a hand against her belly. She couldn't be more than two months along.

She thought about Cecil and the offer he had made her. She'd lain with him and then walked away without a word. He'd be happy about a baby and provide as best he could, but he was a country dirt farmer, probably a sharecropper. With him, there was no way she would ever get back to the life she so loved, and her father would never accept another Carter into their family. *"No land. No schoolin'. Nothin.'"* And maybe there wasn't really a baby. Maybe she was just extra late.

Mary stared at the teacup on the bedside table. Drinking the tea for a few days would bring on her monthly. The baby, if there was one, would be gone. Would she mourn like she mourned her other babies? Would she feel the baby leave her body? Of course, Mary knew she wouldn't feel anything but cramps and maybe a backache, but the thought of giving up this baby... ending the life before it started...

She sighed then cleared her throat and straightened her back. *I gotta do what I gotta do.* She quickly got dressed, found a hat with a short veil and a matching pair of gloves, then she picked up her suitcase and headed for the front door. She didn't speak to Mamie or Bevers as she walked through the house. Out on the porch, she let the screen door slam behind her. *Papa said I could always come home.*

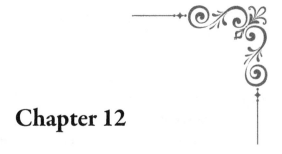

Chapter 12

Mary took a seat on the bench in the colored waiting area out-side the bus and train station. After walking in the heat for fifteen minutes with an aching body and a heavy suitcase, Mary wished she had asked Bevers for a ride to the station. The next bus heading north on Rt. 49 left in two hours. It would stop at Flora, and then Mary would have another three-mile walk to her parents' house. She placed a hand against her belly, and for the first time in what seemed like forever, she felt like crying. Her face hurt, her body hurt, she had a painful journey ahead of her, and... and... and...

At the roar of a bus pulling into the station, Mary looked up. The sign on the front said Chicago. She adjusted her veil and closed her eyes. She wanted more than anything to get on that bus and head back to life in the big city. But she had only five dollars in her pocket-book and hadn't spoken to Mason's uncle Ike and aunt Liz since she moved to Harlem four years ago.

"Miss Mary, is that you?"

Mary opened her eyes. Joshua Floyd stood over her. She sat up straight and adjusted her veil but not before noting the concern ob-vious on the young man's face. "Hello, Joshua." Mary tried her best to sound normal. "What brings you to the bus station this fine day?" She tugged her veil down some more.

"I... uh... was bringing a friend to the bus for Chicago." His eyes darted around for a second, then he sat down beside Mary. "Are you okay, Miss Mary? Do you need anything?"

"Oh. I'm fine." Mary waved off the young man's concern. "Just a li'l bump, that's all. I'm waitin' on the bus to Flora. Goin' to see my mama an' papa."

"Oh... I see. I'mma wait here with you, then. When is the bus coming?" He looked around some more.

Mary looked up at the clock protruding from the wall near the door. "Almost two hours. It's a real short ride to Flora, maybe an hour, but—"

The young man stood up and grabbed Mary's suitcase. "Come with me, Miss Mary. No need to wait out in this heat for two hours. I'mma drive you home."

"Sit down, boy. I'm not goin' home, I'm goin' to Flora." Mary adjusted her veil just as a blast of hot air and smog from the Chicago bus filled the area.

"That's what I mean. I'mma drive you to Flora. If it's only a hour—"

"Now, wait." Mary held up a hand as she slowly stood up. "I cain't ask you to do that—"

"You don't hafta ask. I cain't let you sit out here in this heat, waitin' two hours for a hour bus ride. I got a nice car... well, it's clean at least. We'll take a drive. It'll be fun."

Mary looked around, not sure what she was hoping to see. Waiting in the heat would, of course, be excruciating, and a ride with the nice young student would definitely be better than maybe standing on the crowded bus and then walking from town. "Joshua, are you sure? It's not a short trip..."

He placed a hand on her elbow, leading her away from the bench. "Yes, ma'am. We'll walk to my house and hop in the car. It's not too far; then I'll grab a couple Coca-Colas, maybe get Miz Velma to pack a picnic, and we hit the road to Flora." The young man smiled, showing all his crooked teeth.

"Okay, Joshua. I'd really appreciate that." Mary smiled back at the young man who barely came up to her shoulder. They took a leisurely stroll to the Phi Beta Sigma house, where Joshua's shiny gray Packard sat parked out front. It was an old model, but it was obviously well cared for.

Joshua placed Mary's suitcase in the back seat. "You don't wanna wait in the hot car while I get provisions." He grabbed Mary's elbow and pulled her toward the front steps of the large wood-framed house with the Phi Beta Sigma insignia hung prominently on the front. "There's fans inside, and most everybody is gone."

Mary pulled back. "I don't know, Joshua." She pulled her veil down and adjusted her hat. It don't look right, me goin' in—"

"C'mon, Mary." He pulled her arm again. "Cain't nobody see you with that veil on yo' face. We won't be but a minute. You sittin' out here in the car liable to attract more attention."

Mary conceded he was right and let him lead her up the stairs and through the door. He left her in the front room while he went to find the house mother. Mary didn't know what she expected, but the front room of the fraternity house looked just like any other front room, except all the furniture was worn, and the piano was covered with carvings of what might've been the initials of everybody who ever lived in the house. The heavy drapes were drawn against the afternoon sun, and a few specks of dust danced in the shafts of sunlight that managed to sneak in.

"Now, you know you don't get to bring a woman in here and me not meet her!" A loud woman's voice coming from the back of the house was accompanied by heavy footsteps on the creaky hardwood floor.

"Now, Miz Velma, ain't no need for all that." Joshua Floyd followed the woman into the front room where Mary waited. "She's really just a friend."

"Well, hello there." The older woman, her bonnet slightly askew, offered her hand to Mary but then paused. "Oh... I see... look like you had a little accident."

"Yes, ma'am." Mary tugged on her veil. "Just a bit."

"Mm-hmph. Joshua, go get a rag and some ice for this girl."

"But, Miz Velma, we finna go—"

"Boy, what I say?" Though she was speaking to Joshua, Velma stared into Mary's swollen left eye. "An' pull out that picnic basket and stuff."

Joshua sighed and headed off to do the house mother's bidding.

Mary flinched when Velma reached out and pushed back her veil.

"A little skittish, ain't you?" Velma asked

"No, ma'am. I'm just not used to people reachin' for my face." Mary pulled her veil back over her eye.

"I know what a whoopin' look like. That wasn't no accident." She lifted Mary's veil again. "Did that boy do you like that?"

"Oh, no." Mary almost laughed. "I could whoop him myself. Joshua is a really good friend—"

"Friend, huh? Boy ain't got no business bein' *friends* wit' somebody else's woman, then. He always gettin' hisself in some mess—"

"Miz Velma," Mary interrupted the woman's brewing lecture, "me and Joshua is just friends. For real. He been real nice to me, an' we ain't in no *mess*." She tried to remain respectful, but the motherly woman was getting annoying.

"Whoa!" Joshua came running into the front room, his shoes skidding on the polished floor. "Miz Velma, we just—"

"Calm down, boy." Velma took the dish towel from him. "Women talkin'." She handed the ice rag to Mary. "Keep this on yo' eye for a while. Swellin' should go down some." She turned and headed toward the back of the house. "Send the rag back with Joshua. I'll have yo' picnic packed in just a minute."

Joshua shook his head at the house mother walking away. "I'm sorry, Mary. She treat everybody like they her kids—"

"I noticed." Mary pressed the cold rag to her swollen face. It felt good in the heat. "It's nice to have somebody lookin' out for you." She looked around the room at the carved-up piano and worn furniture. "How many boys live here?"

"Ahem." Joshua cleared his throat and stood up taller. "There's twelve Sigma *men* here in the fall, but right now, it's just five of us."

"That piano look like—"

"Yeah," Joshua said. "We all get to sign the piano when we graduate, since 1927." He smoothed his lapels. "I'mma sign it in December."

Though they were the same age, Mary felt so much older than the young man preening in front of her. In his blue pants and his white short-sleeve shirt, with his ever-present Phi Beta Sigma pin, the short man coming barely to her shoulder looked like a schoolboy playing dress-up.

When Velma came in with a basket of fruit and too many sandwiches for an hour's trip, they said their good-byes and set off on the road.

Mary had to admit, Joshua's car was indeed clean. Not as clean as her husband's car, but it was far cleaner than the band members' cars she'd ridden in and definitely cleaner than the tour buses. Out on Highway 49, Joshua drove not too fast, and they passed a few other people out for Saturday drives. Mary mainly kept quiet and listened to the young man talk. He talked about future plans and maybe heading north. He talked about not having time for a girlfriend and how he wanted to maybe go into business with his uncle, selling Fuller Brushes.

"So, Miss Mary. Can I ask you a personal question?" Joshua kept his eyes on the road as they headed north. "I mean, we *are* friends an all."

Mary took off her hat and veil, enjoying the feel of the wind. "Yes, you can ask me anything. Don't mean I'mma answer, though." She turned up a Coke bottle and took a long swallow.

"Why you marry that old man? I mean, you so young and fine. You could have any man you want. Why him?"

Mary laughed. "I ask myself that every day." She took another drink. "Well... honestly, I thought he was a good man... I mean, except today."

THE RIDE TO FLORA WENT quicker than Mary expected, and as they turned onto the gravel road that led to her parents' house, Mary wished the trip could last a little longer. She found herself enjoying the talkative young man's company even though she'd barely listened to him.

"We goin' about three miles, then turn right. You can see the house from the road." Mary flicked her cigarette ash out of the window. "It's not too late. Mama's gon' try to feed you."

"Of course she is." Joshua laughed. "That's what anybody name '*Mama*' do. They always tryin' to feed me like they think I'mma grow some more. I'm twenty-one. I ain't growin' no bigger."

Mary laughed and agreed with her friend. She took another puff on her cigarette and held it out of the window. The hot late-summer breeze felt good on her arm. They rode in silence for a few minutes until Mary pointed at a house and barn in the distance that stood out above the cotton fields. They turned onto a red dirt driveway and parked in the yard a few paces from the front steps. Mary's papa stood up from his chair on the front porch, while Joshua helped Mary from the car and unloaded her suitcase from the back seat.

"Hmph." Reverend Johnson sucked on his pipe. "You come visit for just a spell." It wasn't a question... it was more like an instruction.

"Yes, Papa," Mary said. "This is my friend, Joshua Floyd. He's one of Will's students. He brung me here so I wouldn't hafta walk from the bus."

Joshua stepped forward. "Pleased to meet you, Reverend Johnson."

Mary's father nodded and headed down the stairs. She watched him walking. His slight limp seemed more pronounced today. "Likewise, young man—"

"Maaaarrrryyy!!" Ellie burst through the screen door and came running down the stairs. Her arms windmilled as she fought to run and keep her balance, and she barreled right into Mary, nearly knocking her off her feet. "Mary, Mary, Mary, Mary, Mary!"

Mary lifted her baby sister in a hug and spun her around. "Ellie, Ellie, Ellie, Ellie, Ellie!" When she stood the little girl back on her feet, they both swayed a little. "Ellie, this is my friend, Mr. Floyd."

"Girl, why you out here screaming like you..." Augusta Johnson stepped out onto the front porch and paused, "... ain't got no sense..."

"Hi, Mama." Mary adjusted her hat and veil as her mother came down the steps.

Augusta looked at her husband then looked again at Mary. "Well, hello, baby." She hugged her eldest daughter. "And who is this young man?"

"Mama, this is my friend, Joshua Floyd. He's one of Will's students—"

"Yeah," Reverend Johnson said. "Young fella didn't want her making the walk from town." He wiped his hand on his shirt then offered it to Joshua. "Much obliged, young man."

"It was my pleasure, sir." Joshua shook Reverend Johnson's hand. "Sister Mary is a real nice lady. Didn't seem right her taking that long bus ride and then walking from town... especially in this heat."

"Do you hafta leave right now, Mr. Floyd?" Augusta asked, fanning herself with a dish towel. "I just put on a pot of green beans and potatoes—"

"Thank you, Mrs. Johnson, but I do hafta hit the road if I wanna make it back by nightfall."

"Well, at least let me make you some sandwiches for the trip—"

"No need, ma'am," Joshua said. "I got plenty sandwiches, but if I could trouble you for a drink of water—"

"No trouble at all. Ellie, go get the man some water." Augusta reached out and patted the little girl's head.

Ellie wrapped herself tighter around her big sister. "Mary, you gonna stay, right?"

"Yes, I'm staying," Mary said, prying her sister's arms from around her waist.

"Forever and ever?"

"We'll see," Mary said. "Now, go do what Mama said." She pushed her sister toward the house.

Ellie ran off up the stairs, and Reverend Johnson picked up Mary's suitcase. "Pretty heavy," he said. "How long you plannin' to visit?"

"Let's not worry 'bout that right now." Augusta waved her husband off. "I'm just glad she's here."

Mary tried not to wince when her mother touched her face. "When we get in the house, I'a get you somethin' to put on that," her mother said.

Ellie came out of the house and down the stairs, holding a teacup. "I got the fancy cup 'cause you're company!" She held the cup out to Joshua. "I didn't even spill it or spit in it."

Joshua took the cup from the little girl, holding it with his pinky up. "Why, thank you, Miss Ellie." He downed the contents in one gulp and made a big show of wiping his lip. "Ooo-wee! That was the best water I ever tasted!"

Ellie smiled a big toothless smile, took the empty cup, and ran back into the house.

"Thank you for your hospitality, Reverend and Mrs. Johnson." Joshua shook hands all the way around. "I'm gonna hit the road now. It's not too long a drive, but still, you know..."

"Thanks again," Reverend Johnson said. "I appreciate you looking out for my daughter."

"Are you sure I can't get you a little somethin'?" Augusta asked again. "It won't take a minute."

"No, thank you, ma'am, but I appreciate the offer." Joshua opened the car door and climbed into the driver's seat. "It was real good meeting everybody!"

Mary and her family stood waving as Joshua Floyd pulled his car out of the yard and turned onto the road. "That young man really likes you," her mother said, still smiling and waving. "Ain't proper you ridin' around with him like that."

"Hmph." Reverend Johnson grunted into his pipe and headed up into the house with Mary's suitcase.

"Aw, Mama, it ain't nothin'."

"Is he why yo' face like that?" Augusta headed into the house. "You messin' 'round with young boys?"

Mary sighed and followed her mother. "No, Mama, I ain't messin' around with nobody." She felt herself tearing up again. For only the second time in her life, she noticed the smell of her old home. The earthy smell of the yard plus the undercurrent of cut hay and the musk of animals. As nostalgic as the fragrance was, Mary was reminded of how much she hated farm smells. In the wallpapered kitchen, she sat still at the table while her mother dabbed at her face with a piece of cotton soaked in witch hazel.

"So, what you do?" her mother asked.

"Nothin'," Mary said.

"You a grown woman now," Augusta said. "But you ain't too old fo' me to get a switch to yo' lyin' tail." She dabbed more of the solution around her daughter's eye and on the bruises on her cheek.

"Really, Mama. I didn't do nothin'. Honest."

"Oh, so he just woke up this mornin' an decided to wale on you? That's what you want me to believe? Did you say somethin' wrong?"

Mary sighed again. "Maybe. I told him a baby was comin'."

Augusta pulled her hand back from her daughter's face. "So he beat you?"

"Kinda." Mary said. "Not really—"

"Dangit, girl! What happened? C'mon... spit it out."

"He say the baby ain't his." Mary felt herself crying, but she didn't sob. "He said get rid of it, and I said no, and when he hit me, I fought him."

"I see." Augusta went to stir the pot of green beans and potatoes. "He got reason to think it ain't his?"

"He say he cain't make babies. He say his stuff don't work." Mary wiped a tear. "None of his women ever even got that way. He say I was whorin' around."

"Mary." Augusta turned to face her daughter. "Do *you* got a reason to think it might not be his?"

Mary wiped another tear and thought again about her husband's cousin Cecil, that one time in the hay. It wasn't but a week or so before her wedding to Will Bevers. She pressed a hand to her belly and looked up at her mother.

"I see," her mother said. "Well, seems like you got a choice to make. Make some cornbread right quick... beans almost ready."

Reverend Johnson smiled as his wife set a plate in front of him. Martha, the third sister, walked around the table, pouring lemonade into the mason jars that served as drinking glasses most days. Ruth, the second sister, helped her mother plate and serve dinner. When everyone was served and seated, the family bowed their heads and offered thanks.

"So, how long you visitin'?" Reverend Johnson asked, digging into his plate of green beans, potatoes, and ham. "Couple weeks?"

"She stayin' long as she want," Augusta said.

"Forever and ever!" said Ellie.

"Hmph... Don't you got a husband at home?" Reverend Johnson smashed his cornbread into the green beans. "Ain't right, a woman leavin' her husband like that. Bible say—"

"Well, we got women stuff to deal with. He can wait a spell." Augusta ended the discussion.

"Hmph." Reverend Johnson shoveled more food into his mouth but said no more.

Mary sat with her family and joined in the dinner-table talk, filling them in on the details of her big house and the fancy church. They all laughed at Mary's tales of Mamie's cooking and listened intently and asked lots of questions about the college.

"I'm not gettin' married to nobody. I'm going to college." Ruth took a drink of her lemonade. "I'm not gon' be stuck with no man."

"What if you meet a nice man at the college?" Martha asked. "Then what?"

"Then nothin'. Still not gettin' married." Ruth took another sip and set her jar down a little too hard.

"I'm goin' to college with Mary," Ellie piped up. "I can live with her and read all the books."

"Of course you can, baby." Mary said. "When you get old enough to read and know all your numbers, you can—"

"Yay!" Ellie cheered. "I know how to read, and I know all the numbers! I can go to college with Mary now!"

Mary listened to her sisters' plans and dreams and felt a pang. Would leaving her husband mean the end of their chances for college? The family wasn't poor, but they hardly had enough to send three girls to college. Would leaving Bevers ruin her sisters' futures?

After dinner, Mary sat in the front room, listening to Ellie read. The little girl read everything in sight and brought out all her books. Her teacher had said she was the smartest girl in her grade. Mary imagined her baby sister really could read the books at the college library. What would become of Ellie without college? Would God punish Mary this time for shaming the family and leaving her husband *and* ruining her sisters' lives?

The next morning, seated on the porch and smoking a cigarette, Mary watched her father head out to the barn to fire up the tractor. His limp was more pronounced, and he moved a bit more slowly than she remembered. Had he always moved that way, dragging a stiff right leg behind him? How had he gotten through the fields for all these years? Since getting the tractor, he'd sold the mules and bought an old truck. Would he be able to get the mules back if he lost the tractor? Would God punish her selfishness for making life harder on her papa and the whole family?

Mary's mother came out onto the porch with a bushel of peas and a bowl and a bucket. "C'mon, girl. Let's get these done. They lookin' real good this year." She set the bowl on the small table and placed the bushel and bucket on the floor. Mary put out her cigarette and took a seat in one of the chairs. She reached into the bushel and began shelling peas into the bowl, dropping the shells into the bucket. The two women worked in silence for a while, Mary realizing her manicure would be ruined and her mother shelling and humming an old gospel tune.

"Mama?"

"Hmmm?"

"What should I do?"

"You don't really want me to answer questions for yo' life, now, do you?"

Mary sighed. "I guess not." Her face still hurt when she moved, and her left eye was still bloodshot. Her sides ached a little less today. "I just..." Her voice trailed off.

"You just what? Don't know what the right thing is? Sound like you might already did the wrong thing... now what?"

"Mama, I want this baby sooo bad... I can feel him in my arms. I can feel him on my titty. I know it's too early, but I swear I feel him move."

"Girl, that's just gas and yo' 'magination."

"I know." Mary sighed. "How long Papa been walkin' like that?"

"Like what? He been walking like he walk since forever. Least long as I know 'im."

"No, it's worse. He's movin' real slow now."

"Oh... well... he slipped and turnt his ankle real bad. But he doin' okay. Didn't lose a step, now that he don't hafta walk behind no mules. But you know, he gettin' old. He's gon' be movin' slower anyway."

Mary didn't look up while her mother spoke. She imagined a pointed look from her mother because she knew she was talking about the tractor given to them by Bevers. She kept shelling peas and listening to the farm sounds... the insects whose chirps and buzzes annoyed her more than anything, the chickens in the yard, and the distant rumble of the tractor out in the field.

"Okay, baby, listen." Augusta interrupted Mary's thoughts. "I cain't tell you what to do, but I can tell you this. Be good to yo'self."

"What do *that* mean?" Mary asked, reaching into the bushel again.

"It means do what's right fo' you in time. Do what'll set right in yo' heart. It don't always mean do what's fun or what's easy. Sometimes, it mean you gotta tell yo' self 'no' cuz it ain't the right time or cuz it might turn bad tomorrow. But always do what'll help you out by and by."

"So you saying I should give up the baby, cuz it's better in the long run?" Mary asked, not looking at her mother.

"Ain't saying nothin' but what I said."

Mary hid her face in her hands. "Please, Mama. Why cain't you just tell me straight—"

"Cuz it ain't my life!" Augusta snapped. "You been a grown woman since you was fifteen years old. Ain't my place to tell you what to do wit' yo' life—"

"But what about Ruthie's and Martha's and Ellie's lifes? What about Papa... and you?"

"Girl, I'm livin' my life, no matter what *you* do. And yo' sisters gon' be however God see fit."

"But, Mama..."

Augusta started humming again. The discussion was over.

AFTER TWO WEEKS AT her childhood home, Mary felt she was no closer to a decision than when she'd arrived. Her heart sank when she looked out from the front porch and saw a familiar car driving up their road. She stood up and waited while her husband parked his car in the yard. Her baby sister, Ellie, jumped up from the porch and ran into the house. Mary lit a cigarette as Bevers cut the engine and stepped out of the car.

"Good to see you, *Miss Mary*," he said. "You look nice. How's everybody doin'?

"We all good." Mary's hand shook as she smoked her cigarette. She didn't know whether it was nerves or anger or what.

"I had Mamie pack up all yo' stuff. It's right here in the car."

"Well, hello, Will." Augusta came out to the porch and folded her arms. "I'd ask what brings you out this way, but I guess I already know." She looked out toward the cotton field and patted her youngest daughter's head. "Ellie, go get your papa. Tell 'em company's here."

The little girl stomped down the stairs and gave the old preacher wide berth before running off into the cotton field.

"Y'all talk. I'mma go get y'all some lemonade." Augusta wiped her brow. "It's sho' hot out here."

Mary watched her mother retreat into the house and tried not to feel abandoned. Her husband came up the stairs and motioned for Mary to have a seat in one of the chairs. Mary took a seat on the top step and took a long defiant drag on her cigarette. Bevers sighed, moved down a few steps, and leaned against the banister.

"Well?" He took off his hat and fanned himself.

"Well, what?" Mary looked up and blew a perfect smoke ring.

"Woman, you know what. Ain't got time to play wit' you," he groused. "You gon' do what I say or not?"

"I'm still thinkin'," Mary said. She looked out in the distance as her papa pulled the tractor up near the yard. She watched Ellie climb down from her father's lap, then she studied her father's slow, stiff movements as he lowered himself down from the tractor. He took a couple of steps and stumbled, falling on his belly. Mary could almost feel the impact of that fall. She stood up and started down the stairs, but Reverend Johnson slowly got to his knees, and then, stepping up one foot at a time, he got to his feet. He dusted off the front of his overalls, took Ellie's hand, and headed toward the house.

Mary sat back down on the step. Not knowing what to call what she was feeling, she settled on *wonder* at the cruelty of God's wrath. For her original sin of shaming the family and dishonoring her parents, God had taken her husband and children. Now, if she didn't sacrifice this child, almost like Abraham almost had to do, the whole family would suffer. She looked up into the cloudless sky. If she could have seen God looking down at her, she'd have spit right in his eye.

As her father approached his front porch, he shook off his daughter's hand and folded his arms. Bevers took a step to the side. "Y'all girls go on in the house," Reverend Johnson said.

Ellie stomped up the stairs, but Mary didn't move. "Papa, it's okay. I'mma go—"

"Gon' in, I say!" he snapped. "We got man stuff to talk about."

"C'mon, Mary," Ellie whispered loudly. "Hurry up!"

Mary flicked her cigarette into the dirt, where her father crushed it out. She looked back over her shoulder as she followed her baby sister into the house.

In the kitchen, Augusta looked up from the pitcher she was stirring. "Oh, is Will gone?" she asked.

"Naw... he's out talking man stuff with Papa!" Ellie climbed up on a chair and took the stirring spoon from her mother. "Lemme do it."

"Girl, git down!" Augusta snapped, taking the spoon back from her daughter.

Mary tried to ignore her mother and sister. She looked out of the kitchen window onto her mother's garden. The trees looked heavy, and the pecans would start falling soon. She made a mental note to harvest some herbs and take some cuttings. She drank a glass of lemonade and went to the bedroom to start packing. She could have another baby... *by and by.*

Chapter 13

Mary didn't quite feel like herself. The cotton root had done its job, and she knew the baby was gone. The bleeding and cramps had lasted almost two weeks. But she was feeling a new sense of determination in her spirit as she accepted her circumstances and developed a plan to have a baby that her husband would accept. Every day, Mary sipped red clover tea and Lydia Pinkham tonic. She fed her husband all the extra meat she could cook, and she reached for him every night. At first, he quickly took his marital pleasure without question. Then one night, Will Bevers denied his wife's advances, and Mary felt a little confused. The following night, he again pushed her away and then again on a third night.

"What's wrong?" she asked, staring at his back in the dark of their moonlit bedroom. "Why you don't want me?" She ran her hand over his shoulder. For a man in his sixties, he was still quite muscular, and if she had actually cared about him, Mary might have found his back and shoulders appealing.

"I'm not stupid. Tha's what's wrong." His clear, deep voice told her he hadn't been asleep. The mattress springs squeaked when he rolled onto his back and pulled the sheet up to his chin. "Woman, you just want me to stud, and I'm damn near seventy. Feedin' me all them heavy meals, wantin' me on you all the time. You must think I'm crazy. I'm not finna let you kill me. Too many old men die on top of young wives. Tha's not gon' be me."

Mary scooted away from him. "Yeah, I do think you crazy," she said. "And I know plenty ways to kill a man, slow or quick. If I wanted you dead, we wouldn't be here talkin'."

"Hmph."

"Listen." Mary reached out and laid a hand on his chest. "You know I want babies, and I ain't never heard of a man's stuff not workin'. Now I *know* my stuff works, so I think if you give yo' God a chance to work a miracle—"

"You think I didn't try? Ain't gon' be no miracles—"

"Abraham was a hundred years old. Ain't that what yo' Bible say?"

"That ain't in God's plan for me."

"Oh... so you think you know yo' God's mind, huh."

Bevers sighed. "I'm a preacher and a teacher, so yeah... I got a good idea of God's mind."

"Well, I know yo' Bible say 'don't deny yo' wife,' and I'm tryin' to be a good wife—"

"*Miss Mary*, if I do it, will you just *be the good wife* and quit talkin' 'bout it?"

Mary moved her hand under the covers and down his belly. "Yes, I will, *sir*." She was still mostly repulsed by the old man, but she closed her eyes and received him. He felt so different from Mason. His touch was rough, matter-of-fact—thoughtless, even. Sometimes, he'd moan "Jesus," and Mary would move and squeeze to hurry him along.

"Woman, I know what you tryin' to do." Bevers groaned as he rolled onto his side of the bed, still panting. "I ain't complainin', but it ain't gon' work."

Mary sat up and turned her body so she sat facing the head of the bed. Then she lay back and propped her feet up on the headboard. "Yo' God make miracles, right?"

"Ha! Only for the righteous. When the last time you was right-eous?"

Mary looked over and rolled her eyes at her husband. "Yo' Bible say—"

"Woman, hush. Only the believers got miracles..." He got out of the bed and shuffled off to the bathroom.

"I hate you," Mary whispered. Then she prayed for God to make her a believer again.

THINGS HAD CHANGED. Will Bevers was a little more indul-gent and a little more polite, and Mary was less quick to challenge him lest he feel she wasn't being *the good wife* and withhold himself from her. As summer turned to fall, though, Mary did not conceive as quickly as she expected, and even her husband expressed disap-pointment... but not surprise.

By October, the college was filled with students, and for Mary, daily trips to the library were as close to being a student as she could get. The history professor who allowed her to visit his class and sit in the back wondered out loud why such a bright, beautiful young lady wasn't taking real classes, and when Bevers found out, he put Mary out of their bed and threatened to beat her again.

"Vashti was put out cuz she didn't obey her husband." the old man chastised Mary. "Bible say, 'If there is anything they desire to learn, let them ask their husbands at home.' Not gon' have you out here shamin' me, goin' up there an' runnin' yo' mouth."

"Well, it's almost time for Ruthie to go to college," Mary said. "Why she get to go and not me?"

"Cuz she a smart girl and she not my wife. An stubborn as she is, she prolly gon' be just as ungodly as all the rest of them girls."

"So, you just wastin' yo life teachin' all them ungodly women, huh?"

"Tha's 'tween them and the Lord. You just better be glad I let you go to the library. You too dumb to be tryin' to take classes. Everything you need to know you can learn from me."

Mary rolled her eyes at her husband and turned the kitchen radio up. The argument was going nowhere. They'd had it before, and each time, Bevers threatened more beatings and restrictions. The last time they argued, he said she could go to college all she wanted, but she'd have to find a way to pay off her daddy's tractor. Mary threatened to get a job, and he reminded her that all she was good for was cooking and cleaning... and ruining her sisters' chances for college.

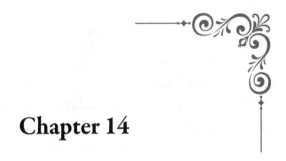

Chapter 14

Not that he could've stopped it, but one of the things Bevers did allow was Mary's continued friendship with Lena Ledell. It was Lena's brilliant idea that they attend church functions and join the sick and shut-in committee and then stop at the Tip Top Club after the visits.

The warehouse-turned-nightclub had its curtains open during the daylight hours, and Mary could appreciate the owners' attempts at decorating. The gray walls were covered with placards and flyers of the singers and other acts that had performed there. There were framed newspaper clippings and movie posters with all the Negro stars. The concrete floor was swept clean, and the worn wooden stage was polished to a shine. There were a few other people in the club—a table of men playing cards and turning up bottles hidden in brown bags and two men slapping down dominoes. While Slim stood wiping the bar and Lena danced with the jukebox, Mary sat at a table, sipping a Coca-Cola and smoking a cigarette... and pretending she wasn't watching Slim watch her.

"So, how you doin', Mary?" Slim asked as he approached her table. He placed a fresh glass of Coca-Cola in front of her and folded himself into the seat across from her. "You lookin' mighty fine today."

Mary nodded thanks and lifted the glass to take a sip. The bubbles tickled her nose, and the smell of whiskey made her smile. "Why, thank you, Slim." She took a sip and tried and failed not to make a face. "It's a little strong." She took a full swallow. The cool sweetness on her tongue followed by the whiskey burn in her throat felt good. "What's up? Why you handin' out free liquor?"

He leaned forward, placing his elbows on the scratched wooden table. "I'mma tell you a secret."

"What?" Mary looked up at him. Even seated, the big man towered over her. She was a little disappointed that he wasn't so attractive when she was sober and in the daylight. The scar on his face went way past his chin, and the bowler hat he wore did little to hide his graying hair. She took another swallow.

"I see a pretty lady, I give her a drink," Slim whispered. "I'm the owner. I do what I want."

"It's enough in here for two drinks." She turned the glass up and drained it. "You tryin' to get me drunk?"

"Maybe a little. You look like you could use some relaxin.'"

Setting the glass back on the table, Mary found herself looking into the man's eyes. Dark and deep set, Slim's eyes reminded her of Mason Jr.'s dark eyes, and suddenly, she wanted another drink.

"Y'all looking mighty cozy over here!" Lena said as she took a seat at the table.

"Well, we *was* gettin' cozy 'fore it got so crowded," Slim said.

Lena pulled out a handkerchief and wiped the sweat from her brow. "How 'bout a drink, Big Daddy?" Lena fanned herself with her hand. "I know you got somethin' good back there."

"I always got somethin' good," Slim said, getting up from the table. He squeezed Mary's shoulder and headed to the bar.

Lena picked up Mary's empty glass and sniffed it. "Yeah, he really likes you. That's the good stuff."

"Lena, you so crazy." Mary laughed.

"Well, if you wanna fool around, I won't tell." Lena pulled out a cigarette and lit it. "Big strong man like him... ooo-wee!"

Mary smiled and shook her head and lit her own cigarette with Lena's lighter. "Girl, you just tryin' to get me in trouble."

"Hahaha! Every woman needs a little trouble sometimes." Lena laughed and nodded toward a group of young men coming in the door. "I know I do."

Slim returned and set a drink on the table in front of Mary. "Your drink is at the bar," he said to Lena as he took his seat. "I made it special, just how you like it."

Lena threw her head back and laughed out loud. "I know you did, Slim." She got up and danced toward the bar. "Y'all kids enjoy your *talk*."

Mary watched her friend dance away and then took a sip of her drink. This one was stronger than the last, making little pretense of having any Coke in it. "You *are* tryin' to get me drunk. You gon' slip me a mickey next?"

"Nah. I'm savin' that f' another day."

Mary shook her head. In spite of a few imperfections, Slim was a handsome man, and if she wasn't married, he certainly wouldn't have to use any tricks. She laughed to herself. The liquor was definitely getting to her.

As the club filled with students and locals, Mary sipped her drink and half listened as Slim shared his life story. His children were grown and had started their own families. His wife had gone to visit her mother in Chicago and said she was never coming back. And he had business partners... silent partners, he called them... but he was the one who actually ran the club.

Without mentioning Mason or her children, Mary told of the sights and sounds and celebrities she'd known in Chicago and Harlem, and she told how she longed to live that life again. They talked for nearly an hour, and when Slim stood up and took her hand, she waved to Lena on the dance floor and followed him out the back door.

Seated in the front seat of a shiny new Mercury, Mary accepted the cigarette Slim lit for her and passed him back his flask. "Mary,

I'm not gon' lie," he said. "I could get real into a woman like you. I know you young, but you ain't like these other young girls. You done seen some stuff."

"What's yo' real name?" Mary asked him. "I know yo' mama didn't name you Slim."

"Well," Slim said, "funny thing is, my mama really did name me Slim. My real name is Edgar, but she always called me Slim on account of I was so scrawny."

"Ha! Like you ever been scrawny." Mary laughed.

"I ain't lyin'. I was so li'l they didn't think I was gon' make it. Then one summer I was thirteen-fourteen, I blew up bigger than Daddy. Hands got so big, arms so long, I didn't know what to do with myself."

"Looks to me like you learned just fine." Mary held her head back and blew smoke rings.

Slim flicked his cigarette out of the window and scooted across the seat closer to Mary. "I guess you ain't got nothin' to say about what I said, huh? I got a strong likin' for you, Mary."

"And I got a husband." She took a last puff on her cigarette and tossed it out.

"I ain't sayin' leave your husband—"

"Good, cuz I'm not."

"I just wanna spend a li'l time with you. You come out to the club. Me and you take a ride somewhere. Maybe even show you my place. I got pictures of my grandkids up, and I can cook you a good meal too..."

Mary stared at his lips as he spoke. They looked full and ripe. Lush. Brown and smooth like his complexion. He probably rubbed Vaseline on his lips every day and never licked them. He was still talking when Mary leaned in. It wasn't a simple kiss. It was a thick, heavy, hungry, complicated kiss. It was not a soft kiss or a warm, moist kiss. It was the kind of kiss that Mary knew was sucking her soul from her body, but since she was going to hell anyway, she wrapped her arms around him and fed on the kiss, caressing the man's tongue with her own like the most delicious treat imaginable. Slim tasted just like he smelled: cigarettes, reefa, and whiskey.

IT HAD BEEN EASY TO take a Monday-morning walk over to the stores on Farish Street. It wasn't as far as she expected. Mary had walked maybe half a mile when Slim's car pulled up beside her.

"Hey, Miss Mary, need a ride?"

Mary looked around before approaching the car. The street was practically empty save for the delivery boy rushing into the grocer's, and she doubted anybody was looking at her anyway. She quickly climbed into the car and settled herself, folding her hands in her lap.

"Where you headed?" Slim asked. He flicked the ash from his cigar into the ashtray.

Mary looked at him, and the words came out before she knew she'd made the decision. "Your place," she said.

Slim coughed and smiled but didn't ask twice. Inside the empty club, Mary followed him up the narrow metal staircase in the back corner. She didn't know why, but she was in a hurry. Upon entering the small space, she quickly shed her coat and hat. "What's to drink?" she asked. She looked around the one-room apartment, guessing that the privacy screen hid his bed area.

"You know I got a li'l everything. What you want?" Slim stood with his back to the door, his arms folded.

"I think you already know what I want, Slim." Mary unbuckled her patent-leather belt and started unbuttoning her dress. "You gon' help me, or I gotta do this all by myself?"

The big man didn't hesitate. He crossed the room to Mary in a few steps, peeling off his jacket and suspenders. Mary's hands trembled as she tried to work on her buttons, but when Slim pushed her dress and slip back off her shoulders and down over her hips, she shimmied out of the expensive garments and pushed them away with her foot. When he lifted her into his arms, she wrapped her legs around him and pressed her lips to his, reveling in the familiar taste. And when he laid her down, there was no turning back.

Lying skin to skin with Slim felt as natural as breathing. And Mary didn't just lie back and give herself—she took from him with every part of herself. In Slim's bed, she touched and tasted and held on to him, taking the pleasure she had long been denied in her own bed. They matched panting breath for panting breath, hungry kiss for hungry kiss, frantic touch for frantic touch. Pressed under the weight of the powerful man, Mary felt alive for the first time in months.

MARY AWOKE ALONE IN bed to the smell of something cooking. In the chilly room, she pulled the quilt from the bed and wrapped it around herself. From the former warehouse office, Mary looked down on the club, watching the patrons trickle in: soldiers, students, and a few locals. The latest tune poured out of the jukebox, and the dance floor was filled with the wild gyrations of people dancing like they hadn't a care in the world. After America joined the war, the Tip Top Club, like everything else in Jackson, was all decked out in red, white, and blue. The few soldiers on active duty wore their uniforms, and the women were all extra fancy. The dancing was wild and free, and Mary thought it looked like an end-of-the-world party.

Slim came up behind her and slid his arms around her, resting his chin on the top of her head. "What you thinkin' 'bout, Mary?"

She wanted to kick herself... and Slim. She'd fallen asleep, and he hadn't woken her. "How I'm gon' get outta here?" she asked. "I'm not sneakin' out no back doors. Only whores sneak out the back door. You should'a woke me up." She enjoyed the feeling of his strong arms.

She felt protected and powerful at the same time. At home, her husband never touched her outside of bed... except when he was angry.

Slim chuckled. "Woman, I been wantin' you in my bed for months. I wasn't 'bout to kick you out. Besides, you real pretty when you sleep. We close at sunrise. I could take you home then. You be in bed before yo' old man wakes up."

Mary pulled away from him and walked over to the bedside table. She picked up Slim's cigarettes and lit one. She took a long drag and blew the smoke out in a thin stream. "Only whores let the sunrise catch 'em."

"Then we goin' out the back door. Soon as it get dark, I'll drive you home." Slim walked over to the small electric stove and stirred a simmering pot. "Now, come get some of this stew. I told you I could make you a good meal."

"LET ME TAKE YOU TO Chicago. See the bright lights and the live bands... all the fancy people in the fancy clubs..."

Mary looked at the big man propped up on his elbow lying beside her. "It's too cold right now. It don't get warm there 'til May." She took her index finger and traced the scar that went from the corner of his mouth to down under his chin and stopped just past his collarbone. "When you gon' tell me how you got this scar?" she asked. She liked Slim, and the scar intrigued her. She imagined he'd gotten it in a bar fight or something. She knew he wasn't much more than a run-of-the-mill, small-time hoodlum who dreamed of the high life like she used to.

"Mary, why you wanna hear my whole life story? Tha's all old stuff." Slim ran a calloused finger over her lips, down her chin, and down between her breasts. "It don't count no how."

"I see." Mary pushed his hand away, scooted over, and turned her back to him. "Must got somethin' to do with a woman. Hmph."

"Now why you think that?" Slim ran his hand over Mary's shoulder and down her arm. "Damn, you the finest woman in the world. How did I get so lucky?"

"Man, you done told me yo' whole life story already. I know all about yo' kids and grandkids. You talk about school and playin' in the creek. Hell, you told me so much about yo' mama, I'll probably know her if I see her on the street."

"Fine." Slim huffed. He laid on his back, and Mary turned to face him. "My wife did it."

"Yo' wife? The one in Chicago?"

"Yup. She took a razor to me when I was asleep... thought I had another woman."

"Did you?"

"Do it matter? Woman tried to take my head off. I had to fight her to get the razor."

"So, you tellin' me yo' wife tried to kill you cuz you had a woman... and you wanna take me to visit her?" Mary rolled over and reached for a cigarette and lighter.

"Chicago is a big city. Ain't like we gon' see her."

"Man, you crazy."

"Then let me take you to New York. You can show me around Harlem."

Mary rolled her eyes and took a deep drag on the cigarette. "You know I'm not leavin' my husband."

"You ain't gotta leave 'im right now. Just say you goin' to see yo' mama for a week—"

"I say that, and he'a wanna drive me."

"We can leave when he ain't home. Wait 'til he go to work. Leave a note—"

"Nope... he'a show up at my mama's house to get me on Sunday, then what?"

"Girl, I can see it now... walkin' up in them clubs in Harlem with you on my arm in one of them slinky red dresses with feathers, high-heel shoes, diamonds and pearls..."

"I said no." Mary exhaled slowly and put out her cigarette. She imagined she could have a good time with Slim in Harlem. The lights and clubs on Seventh Avenue would suit him just fine. But her heart hurt whenever she actually considered going back there. Mary refused to dream again. She and Mason had done that, and now Mason was dead. "Slim. I'm not goin' nowhere with you right now past this bed and this room."

Slim sat up on the side of the bed. He reached back and patted Mary's hip. "C'mon, let's get movin'. Gotta open up the club in a hour."

Mary stretched and sat up in the bed. She imagined life with Slim might be fun. Running a fancy club with him somewhere in Chicago. She wondered if he had a talent. Maybe he could be the MC. She'd bet he cleaned up nicely... probably looked good in a suit. Maybe one day, after her sisters got through college, after the old preacher died... she'd allow herself to dream again.

LUCIOUS GIBBONS WAS a local boy who made good, and when he rolled into Jackson in his big, shiny car with the whitewall tires, it set the whole town talking about him. Rumor was he had connections in Chicago, and most of the local gamblers and gamers gave him a wide berth. He wasn't big or tall, but his ego was, and Slim cautioned Mary to avoid him. "That boy think he somethin', always causin' trouble in here."

Sure enough, the first evening Mary saw him at the club, there was trouble. She and Lena sat at a corner table near the back, sipping their "Coca-Colas" and watching the young people cutting up on the dance floor. It was still early, the sun just setting, when Lucious Gibbons entered the club. With his processed hair and baggy, oversized suit, he looked out of place among the soldiers and students. He and his companion walked over to a table near the dance floor and tipped two young men out of their chairs. The boys jumped to their feet, ready to fight, but Slim placed his great bulk between them.

"Don't want no trouble in here now, Lucious." Slim kept his voice even, but the dancing had stopped, and most of the room could hear him.

"My apologies." Lucious laughed and looked around the room. "I didn't think this table was taken."

One of the students made ready to speak, but Slim held up a hand, cutting him off. "Y'all boys meet me at the bar," he said to the two young men. The young men walked away, and Slim stood looking down at Lucious. "We don't have no trouble in here. Got a good thing goin'. Ain't lettin' nobody mess it up. Understand?"

Lucious smiled and motioned for his friend to sit down at the table. "Easy, big fella." He reached up and brushed invisible dust from Slim's shoulder. "I'm just here for a good time." He pulled a chair from a nearby abandoned table and sat down. "When does the show start?"

"Only shows on Friday and Saturday." Slim leaned down and placed his hands on the table. "Not playin' with you, boy. You don't impress me one damn bit."

Lucious stopped smiling as Slim walked away.

Mary sat at her table, watching the scene. She'd known men like Lucious in Harlem. They liked to cause trouble, making a fuss, grabbin' at the women, and fightin' the bouncers. "Lena, we need to go," she said, crushing out her cigarette and quickly downing her drink. "That man ain't nothin' but trouble, and I can't be caught up in no mess—"

The sound of breaking glass drew their attention again to the troublemakers. A young college girl struggled to free herself from

Lucious's lap, and her boyfriend stood trembling while the other man held a razor to his throat.

"Aw, baby girl, quit actin' a fool. All I want is just a little kiss."

"Lucious!" Slim's voice was heard over the music, and all action stopped. "Let that girl alone." He moved through the sparse crowd and towered over the seated man. "It's time for you to go."

Lucious pushed the girl from his lap, and she landed in a sobbing heap on the floor. "Aw, she all right. I was just havin' a li'l fun."

Mary stood up from her table and pulled at Lena's arm. She'd seen too many club fights, and the last thing she needed was to have to explain how she got caught in a bar fight when she was supposed to be visiting shut-ins. "C'mon, Lena—"

The fight did happen, but it was quick. Slim easily disarmed and disabled the friend then flipped the table over and pinned a stunned Lucious under it with his foot. "I said it's time for you to go. Don't make me hafta help you to the door."

Patrons seated near the commotion looked on and laughed, and a few people cheered for Slim as he lifted the table off Lucious and grabbed the front of the prone man's fancy jacket. It seemed nobody recognized the loud *bang* until Slim froze and then toppled over. Then all hell broke loose.

With people running and screaming, Mary let go of Lena and watched the friend slide a smoking gun into a holster under his coat. The man then pulled a screaming Lucious from under Slim's bleeding body, and they joined the crowd fleeing the club. With people pushing out the back and front doors and Lena pulling on her arm, Mary moved toward Slim.

"Mary! We gotta get outta here!"

Mary kept moving toward Slim. Big, strong Slim... powerful Slim... shot Slim... fallen Slim... She knelt beside him, bloodying her skirt.

"C'mon, girl," Lena coaxed, pulling up on Mary's arm. "Ain't nothing to do for him."

Mary looked down at his fluttering eyes and reached for his hand. He was warm, and his finger twitched as his still-beating heart pumped his blood out onto the concrete floor.

"Mary, we get caught in here, that old preacher gon' skin you alive!"

Mary couldn't move. She barely heard Lena. And when a pair of strong arms lifted her around the waist, she let Slim's hand slip from her fingers as a young man carried her out to Lena's car. Slim should've been her ticket back to the good life. After her sisters got to college... maybe if the old preacher died soon, she and Slim would pack up and go... Chicago, New York, anywhere... anywhere... anywhere...

Chapter 15

Mary would never have said she loved Slim, but she did quietly mourn him. When the Tip Top Club reopened a month later *under new management*, Mary shared a flask with Lena, and in the parking lot, she had a smoke for Slim. Lucious Gibbons and his friend had managed to get out of Jackson without being caught.

When she felt the familiar flutter in her belly, it was bittersweet. She imagined a son, a scrawny little boy growing to a giant of a man. And she ignored the questioning looks and the whispered gossip, and Bevers thanked God and celebrated the miracle. And Mary swore to the God she no longer believed in that if she had a healthy baby, she would worship and sing his praises and be the perfect preacher's wife... but Mary knew without a doubt that the baby she carried was not her husband's and that she would take the secret to her grave.

"Mary, talk say you was out there with that man was killed in the club." Will Bevers lay in bed beside his wife. "Folks sayin' I'm too old."

Mary stared into the darkness and pulled the quilt up to her neck. "You got yo' miracle. What else you want?"

"I want the truth. Ain't gon' beat you. I might want to, but I'm too tired."

Mary rolled onto her side and looked at the old man. "Why you cain't just be happy? Baby is coming. God answered yo' prayers."

"I just think it's mighty funny that 'God' answered my prayers after you and Lena been sneakin' off to that club when you s'posed to be doin' the Lord's work."

If he had been looking at her, he'd have seen Mary's eyes go wide. Mary sighed. "Yeah, we went there sometimes—"

"A lotta times from what I hear."

"Well, how I'm gon' be foolin' around inside the club with Lena and a whole lotta other people watchin'?"

The mattress squeaked as Bevers shifted in the bed. He moved his hand under the covers and placed it against Mary's belly. "I know one thing," he said. "If it ain't mine, God ain't gon' let you deceive me for too long. God punishes sinners and liars."

Mary placed her hand over her husband's. "It's gon' be a scrawny little boy that's gon' grow up to be a big, strong man. You'll see."

MARY GUESSED SHE WAS four or five months gone when the cramps started. She cried and prayed, and Bevers drove her fifty miles to the colored hospital in Yazoo City, but the doctor said there was nothing to be done.

On the long drive home, Mary couldn't enjoy the late-spring sunrise. She was touched by memories of Monday-morning rides taken with Slim, and she wished for a cigarette. She rolled down the window and let her hand surf on the wind.

"Woman, I told you God wasn't gon' let you deceive me."

Mary looked over at her husband. A single tear rolled down his cheek.

"Now you hurtin' and bleedin' cuz you a liar and a whore."

"You wrong, Will." Mary hung her head. "Doctor said these things happen. Sometimes, it's somethin' wrong with the baby—"

"Yeah, somethin' wrong, all right. You think I'm just a old fool. Well, I ain't! Ya hear me?" He pounded the steering wheel as the car picked up speed.

Mary held on to the door handle. "Will, maybe God saw fit—"

"God will not be mocked! Don't you dare talk to me 'bout God!" Tires squealed as the car took a sharp curve.

"Will, please! What good is killin' us? Slow down!"

Bevers slowed down and pulled the car over, and Mary watched the old man cry. She reached out and laid her hand over his. He pushed her away. "Don't touch me," he whispered.

Mary didn't know what she felt. She didn't love him or even like him. She didn't really care about him at all, but her heart ached at the pain she'd caused him.

"Listen, Mary." Will spoke so quietly that Mary had to strain to hear him. "We both know God took that baby cuz he knew you was wrong, and we both know God ain't got no miracles for me. If you ever get that way again, try to trick me again... me and God gon' know you did wrong, and I'mma beat it outta you then put you out. Understand?"

And just like that, Mary believed in God again and in the thoroughness of God's wrath.

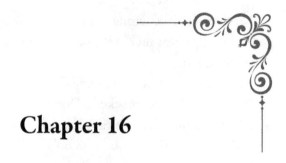

Chapter 16

Mary blew out a puff of smoke and looked across the kitchen table at her younger sister. Seventeen-year-old Ruthie sat with her arms crossed, angry, defiant. Her hand-me-down white dress was trimmed in lace, her hair braided with flowers.

"I'm not going back there!"

"That's your husband." Mary took a long drag and blew it out. "You'll get used to it."

"I'm not finna get used to nothin'. You don't know what he wanted me to do. I kicked him in the—"

Mary nearly dropped her cigarette. "Tell me you didn't do that. He gon' sho' beat you half to death."

"Nope, he ain't." Ruthie reached for Mary's cigarette pack. "I told him I'a cut 'im into a woman when he went to sleep." She tapped the cigarette on the table and lit it with Mary's lighter. She took a puff and coughed. Her face contorted into an ugly grimace, but she took another puff.

Mary watched her sister trying to be grown-up and almost laughed. Their six-year age difference felt like eons, and she wanted to slap the cigarette from her little sister's hand. "Girl, you gon' waste my cigarette and make yourself sick. Smokin' don't make you grown." She took a long drag on her own cigarette and then blew smoke rings.

"He told me to get out and not come back. I can stay here, right?"

Mary knew the question was coming, and she'd promised her sister she'd always have a place for her, but now wasn't a good time. "It ain't right to leave yo' husband like that. A good woman works it out. You stay and learn what he likes." She took another deep drag on her cigarette and kept talking with smoke pouring out of her mouth. "You know how you supposed to do. Why you cain't do right... always so willful..."

"Well, looks like you kinda willful too." Ruth nodded toward Mary.

Too prideful to be ashamed or even blush, Mary waved off her sister's dig. Her black eye wasn't that bad. The old preacher had beaten her a lot worse for a lot less. "My willfulness ain't what we talkin' 'bout right now. What's Papa gon' say he find out what you did?"

"Papa ain't gon' say a damn thing." Ruth took another short puff of the cigarette. She didn't cough this time. "Wha's he gon' do? Drive his tractor all the way from Flora to get me with a switch?"

Mary stood up from the table and went to the stove for more coffee. "Well, I'll talk to the old man about you stayin' here, but then what you gon' do?"

"Didn't you marry him so I could go to college?" Ruth held out her cup for a refill.

"Hmph... He told me I couldn't go to college since I didn't finish school."

"Well, I finished school; I'm ready for college."

"We'll see what he says, but I wouldn't get no hopes up."

That evening, at the dinner table, Will Bevers quizzed his young sister-in-law on her plans and readiness for the rigors of academia, and much to Mary's surprise, her sister showed perfect manners in answering his questions.

"Yes, sir, I am ready. I got perfect marks in all my subjects." Ruthie sat up straight and looked Bevers in the eye when she spoke. She'd changed out of her wedding clothes and had squeezed herself into one of Mary's dresses. The pearl buttons were pulled tight, and Mary hoped they wouldn't pop off.

"Well, college classes ain't like them little classes you took out in the sticks."

"I know. That's why I studied from college books, and my teacher got me some books from the white school. Even if I don't know everything, I can learn fast."

"Okay, fine." Bevers pushed his plate toward his wife. "Mary, put me some more greens and cornbread on here." He looked at Ruthie. "What you good at? Can you cook like yo' sister?"

Mary got up from the table and took her husband's plate to the kitchen. She wasn't sure how she felt about Ruthie going to the college. Of course, she was happy her sister had the chance, but what good would it do? Now that Ruthie was married, did she even need to go to college? Back in the dining room, she placed her husband's plate on the table.

"So, what about yo' husband?" Bevers asked as he dug into his plate. "He got some say. Maybe he don't want you there around all them young men."

Mary and Ruthie exchanged glances. "He tore up the paper and put me out," Ruthie said. "And I don't want him no how. I only married him so I could get here to Jackson."

Mary kicked her sister under the table.

"Mary, you supposed to kick her *before* she say something stupid." Bevers laughed. "Ain't nothin' wrong with tellin' the truth. If all you wanted was a ride, though, we would'a came and got you."

"I didn't mean it like that," Ruth said. "I thought I wanted to get married, but I don't. I just wanna go to college and maybe be a teacher and see the world."

"See the world, huh?" Bevers scooped collard greens into his mouth. "That's mighty ambitious. But you stubborn as hell. I'a be surprised if you don't actually do it."

Ruthie smiled. "So I can stay here and go to college, right?"

Mary sat listening to the exchange, knowing that Bevers had to say "yes." After all, that was the reason she married him. That was the reason she rarely fought him back now. And that was the reason she kept her bargain with God. She would be the good wife and secure her sisters' futures, and after the old preacher died, God would restore to her all that she had lost.

SINCE THEY WERE NO longer trying to conceive, Bevers was far less patient and quicker to strike Mary for any perceived disrespect. Sometimes, she fought back, but he always reminded her of what she had to lose. The hardest thing for Mary, though, was keeping her fights with Bevers quiet lest Ruthie hear and come running. It wasn't like they fought every day, and when they did fight, Mary never cried. She considered the beatings part of her continued penance... for current and probably future sins.

"Woman, why you always gotta act up?" Mary tried to duck out of the way of Bevers's aim and backed herself into a far corner of their bedroom. The slap landed on her ear, knocking the Sunday hat from her head. When she straightened up, before she could shield herself, a blow landed against her left cheek. "Bible say women s'posed to be quiet in church, and you all'a time be runnin' yo' mouth." Another blow, this time a backhand to the right side of her face.

Mary knew there would be swelling and probably a black eye. She quietly sank to the floor, making herself as small as possible, shielding herself with her arms. Though sometimes a grunt or groan escaped, she remained curled in a ball in the corner, not talking back... not crying out... silent.

And Bevers, it seemed, took his time carefully aiming, slapping and punching his wife until he grew tired.

But Mary didn't cower in that corner. There was no fear in her, only resignation. She stayed crouched in the fetal position, protecting her face, whispering prayers for the old preacher's death, and she endured. She'd suffered a lot worse, and if an occasional beating was the cost of providing for her family and returning to the life she missed... so be it.

AT FIRST, MARY HAD worried about having her stubborn, bossy sister in the house, but Ruthie mostly kept to herself and concentrated on school. When her husband came to visit and tried to talk her into coming home with him, Ruthie threatened to kick him again. In church, she ignored the attention of all the young men, and when Joshua Floyd was home on leave from the navy, he tried making friends with her, but Ruthie wanted no part of anything social. "Ain't got time for friends," she'd said.

Mary initially blew off her sister's concerns and told her not to worry about *married folks' business*. She covered her bruises and explained away bumps and falls, but soon, she noticed her sister being a little more protective and a lot angrier.

"Mary, Papa never fights Mama." Ruthie stirred cornbread batter and poured it into the greased skillet.

"You don't know that," Mary said.

"You ever seen Mama with a black eye?" Ruthie asked. "No. Not one time... ever." Ruthie placed the heavy skillet in the oven. Even though it was late September, the heat was still oppressive.

"Well, ain't no way to know—"

"I know 'married folks' business' don't mean fighting all the time. And you don't even fight back. I hear him fussin' and swingin', and you don't make a sound—"

"Ruthie, hush." Mary stood at the sink, washing dishes. "You don't know nothin' 'bout being married. Bible say—"

"What Bible say you gotta take a whoopin? I know mine don't."

Mary shook her head, dropping a bit of cigarette ash into the dishwater. "Ruthie, I'm fine. I be sassin' him sometimes on purpose... rude... disrespectful—"

"Then he can be rude right back. Ain't no man ever hit me—"

"Ain't no man ever touched you at all, little girl." Mary laughed at her sister's bravado.

"Well, you know what?" Ruthie folded her arms and turned to face her sister.

"What?" Mary grabbed the cornbread-batter bowl and rinsed it before putting it into the dish water.

"Next time I hear him fighting you, I'm gon' kick his ass."

"I don't know, Ruthie." Mary laughed. "He might be old, but that old man is strong. He might whoop us both."

"YOU BEEN BACK AT THAT club!" Bevers slammed the front door, placed his hat on the hat rack, and followed his wife through the front room and into the dining room.

"No... I ain't been there since the last time I told you I went." Mary moved around the dining table, out of her husband's reach. She wasn't particularly afraid of him, but she was tired. She didn't feel like fighting or being his punching bag this afternoon.

"Mother Berry say she ain't seen you." Bevers stomped around the table after his wife. "And Miss Luella said you left her house after fifteen minutes." He reached for Mary's arm, but she snatched away.

"Mother Berry cain't remember her own name half the time." Mary stepped out of his way again. "And Miss Luella's house smell like a tomcat! Cain't nobody stay in there more than fifteen minutes!"

"Woman, what I tell you? Don't you lie to me!" He reached out and caught Mary by her hair. Mary closed her eyes and raised her arms to shield her face from the inevitable blow.

"You let her alone!"

Bevers let go of Mary's hair, and she opened her eyes to see her husband, arms flailing, staggering under the weight of Ruthie on his back with her arm around his neck.

"You son of a bitch! Don't you hit my sister no more!"

Bevers struggled to pry Ruthie's arm from around his neck while she twisted and turned, biting into his shoulder, and wrestling him to the floor in the kitchen doorway.

"Ruthie, stop!" Mary tried to pull her sister off the old man, but once he was down, Ruthie sat on his back, punching and pounding him. "Ruthie, please! I'm okay!" Mary pushed against her sister to no avail.

Ruthie clawed at his ears and pummeled the side of his face. "I told you I was gon' kick... his... ass!" She caught his arm and twisted it around his back, stopping only when Mary threw a vase of water in her face.

"God, Ruthie, stop!"

Ruthie stood up and kicked the old man a few times until Mary placed herself between her sister and her husband. "And every time you swing at my sister, I'mma kick yo' ass again!" Ruthie kicked him in the shoulder.

Bevers struggled to get to his knees. "Get out of my house." He panted and groaned. "Get the hell outta my house right now!"

"Fine with us!" Ruthie kicked him again, and he collapsed to the floor. "C'mon, Mary. Let's go."

"Ha! She ain't goin' nowhere." Bevers got to his knees again and stood up, his nose and mouth bloodied. "Mary stayin' right here. Ain't that right?"

"No, she ain't! We both finna get the hell outta here, right, Mary?"

Mary looked from her angry sister to her beaten-up husband and back again. Bevers used a handkerchief to wipe his bloody face, and Ruthie looked as triumphant as Jack Johnson after a title fight.

"Nah, Mary ain't goin' nowhere," the old man said. "She ain't leavin', and she know it." Bevers smiled a little. "But she can if she want to." He looked Mary in the eye. "I ain't stoppin' her." He walked into the bathroom and slammed the door behind him.

"C'mon, Mary. Let's get packed. We can be outta here lickety-split." Ruthie placed a hand on Mary's shoulder, pushing her toward her bedroom.

Mary ran her hands through her hair as she turned away from her sister. She didn't know how she felt. Seeing her sister fighting Bevers, she had been scared for Ruthie—scared the old man would get loose and hurt her little sister. Then she was scared Ruthie might accidentally kill him... give him a heart attack or something. But now, after the heated moment had passed, Mary was again faced with a devil's dilemma.

Of course, she couldn't leave with Ruthie. She didn't want to go back to Flora, and what about Martha and Ellie... and Papa? But there was no way she could talk Bevers into letting Ruthie stay now. Where could the girl go alone? Back to her husband, maybe? Mary walked around the dining room, tuning out her sister's urgings for her to leave.

Bevers came out of the bathroom and paused. "Y'all still here?" he asked. "I told you to get out. You got ten minutes to get outta my house 'fore I start tossin' you and yo' stuff out —"

"I been ready to go since I got here," Ruthie shot back. "And I ain't scared of you!"

"We can go another round if you feel like it." Bevers stood facing his sister-in-law. "You ain't gon' catch me by surprise this time. I'll whoop you like a man."

"Yeah, you might," Ruthie said. "But you ain't gon' hit my sister no more—"

"Y'all stop!" Mary placed herself between them, facing her husband. "Will, please—"

"Woman, you crazy. Don't even ask." He looked at his pocket watch. "She got nine minutes to get out." He turned and headed to their bedroom. "And you got a lotta stuff to pack if you goin' with her."

"Mary, you go get packed," Ruthie said. "My stuff ain't never been unpacked. It'a only take me a minute."

Mary didn't move when Ruthie rushed past her and headed to her own room. Then she went into the kitchen, opened a window, and lit a cigarette. The weather was warm for December. The cool breeze blew into the kitchen, and Mary closed one eye as the smoke rose in her face. There hadn't been a real frost yet, so there were still collard greens in the garden. A bright-red bird landed on a bush. Mary watched it until it flew away.

"You not comin' with me, are you?"

"No, Ruthie, I'm not." Mary inhaled deeply and breathed the smoke out slowly. She didn't turn to face her sister.

"Why, Mary?" Ruthie pleaded.

"Ruthie, Mama told me to be good to myself. That don't mean do what's fun or easy. It mean do what's gon' feel right in the future. Do what you ain't gon' regret one day. If I leave my husband, the whole family loses—"

"Bullshit, Mary! We can go up north and get jobs and take care of everybody. I'll even get two jobs—"

"No you won't. You gon' go back to Flora and—"

"Mary, I'm not goin' back to Flora. I'm goin' to the bus station, and I'm goin' to Chicago."

"It's too cold there right now." Mary finished her cigarette and lit another one. "That winter wind gon' freeze yo' bones."

"Then I'll get two coats and a scarf, but I'm goin'."

Mary smoked quietly for a minute and then sighed. "I know you goin', Ruthie. And you gon' see the bright lights and the big city, and then you gon' see the world." Mary took a deep drag and blew out a thin stream of smoke. "I know you gon' do all that. An I'm gon' come visit you, and we gon' have a li'l fun for a while."

"Mary, please... That man is gon' hurt you real bad one day."

"It won't be too bad," Mary said. "I know how I'm s'posed to act. I just don't care sometimes." Her hand trembled a little as she smoked her cigarette. She still couldn't face her sister. "You better get goin'. The bus to Flora leaves around three. I don't know when the Chicago bus run."

Ruthie put down her suitcase and went to her sister. She wrapped her arms around Mary's waist and laid her head against her back. "Mary... I'm gon' go get me a place, and when you get tired of this mess..."

"Yeah, I'mma come stay with you... just like I said I would." She laid a hand over Ruthie's. "You write me a lotta letters and postcards, okay?"

"I will, Mary."

"And you watch out for those fancy men tryin' to get you in trouble... women, too, okay?"

"I will." Ruthie let go of her sister and picked up her suitcase. She headed out of the kitchen.

Mary put out her cigarette and followed Ruthie through the dining room to the front door. "You need money? I got about—"

"Nah, I got plenty money saved up."

At the front door, Mary hugged her little sister. "Ruthie, please be careful. I know you wanna see the world, but it's bad things and bad people..."

"And I'm smart, and I know how to stay outta trouble. Maybe I'll find the college in Chicago and go there."

"I know you will." Mary squeezed tighter. "Bye, little sister... be careful."

"Bye, big sister. You be careful too."

Mary closed the door behind her sister and stood with her ear against the door, listening to Ruthie walk across the porch and down the steps. She thought she could hear her walking down the path to the sidewalk, and she listened until there was nothing but silence.

"I knew you was gon' make the right choice, *Miss Mary*."

"Leave me alone." Mary leaned her forehead against the door. She knew she should be crying, but she found she had no actual sadness. She was envious of her sister's freedom. Freedom she herself had just turned down. When she heard her husband come up behind her, she braced herself. He was probably going to say she had sassed him, but he laid a hand gently on her shoulder.

"That girl gon' be just fine," he said. "She tough like a man."

After Bevers walked away, Mary stood up straight. She brushed her hair back with her fingers and headed to the kitchen to see what Mamie had left for Sunday dinner.

Chapter 17
March 1945

Mary looked out into the backyard, listening as her husband left for work, the front screen door slamming behind him. She poured herself a cup of coffee and took it through the house out to the front porch. She knew her neighbors but mostly kept to herself, reading letters from Ruthie and having her coffee and cigarette on the porch swing on the days she was home alone. Sometimes, when a person walked by, Mary would take a long sip of coffee so she wouldn't look like she was staring. The lady across the way, Sylvia Mabry, spent a lot of time with the grocery boy when her husband wasn't home. Loreen, the maid down the way at the Watsons', was a terrible gossip, and she listened in on people's phone calls. Hazel Thomas, the snooty ol' biddy, was a dean's wife and made sure everybody knew it. All in all, the neighborhood and its people bored Mary.

Watching the few cars go by, Mary took a sip of her coffee and a puff of her cigarette and counted the people out and about just beginning their day. Right on time, the boy from the grocery store came down the street, heading to the Mabrys'. A couple of girls rushed by, heading toward the college, and an old man with a cowboy hat and a satchel ambled slowly up the street. At first, Mary paid no attention to the young man walking by, but by the third time he passed, she noticed he carried a notepad and had an instrument case strapped to his back. He was scribbling intently while he walked. When she went inside to refill her coffee, she came back out, and he was passing by yet again. As she returned to her seat on the swing, the young man slowed down at her gate.

"Hey!" Mary called out to him. "You been roundin' this block all mornin'. You lost?"

The young man looked up from his notepad. Mary thought he looked scared, like he was about to change his mind and run away. His brown pants were too short but bunched up at the waist, like they were made for somebody bigger and shorter. His white shirt was wrinkled and curled at the collar. He had a box of colored pencils showing in his shirt pocket.

"Uh, no... no, ma'am," he stuttered. "I... I... g... got something for you." He tore off a sheet from his notepad and held it out to Mary.

She placed her coffee cup on the seat beside her and carefully steadied the swing as she stood up. Coming down the stairs, she saw the young man had a nice smile. She took the paper from him. "Well, this is nice." She looked at the perfect pencil drawing of the purple flowers growing in her front yard. With fine details and soft colors, it looked almost like a painting.

"I... I wanted to bring you flowers, but I didn't think it was a good idea to take 'em from your yard."

Mary held the drawing out at a distance. "You a good artist. What's your name, artist?"

"H... h... hi. I'm John Dixon." He offered his hand, but Mary didn't shake it.

"You go to the college, John Dixon?"

"Yes, ma'am."

"Strong young man like you, why you not off fightin' in the war?" Mary looked at the drawing again.

"I... I g... got a short leg." John Dixon shrugged. "They wouldn't take me. My brothers went, though."

Mary watched his shoulder rise and fall as he shifted from one foot to the other. "That's too bad." She put the drawing into her apron pocket and fished out a cigarette. She looked at him some more. He had deep hooded eyes, so dark you couldn't see his pupils, and his nose was a little too wide and a little too thick, with a pox scar on the end. His lips, a shade darker than his deep brown complexion, looked like he licked them a little too much. "John Dixon, gon' down the block a bit and then come 'round back and have a glass of lemonade with me." She lit her cigarette and motioned toward the end of the block.

He smiled, showing all his teeth. "Th... th... that would be real nice."

Mamie was off on Mondays, so Mary had the house to herself. In the kitchen, she poured two glasses of lemonade and stepped out onto the small back porch. It was more like an extra-wide step than a porch, and John Dixon stood waiting with his arms folded, looking at the basil that grew by the back door. She'd invited him to come around to the back because it wouldn't look good to have the young visitor looking like he was courting her on the front porch. There was enough gossip in the neighborhood as it was.

John took the glass that Mary offered, then he took her hand to guide her down the three steps to the dusty ground. Mary took a seat on the top step and patted the step beside her. John sat on the second step, his shoulder brushing against her leg.

"So, John Dixon." Mary took a sip of her lemonade. "Why you bring me those pretty flowers?" She looked him in the eye until he looked away.

"Um... um... I see you got a lotta p... p... purple flowers." He took a deep breath and closed his eyes. "I thought you might like 'em," he said slowly. "I thought you might like purple flowers."

"Yeah, I love purple. Where you from, John Dixon?" Mary drained her glass and set it on the step beside her. She felt around in her apron for another cigarette.

"Natchez."

Mary noticed he didn't stutter when he tried to speak slowly. She imagined he'd be hard to understand if he got excited. "You got a girl in Natchez?"

"No, ma'am," he said. "They only want soldiers."

"Not me." Mary looked at the young man, who was probably just the right age for her sister Ruthie. "I think the soldiers are good and all, but I wouldn't want my man to come home shell-shocked without his arms or legs. Count yourself lucky. How old are you?"

"I'm twenty. Um... ma'am...?"

"Yes?" She reached into her apron pocket and found her lighter. She offered a cigarette to him, but he declined.

"No, thank you. Um, ma'am..." He set down his empty glass. "...um... What's your name?"

"Ha-ha." Mary laughed a little. "I guess I didn't introduce myself. John Dixon, I'm Mary Bevers. Tell me about that horn on yo' back. What you play?"

"It's a trumpet, but I play piano too."

"You any good?"

"Y... y... yeah. I'm pretty good." He sat up a little taller. "I play at the Crystal Palace on Friday and Saturday."

"I knew a trumpet player once. He played in clubs all over. Got caught up in devilment and died." Mary looked at the young man some more. Wide shoulders, broad chest, and the wrinkles on his shirt were sharp creases, like he'd tried to iron it himself. So he really *didn't* have a girlfriend.

"Oh, that's sad," John said. "You related to Professor Bevers, right?"

"Yep." Mary took a long drag on her cigarette. "He's my husband."

John's eyes went wide. He jumped up from his seat, nearly knocking Mary over. "I... I... I'm sorry, ma'am. I... I... thought he was your d... daddy." He backed away from the porch as Mary stood up. "I... I... d... didn't mean no d... d... disrespect—"

"Boy, calm down."

"I'll be goin' now, Mrs. Dixon... I mean Mrs. Bevers." He slapped himself on the forehead. "Thank you for the lemonade. You can tear the flowers up—"

Mary raised a hand, silencing him. "I'm keeping my flowers, and you gon' come back and bring me some more next Monday at ten."

"I... I... I don't know, Mrs. Bevers." John ran a hand over his hair. "The professor is tough. He could have me kicked outta school if he saw me around you—"

Mary silenced him again with a finger. "Next Monday at ten. We gon' have coffee and sweet rolls." Mary picked up the glasses and turned to the back screen door. "Get the door for me."

John maneuvered himself around Mary on the wide top step, barely touching her waist when he reached for the door handle. He opened the door, and Mary stepped through, brushing his hand with her hip.

Setting the glasses on the nearest counter, she turned to face him. "When you come next Monday, just come to this door. Don't wanna start gossip."

"B... b... but M... M... Mrs. Bevers..."

"Aw, come on, John. I'm bored in this house. Ain't you like sittin' with me?"

"Y... y... yes, ma'am... But—"

"I'm married to a grumpy old preacher, and I need to talk to a fine young man sometimes." Mary looked into his eyes through the screen. "So you come see me, right?"

John ran his hand over his hair again and sighed. "Yes, ma'am. I'll see you next Monday." He turned to leave.

"Oh, John Dixon!"

He turned back to her.

"Don't call me Mrs. Bevers. My name is Mary."

THE FOLLOWING MONDAY, Mary watched with supreme annoyance as her husband reached for a third sweet roll. She had set the dough in the icebox overnight, and she'd gotten up extra early to cut it up and let it rise. The hot rolls had been ready at nine, and at nine-forty, Will Bevers was getting a third roll from the pan.

"*Miss Mary*, this is the best sweet roll I eva had."

Mary smoothed her apron and watched the clock. "Ain't you gon' be late?"

"I s'pose I am," the old preacher said. "But these rolls won't let me go." He took a bite. "I just don't know how you do it."

Mary picked up his lunch pail and held it out to him. "I'll save you some for later. Want me to bring 'em to your office?"

"Naw." He took his lunch pail from her and headed out of the kitchen. After pausing to brush his mustache and grab his hat, he got as far as the front door and turned back. "Where's my satchel?" He stalked back through the house, heading for his office.

Mary stood watching from the kitchen doorway, praying John Dixon wouldn't be early. Bevers emerged from his office with his satchel and headed out of the house without a word.

"Yeah, you have a good day too," Mary said to the closing door. She went out to the front porch and watched her husband head down the street toward the college. She wondered again if that mean old man was truly supposed to be her blessing. After four years of marriage, she didn't feel blessed at all.

The knock at the back door came at exactly ten. Mary put out her cigarette and went to answer. "Hello, John Dixon. You right on time." She pushed the door open and held it for him. "Come on in."

"Um... um... Miss M... Mary..." He stepped back from the door and shoved his hands into his pockets. "I th... th... think we... we... we should sit outside."

Mary laughed a little. The poor boy looked terrified. "Well, okay. You sit down on the step. I'mma get a tray." She tried to keep the amusement out of her voice. "Did you bring me more flowers?"

"Y... y... yes, ma'am." He nodded, pulling his notepad from his shirt pocket.

"Good." Mary quickly gathered two sweet rolls and two cups of coffee on a tray. She used her hip to open the door, and John Dixon stood up from his seat on the step.

"Lemme get that for you." He took the tray from her hands, their fingers briefly touching. His hand shook a little.

Mary sat on the top step and accepted the tray onto her lap. "Don't sit way down there. Sit here by me." She patted the step beside her, and the young man sat down as close to the opposite side of the porch as he could get. Mary handed him a cup of coffee. He reached for it with trembling hands. She pulled the cup back and set it on the step between them and then took his hands in hers. They were rough, and his nails were dirty, the hands of a hard worker. He tried to pull away, but Mary held tighter. The night before, under her husband's uninterested touch, Mary had wondered if the young man's hands would feel different.

"Boy, you brought me flowers and had lemonade with me. What you scared of?"

"I'm scared of your husband, Miss Mary. I can get kicked outta school. And... and..."

"But you like me, or you wouldn'a came today." She let go of his hands. "Lemme see my flowers." He passed her his notepad. The small page was covered with perfect purple roses. Mary stared at the picture then looked at the artist. "These real pretty, John."

"Th... th... thank you. I... I... like you just fine. But Professor Bevers is... is..."

"A mean ol' cuss, ain't he?" Mary laughed. "Tha's why I need some company." She scooted closer, placed a hand on his knee, and squeezed. "He ain't gotta know. We just gon' be two friends havin' coffee and sweet rolls." She scooted even closer and nudged him with her elbow. "Tell me about Natchez. What you leave back home?"

Mary sipped her coffee and listened to John Dixon talk about his life and family in Natchez. He had two married sisters and four brothers all in the service. One overseas, two in Gulfport, and one up north in the navy. His parents were sharecroppers but did okay for themselves. All of his siblings sent him money for school, and he told of being the great hope of his family... He would finish school and go north with his college degree and bring his family with him.

"So, where you goin' up north?" Mary asked. "I lived in Chicago and New York."

"Really? Y... y... you don't sound like a big-city girl. Why you come here?"

"Big-city life is hard." Mary put down her coffee cup and dug a cigarette out of her apron pocket. "It got too hard on me, and I came home. But I'm ready to go back, though. I miss the bright lights and the music." She lit the cigarette and took a long drag.

"I... I... I'm goin' to Chicago. Maybe play in a club or something. I hear you can play on the streets, and people just give you money." John Dixon passed Mary his empty cup. "I should go now." He stood up and took a deep breath. "I like talking to you, Mary."

"Good." Mary held her hand out, and he helped her to her feet. "Then I'll see you next Monday and the Monday after that."

"Yes, ma'am, you will." He smiled at Mary.

She reached for his hand again. "Your hands are so rough." She touched the pads on his fingers. "Strong... manly." She laid her palm over his. "You got fine hands, John Dixon. You go on now. I'll see you next week."

The young man turned and headed for the back gate. Mary watched his retreat... He moved not at all like the shy boy who trembled when she touched him. His slightly lopsided gait made his shoulders sway when he walked. She waved when he looked back at her. When he bumped into the gate, she laughed and went into the house.

Mary turned on the radio on the kitchen table, caught the ending of a soap opera, and turned off the beginning of the news report. The war was going well, but Mary paid it no mind. The president said the Allies were winning, and Mary had no one she cared about in the fighting. She imagined Mason might have gotten drafted, had he lived... but she doubted he would've gone. Did the army even take dope addicts? She turned the dial until she found a song... a slow blues. She slow-danced herself around the kitchen with the broom and promised herself a slow dance with John Dixon on his next visit. She'd insist that he come in, and she'd get to feel his strong young arms...

THE NEXT WEEK BROUGHT rain, and Mary waited in the kitchen, but John Dixon didn't visit. The Monday after that, however, the young man appeared at the back door with real flowers. He stepped back when she opened the door.

"I... I... I'm sorry, Miss Mary. I didn't th... th... think you wanted to sit out in the rain last week."

"Well, it looks like rain today, so you hafta come in and sit here in the kitchen." Mary held the door for him, and John Dixon didn't move. "Come on, boy. Don't be like that. We just two friends having coffee." She watched the boy's uncertainty for a full minute, then she reached out and took his hand. "I promise it'll be only for a while. Just one cup of coffee, okay?"

He sighed, one shoulder drooping lower than the other. "M... M... Miss Mary..." He looked her in the eye. "Y... You gon' get us both in tr... tr... trouble."

She pulled his hand, and he hesitated for another moment, but then he followed her into the kitchen. "Sit down over there." She pointed at a chair by the icebox, placed a hand on his arm, and squeezed. His muscles were tense... solid. While Mary served the coffee, he sat on the edge of the chair with his hands on his knees. "I bet you was a good little boy," Mary said. "Sittin' up so straight." She placed a cup of coffee in front of him and another in front of the chair beside him. "So, tell me some more about college. You got a girlfriend there?"

"Um... naw... I'm not a soldier."

"But you a fine, strong man. I know somebody lookin' at you."

"W... w... well if it i... i... is, she ain't talkin'."

Mary and John spent nearly an hour talking about school and radio stories and music. She turned the radio dial whenever a commercial came on, and they laughed at Abbot and Costello's *Who's on First*, and when a Tommy Dorsey and Frank Sinatra song came on, Mary stood up and took John Dixon's hand.

"You gotta dance with me. Just for a minute."

"I cain't dance, Miss Mary," he said. "I'm all lopsided." He resisted, but she pulled harder.

"Come on." Mary stepped close to him and placed his hand on her waist. "It's easy." She looked in his eyes and blinked slowly. "C'mon, John."

John stood up from his seat. "I should be goin' now."

She held his hand against her waist and reached for his other hand. She swayed from side to side. "You like dancin' with me, don't you?"

He swallowed hard. "Yes, ma'am."

"John, stop callin' me 'ma'am.' I'm only five years older than you." She stepped a little closer, and he backed up against the table. "Do it right. You gotta hold me close."

"Miss Mary..."

She pulled his arms around her waist and leaned against him, resting her head against his chest. His heart was pounding.

He trembled, but he pulled her closer.

"This the part where you kiss me." She lifted her head, offering her lips.

He stared at her, and Mary could see his fear and uncertainty. She stood on tiptoe and gently pressed her lips to his. "See." She kissed him again. "It's easy." She pressed her mouth to his again, parting her lips as he finally relaxed and returned the kiss. He moved his hands up to her back, pulling her against him, surprising her with the strength of his embrace and the passion of his kiss.

When they parted, he pressed his forehead to hers. "I g... g... gotta go," he said.

"I know. See you next Monday, right?"

"Yeah." He kissed her again. "Yeah, I... I'll see you next Monday."

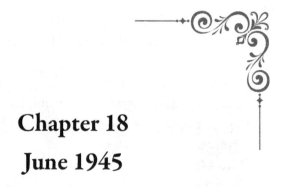

Chapter 18
June 1945

"So, when is graduation?" Mary sat down at the kitchen table beside John Dixon. In the weeks since his first visit, as the weather heated up, he continued to bring her hand-drawn flowers every Monday. He had relaxed a lot lately and now sat comfortably, resting an arm over the back of Mary's chair.

"December." He drummed his fingers on the table. "I'm goin' to Chicago the same day. I'm ready to get outta here."

Mary sipped her coffee. Over the past few weeks, their hour-long visits had slowly fallen into a routine: coffee and chitchat, slow dancing, and then long good-bye kisses. Mary refused to let herself care for the sensitive young man, but she did wish they could visit more often than just Monday mornings. She listened to him talk of his plans of moving to Chicago, playing in clubs, and maybe becoming a war correspondent for the *Chicago Defender*. He talked about not wanting to be a teacher and instead being a musician, how much he was liking art since he started drawing flowers, and maybe one day drawing a picture of Mary.

Mary laughed. "You want me to pose, or do you want a picture?" She stood up from the table and reached for his hand. "I think I'mma give you a picture."

He didn't move from his seat. He pulled her into his lap, wrapping his arms around her, nuzzling her neck. "You smell so good, Mary."

Mary smiled. She had many perfumes, but on Mondays, she just used a generous dab of vanilla. "It's just a little something I know you like." She kissed him and felt his hands moving over her back. "Mmm... You ever been with a woman, John?"

She felt him freeze and his back stiffen. He pulled away from her, and she stood up. He looked up at her. "Y... y... yeah. We broke up when I came to college. She... She wanted me to go off to war." He hung his head briefly then looked up again. "She wasn't nowhere near f... f... fine as you."

Mary pulled him to his feet and wrapped her arms around his neck. She kissed him again, this practically innocent boy. He held her close and kissed her back. She moved herself against him, feeling his muscles tense. "Treat me like a woman, John," she whispered. She stepped back, took his hand, and turned to lead him to the bedroom she shared with the old preacher.

John gently pulled his hand from hers. "Mary, this ain't right. I c... c... cain't just lay with a married woman—"

She laid a finger over his lips. "I'm married to a tired old man, John Dixon, a real tired, real old man. He only wants me to cook and look pretty and nurse him when he's ailin'. I ain't no more woman to him than that there chair." Mary took John's hand again. She let her hunger and desperation show on her face. John Dixon was a good man. Mary had never known a truly good man other than her father, and she truly felt this young student was the blessing God had in store for her. She took his hand again. This time, he didn't pull away.

Mary was surprised how much the young man reminded her of Mason... his touch... his kisses... his strength... even his scent. But there was a difference in their energy. Where Mason had been sure, almost selfish in taking his pleasure, John was tentative and concerned with Mary's pleasure. He touched softly and gently... He tickled and teased. His movements were slow and easy, almost languid. And when they were spent, Mary was positive he wasn't as innocent as he had seemed.

Mary propped herself up on an elbow, her arm resting on a pillow, her head on her hand. She watched the young man dress himself. His lopsided stance flexed well-toned muscles, and his dark skin still shone with sweat.

"I g... g... gotta go, Mary." He leaned down and kissed her forehead.

She didn't want him to leave. She wanted him to stay and take an afternoon nap with her, but it was time for him to go. The last thing she wanted was her husband coming home early and catching them—not for her sake but for John's. Out loud, she sighed. "I wish you didn't." She stood up from the bed, and the young man respectfully averted his eyes. "Too late to be shy now." She kissed him again until he pulled away. "Next Monday, we'll talk and kiss, do it some more, okay?"

"Mary, this ain't right." He buttoned and tucked in his shirt. "I ain't touchin' you like that no more. Professor come home early, I'm kicked outta school, and he'll shoot me too."

Mary pulled on a robe. "Then we can go someplace else. We can take a ride out to the country and..."

He placed a finger to her lips. "I'll see you next week," he whispered.

Mary followed him through the kitchen to the back door. Watching him walk through the yard to the back gate, she noticed he walked a little straighter today.

Chapter 19
September 1945

Dear Mary,

How are you? Tell the truth, are you hurt or anything? I will come back and kick his ass again. Just tell me when. My job is ok. It has a lot of ups and downs, ha ha! Sometimes I meet real nice people and somebody gave me a card and said I should be a model! Maybe I will leave this elevator job and go work for that new Ebony *magazine. Have you seen it? You know what? I think I will. Anyway, school is going well. I will be a real teacher pretty soon. I'm starting to think I might not like it but we will see. I get letters from Martha a lot. She said Papa wants her to get married but she thinks it might be too late if you know what I mean. He even said she could marry that soldier boy, Leroy Wilson. Well whatever happens, I hope they do it soon. Ellie—I mean Miss Elizabeth—wrote me a letter too. All she talks about is how smart she is. She uses big words that I don't even know and I go to college. She really thinks a lot of herself.*

Mary, I know why you didn't come with me, but you still should come visit. I have a nice flat and a real soft couch

*for you, or you could take the bed and I take the couch. You
know I love the lights just like you said I would. I think you
should come in the spring when it's real pretty and not too
hot. Please come to visit. I can even buy you a ticket. Just
think about it.*

Love, Ruthie

*P.S. Chicago Teachers College has some fine men. You would
love it here!*

M ary read the letter twice and then stuffed it back into the envelope. No, Bevers would never allow her to go. She wasn't
going to visit Chicago until she could move back there for good.
Ruthie always gave her updates on the family, like she was the only
one with the information. Of course, Ellie was smart. She was a smar-
ty-pants too, always acting like she knew more than everybody. Mary
thought it was very disrespectful when the not-so-little girl correct-
ed their parents. And Martha... Mary was honestly worried for her.
The fifteen-year-old wanted to marry a soldier probably going to war,
and she was having a baby. Mary had been that young when she married Mason, and look how her life had turned out.

Mary went to church most Sundays, sometimes with a veil or
pancake makeup to cover a bruise. At home, she did most of the
cooking and a little of the cleaning. She kept herself as pretty as she
could and still visited the college library at least twice a week. But after four years of pretending, Mary could never quite call herself *the
good wife*. In the three years since Slim's death, she'd avoided the Tip
Top Club, but she and Lena Ledell still found ways to have ungodly
fun.

On Monday mornings, when she wasn't home alone, Mary hung
dish towels over the back banister; that way John Dixon knew not to
visit. On this particular Monday, Mary sat in the kitchen with Lena,

sipping coffee and discussing the news of the day. Since the war had ended with the Allied victory in Japan, there were celebrations every-where. The Crystal Palace Ballroom had a big event planned, and Lena had brought over party dresses for Mary to try on.

"All you hafta do is tell him it's his patriotic duty to take you. We gettin' too old to be sneakin' out to the clubs, and the Crystal Palace ain't no shady juke joint like the Tip Top Club—even though I love that place." Lena put down her cigarette and stood up to refill her coffee cup at the stove.

"Lena, he ain't gon' take me nowhere near a dance hall." Mary tore apart one of the sweet rolls she'd made for John Dixon's canceled visit.

"C'mon, Mary." Lena returned to her seat and switched on the radio. "You ain't been out since that fight with the crazy lady at that country hole-in-the-wall. Half the church is gonna be at the Crystal Palace. As the pastor, he should be there to look out for his flock. You gotta at least ask him."

Mary took a bite of the roll and laughed a little. "Yeah, I'mma ask him. If you get the deacon to mention it, maybe that'll help. I mean, I do wanna go, but I'a probably be better off sneaking than askin'."

"Then you come to my house, and we'll get dressed and go. Lee'll love havin' a fine woman on each arm. Ahahaha!" Lena took a puff of her cigarette. "And that gold dress is a showstopper on you. I wish I had your curves."

The women sat talking until Bevers arrived home for lunch just after noon. He came into the house in a good mood, even asking Lena to stay for lunch.

"Nah, thank you, Pastor. I gotta get movin'," Lena said. "I hafta get dinner on, since I don't have a maid like some people." Lena laughed again. "You do what I said, Mary," she said as she went out the back door.

Mary plated her husband's favorite lunch—ham sandwich, potato salad, and fruit with a glass of lemonade—and served him in the
dining room.

"So, them signs up all over," Bevers said between bites of his
sandwich. "That dance hall havin' a big party. Whole church is goin.'"

"I know," Mary said evenly. She knew her husband was about to
forbid her from attending. She sighed and resigned herself to either
sneaking or not going at all.

He took a swallow of his drink and set the glass on the table. "I
got us tickets. We goin.' You got somethin' to wear, right?"

Mary sat staring at the man seated at the head of the dining
table, devouring his lunch like he hadn't just said they were going to
a nightclub.

"I ain't gon' dance or nothin'," he said, "but I figure we should
show up for a little while. Lotta important folks gon' be there."

"Yeah, I got somethin' to wear." Still stunned, Mary took a swallow of her lemonade. "What you gon' do sittin' in a dance hall, watch
me dance?"

"You ain't gon' be doin' no dancin.'" He took a bite of his sandwich and chewed for a few seconds. "Don't look right, a preacher's
wife out there shakin' her tail on the dance floor. I'm goin' to put
in appearance, keep a eye on my congregation. I know they gon' be
drinkin' and smokin' and all kinds of sin. Maybe with us there, folks
won't act so crazy."

"So you goin' just to ruin everybody's fun, huh?"

"Tha's the plan," the old man said. "That's the plan."

AS SHE CLIMBED THE stairs to the second-floor ballroom, the
first thing Mary did was look for the exits. Since the fire in Natchez
a few years ago, Mary wasn't too keen on crowded nightclubs, and
the Crystal Palace Ballroom was packed. Women in shiny dresses

they'd never wear to church and men in fancy suits with wide shoulder pads. A thick cloud of cigarette smoke clung to the high, chandeliered ceiling in the large room lined with gilded mirrors. The band was loud, and the dance floor was jumping. A man in a black tuxedo led the Beverses through the crowd to their table, where the Ledells were already seated. Lena made no attempt to hide her silver flask sitting on the table.

Lee Ledell stood up and shook the pastor's hand and kissed Mary's cheek. A cigarette girl in a short, fluffy skirt stopped at their table, and Mary watched the good deacon blush and buy a pack of Luckys. Bevers pulled his pipe from an inside jacket pocket and sat back in his chair. "Ain't gon' be here more than a hour," he said to Mary.

Mary nodded just as the band struck up their version of Duke Ellington's "Take the 'A' Train." Lena grabbed her husband's hand and headed to the dance floor.

"Don't even ask," Bevers said.

Mary smiled as the trumpet soloist stood up, and she almost called out to John Dixon. He was really good and looked nice in his fancy jacket.

Sitting at the table and sipping a Coca-Cola, Mary tapped her foot to the music and let herself be transported back to her nights at Harlem clubs. The big-band music and jitterbug and swing dancing... It was all she could do to keep her seat. And watching John Dixon up there on the bandstand, she felt a pang. She had always been so proud of Mason in his white tuxedo jacket and slicked-back, processed hair. She always thought he could've been the band leader. And now, watching John Dixon play lead trumpet, Mary felt the pull of the glamorous life she once lived and renewed her vow to get back to the big city as soon as Ellie was safely finished with college.

"Bet you like this music, don't you?" the old preacher said.

Mary didn't turn to look at her husband. "Yeah, it's good." She opened her purse and pulled out her fancy beaded cigarette case.

"Oh no, you not gonna sit up in here and smoke where folks can see you." Bevers reached over and snatched the case from Mary's hand. "It ain't seemly, the first lady smokin' in public." He slipped the case into his inside jacket pocket.

Mary stared at her husband sitting there smoking a pipe in a nightclub, chastising her about cigarettes. "Old man, you crazy." Mary got up from the table and headed in the direction she assumed was the ladies' room. She greeted a few people, exchanged compliments on dresses, and ran into the cigarette girl. She paid a nickel for a single cigarette and headed into the ladies' room to enjoy her smoke.

Coming back out into the club, Mary fought against the call of the music and the pull of the dance floor. She leaned against a pillar and tapped her foot to the music, careful not to shimmy like the dancers. A young man in a zoot suit approached her and reached for her hand. Before Mary could decline, a church lady appeared and swatted him. "Tha's the first lady, you idiot! You know she cain't dance."

"Hmph... I bet she can," the young man said, skulking away.

"Sister Mary," the older woman said. "Maybe you shouldn't be standin' so close to the dance floor. Folks bound to think you waitin' for a invitation. And you know how these young boys be all mannish actin'."

Mary sighed and looked around. The young man stood with friends, pointing in her direction. "Yeah, I guess you right, Sister Brenda," she said. "But the music is *so* good." She tapped her foot and snapped her fingers again.

"It's good, all right, but it still ain't proper."

Mary silently applauded herself for not rolling her eyes at the up-pity woman in the way-too-low-cut dress, and while heading back to her table, she let her hips bounce a little as she walked.

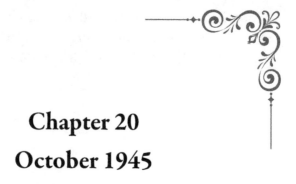

Chapter 20
October 1945

Holding the postcard from Ruthie, Mary didn't know whether to laugh or cry. It was a picture of a giant fish at the John G. Shedd Aquarium in Chicago. Mary hadn't gone to the aquarium when she lived there, but Ruthie seemed to have visited every site to see in Chicago. On the postcard, Ruthie had written that she'd been dreaming of fish. Mary understood that meant Ruthie was playing *policy*... and that somebody was having a baby. Since Martha's little Ricky was only a month old, Ruthie had written that the dream was probably a leftover, and it was just a superstition anyway.

Even as she tried to fight it, Mary had to admit that she had true feelings for John Dixon. Not feelings like for Slim or even for Mason. She hadn't been looking for love when she asked John how he felt, but whenever he told her she was the finest woman he ever saw, she found love anyway. She often fantasized about life with him, not life as a musician's woman but real regular life... as a wife. She imagined cooking for him and keeping his house and even washing his shorts. And in her dreams, she saw him holding their babies. She saw little boys in light-blue sailor suits and a little girl in a fluffy light-blue dress. She saw them seated at the dinner table, like in the movies, with John Dixon at the head. Mary often awoke, shaking off such dreams. Unless the old preacher died soon, there was no chance of those dreams coming true.

SEATED ASTRIDE HER lover in the bed she shared with her husband, Mary lay against John Dixon's chest, bathed in sweat, reveling in his warmth. She was almost asleep when he patted her back and kissed her forehead. "I gotta get goin', Mary," he said.

"I know," Mary groaned. She kissed his lips and then sat up. "I hate that you leavin' town so soon. I wish I'd'a met you when you first started school."

"I do too." John moved a little, and Mary climbed off of him. "I guess I should'a spent more time at the library."

She slipped on her housecoat and sat on the bed, watching John dress himself. She loved the young man's body, the way his muscles flexed when he moved, short legs and all. His shoulders were broader than Mason's had been, even broader than the old preacher's. His chest had a sparse sprinkling of coarse curly hairs, and his belly was smooth and lean with muscles that rippled when he turned or stretched. And soon, he'd be graduating and then taking a bus north the same day. He'd be gone. She sadly wondered who would be enjoying his body in Chicago.

In the kitchen, Mary kissed her guest goodbye. She lit a cigarette and watched him walk out of the back gate. Not for the first time, she wondered if her neighbors had ever noticed his comings and goings. She mostly doubted it. If they had, between Mamie and Lena, surely, she would have heard gossip by now. Since her visit to the Crystal Palace, Mary had been seriously entertaining the idea of going with John Dixon and starting a new life in Chicago. Ruthie had quickly found a job as an elevator operator in a department store and was doing well for herself. And Martha still wanted to finish school. Mary could get a job while Ruthie finished college, and they could work together to pay for school for Martha, then the three sisters could pay for Ellie's education. What about Papa's tractor? Could the sisters afford a new tractor while paying for college? *Of course not.* She blew out a stream of smoke and tried to push the idea out of her head.

In her bedroom, Mary changed the sheets and switched out the quilt. It had been more than ten years since she'd lived in Chicago, but she still remembered the night life and the lights and the high living. Those two months with Mason's band at the Regal and Club DeLisa had been her introduction to big-city nightlife, and she had loved it. Would John Dixon like playing his horn in Chicago clubs? Would he want to spend days making love and nights making music? Mary laughed at herself. How could she work to pay for her sisters' college and be a layabout housewife following the band? And what if he decided to leave her home alone with babies while he traveled? What if John Dixon didn't want babies? She'd be sure to ask him on his next visit. She laughed a little. Was she really considering going with him?

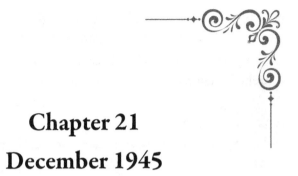

Chapter 21
December 1945

Standing naked and looking into her vanity mirror, Mary could see major changes in her body. Her facial features had darkened and thickened. Her belly stuck out a bit. She hadn't had her monthly since the summer, and her breasts felt swollen and sore. Of course, she was happy to be having John Dixon's baby, but what of her husband's promise to beat a baby out of her and put her out? What of her sisters and her papa? What of God's wrath for conceiving another child in sin? Could this baby even survive?

At night, Mary lay awake listening to her husband's light snoring, his slow breathing, watching his chest rise and fall. She wondered what would happen if she pressed a pillow over his face and sat on it 'til he stopped moving. Nah, he was too strong. He'd throw her off easily. But what if she made some extra-good greens and added some daffodils and other things? The sickness might be enough to weaken him gravely, and then nobody would be surprised if he stopped breathing one night. She rolled over and pushed the sinful thoughts out of her mind. If God's wrath for adultery was painful, what would be the price for murder?

MARY STOOD LEANING against the sink, watching John Dixon process the news. She took a long drag on her cigarette, flicked it into the sink, and rested a hand on her tightened belly. Her flowered housedress hid her condition easily, and her husband hadn't seemed to notice a thing. John paced back and forth in the Beverses' kitchen, running his hand over his hair and looking up at Mary occasionally.

"I... I guess I could take you to... to... to Chicago with me." He took her in his arms. "I'a make sure we have a r... r... real good time and a real good life." He kissed her forehead. "I'a take you everywhere I g... g... go."

Mary laid her head on his shoulder, enjoying the fragrance of his aftershave. "You know I wanna go with you, but I got other people to think about. You don't wanna take on all of my burdens."

"W... w... well, you found a husband to pay for c... c... college; why cain't yo' sisters?"

Mary looked up at him. She wanted to pat his head and call him a poor little fool. Young men who could pay for college didn't want farm girls, and old men who could pay didn't want college girls. "My husband is sendin' two of my sisters to college and payin' for my pa-pa's tractor. I cain't walk away from that," Mary said. "And you ain't gon' make enough money to pay all that—"

John Dixon kissed her, silencing her protest. "Y... y... you don't know that." He smiled. "I might make a record. Y... y... you never know. And I c... c... cain't stay here. My family countin' on me to get outta Mississippi."

"John, if I leave, my family loses everything." Mary crossed her arms and hugged herself. She couldn't bring herself to tell him about her husband's promise of a beating. What good would it do? Mary imagined John stuttering at the old man and suppressed a sigh. Ruthie would be more protection than her gentle lover.

John Dixon took her in his arms again. "We g... gon' g... go to Chicago, and I'mma get two jobs. An' you can get a job somewhere, maybe a maid or something where you can take the baby with you...

an' we gon' be just fine." He kissed her lips gently. "We gon' pay off yo' papa's tractor, and we gon' work it out."

"What about music? Do you really wanna give that up?" Mary turned her head, and his kiss landed against her cheek.

"I'a always make music, even if it's only for you."

Mary laid her head against his shoulder and wiped a tear. This was not what she wanted. She didn't want a plain old hard life. She wanted John to take her away to Chicago to live her dreams of big-city life and taking care of her family. She wanted him to bring the band home and have jam sessions 'til morning. She wanted sparkly dresses and dancing and reefa and brown liquor...

"John, you really want me to go with you... really?"

"Right after graduation, I'mma c... c... come get you, and we gon' take the *train*. We ain't gon' take no crowded bus." He started unbuttoning her housedress. "We gon' get m... m... married soon as we get to Chicago, and we gon' have a good life."

MARY HADN'T GONE TO church that day, and Bevers was supposed to have gone straight to the college after church, but instead, he came home and caught her packing. Through her open housecoat, with the afternoon sunlight filling the bedroom, he had seen her growing belly. This time, Mary did try to cower and protect herself. She tried to run and to fight back. She begged, and she pleaded, and she prayed out loud... but the beating didn't stop.

"Everybody see you gon' know you a whore!" He pounded and kicked and stomped her. "Tol' you I was gon' beat it outta you!" And when his hands closed around her throat, Mary closed her eyes and prayed not to die.

And she didn't die. She opened her eyes and looked up from the floor at her panting husband leaning over her, seated on her belly.

"Get out," he said. His voice was low, almost a whisper. "You did wrong. And now you gon' leave here with what you came with."

"I'm goin'," Mary groaned. She wanted to shout at him, but her mouth was swollen, and her throat burned. "Me an' my man gon' go to Chicago today, an' when he see what you did to me, he gon' whoop yo' ass." Mary's words came out slurred through swollen, bloodied lips, but she was sure he understood her. She tried to push him off, but every part of her hurt. Her left arm hurt so bad, she wondered if it was broken. Her sides and her belly cramped and ached deep inside. When Bevers stood up, she tried to get up again, but he stepped on her belly as he stumbled out of the room.

Mary cried as she struggled to get up from the bedroom floor. In her heart, she knew John Dixon would not fight the old man. He'd never even commented on her bruises or blackened eyes in all the months they'd been together. At most, he'd maybe raised an eyebrow and kissed her injuries. She rolled onto her side and propped herself up on an elbow. It hurt to breathe, and when she coughed, she tasted blood. Her vision blurred as the flesh around her eyes swelled. She pressed a hand to her aching belly and cried some more. The sharp pains terrified her. Would John Dixon still marry her if there was no baby? Losing this baby could mean losing everything. No husband and no help for her family. Her whole life would have been for nothing.

Mary struggled to her feet, moved slowly to the bed, and sat down beside her open suitcase. She wanted to lie back on the bed, get under the covers, and rock herself to sleep, but everything hurt too bad. She heard the front door slam. Bevers was headed to the college for the graduation ceremony. She didn't know how long a college graduation lasted, so she finished packing her suitcase, careful to take only the old clothes and things not provided by her husband.

Seated on the sofa in the front room near the big radio, Mary sipped mild ginger tea to ease her nausea and waited for John Dixon.

Her attire was simple—her old brown dress and a summer hat. She covered her bruised face with a silky white scarf her mother had given her. While she waited, Mary flipped through a two-week-old edition of the *Chicago Defender* newspaper. Though the paper was basically banned in the South, it wasn't hard to get a copy. Anybody who came to town on the bus or train seemed to have one, and issues of the weekly paper were shared around the church regularly. She read of the goings-on in Chicago and imagined the freezing winter weather waiting for her there. Flipping through the classified ads, she marked the Rooms for Rent section and wondered if she and John Dixon would need papers saying they were married to stay in the same room. She skipped the Help Wanted section because John Dixon was a good musician, and he'd get hired as soon as he walked into any Chicago club.

Despite her pain, Mary dozed off, and she was awakened by the opening of the front door. It was almost sunset, and the graduation ceremony was obviously over because her husband was home.

"Why you still here?" Bevers asked as he hung up his coat and hat. "I said get out. Ain't you s'posed to be headed to Chicago?" He stood, scowling at Mary.

"We goin' after the graduation," Mary said, "soon as he get here."

"Then go wait outside for him. Hmph. Graduation was over a hour ago." Bevers headed toward his office. "Ain't nobody comin' f' you."

"To hell wit' you, old man," Mary mumbled under her breath, and she slowly stood up from the sofa. Her sides and belly still ached, and taking deep breaths caused even more pain. She made her way to the foyer and donned her warmest coat and a winter hat. Suitcase in hand, she stepped out into the chilly December air and took a seat on the porch swing to wait.

John Dixon arrived in his graduation cap and gown, his trumpet playing a fanfare. He scooped Mary up into his arms and kissed her long and hard. At the train station, the conductor announced, "All aboard," and the blast of the train whistle filled the air again and again...

Mary opened her eyes. She was still on the porch swing. She'd dozed off and had been awakened by the sound of the train whistle in the distance. The sun had set, and the air had turned colder. She wanted to look at her watch, but it had been a gift from her husband, and she'd left it in the jewelry box on her night table. She sat back, moving the swing back and forth, her toes barely touching the porch. She had to stay awake. John Dixon would be there any minute, and she was ready to go. She laid a hand on her belly. She hadn't felt the baby move all day, not since the fight... the beating. She blinked back tears and tried to think good thoughts. The little boy would grow up fine... big and strong... smart... handsome... perfect...

Mary opened her eyes. She'd dozed off again. The temperature had dropped even more, and she shivered. The cloudy night sky was almost perfectly black. She could see neither moon nor stars. She thought about going back into the house to see what time it was and maybe warm up a bit. Or maybe she should walk to the train station. *Was she supposed to meet him there?* Mary stood up and paced back and forth on the porch. She was stiff and still ached all over, but she moved around, trying to warm up.

The front door opened, and Bevers's long shadow appeared framed in a rectangle of yellow light that fell onto the porch and down the front stairs. Mary paused her movements and faced her husband's shadow.

"I see you still here." he said. "Mighty cold, ain't it?"

The smell of his pipe tobacco wafting through the screen door reminded Mary how warm it was inside the house. "It's not that cold." Mary said, willing her teeth not to chatter. "It's gon' be even colder when I get to Chicago."

"So, you waitin' on a college boy, huh?"

Mary didn't respond. She blew into her gloved hands and flexed her fingers.

"Well, all the ones graduated is all gone. Most of 'em went home, but a few did head north. Like I said, ain't nobody comin' f' you."

"John Dixon *is* comin' for me." Mary wished she had a cigarette, but she didn't want to open her coat in the cold. "He probably had things to take care of." She stepped closer to the door.

"Ahaha! Tha's who you waitin' on!" The old man laughed until he had a coughing fit. "Woman, you dumb as hell! He ain't comin' f' you. Him and his girl left for Chicago right after graduation. Hmph. Shook my hand and everything."

"You a liar!" Mary spat. She sat back down on the porch swing, feeling the cold wood through her coat and clothes.

"Only John Dixon graduate today got a limp. Haha! Tha's him, right?"

Mary pressed her hands to her ears to block out her husband's laughter.

"Well, it's too cold to be standin' in this door. You keep waitin'. Maybe they'a come back for you. Ahahaha!"

Mary hung her head as her husband's laughter receded behind the closing door. She opened her coat and dug a cigarette and her lighter out of her dress pocket. She fiddled with the lighter until she was forced to remove a glove to light her cigarette. She inhaled, letting the warm smoke fill her lungs, and when she exhaled, the smoke came out with deep, choking sobs. She finished her cigarette and lit another and then another, rocking herself on the swing until her hands were numb and she couldn't hold a cigarette for the shivering.

The night was eerily silent when she heard the front door open again. She braced herself for more of her husband's ridicule. He came out to the porch in his coat and hat. Mary could also see he still had his nightclothes on. "Bring yo' silly tail in the house," he said. "Too much talk in the mornin' if folks see you froze to death on the front porch." He turned and went back in the house, leaving the front door open.

Mary lay there on the porch swing and sobbed. She finally felt the baby move again, and she sobbed even more. When she had asked John Dixon if he really wanted her to come with him, he'd told her they'd have a good life and take care of her family. He said there'd be fun and music and high living. He'd told her they'd have the life that she dreamed of... but he'd never said "yes."

Chapter 22
December 1945
Flora, Mississippi

When Will Bevers brought Mary to her parents' house, Mary couldn't help smiling in spite of her pain. A large extension had been added, making the house more befitting a minister of *Elder* Charles Johnson's status. Bevers reminded Mary that it was her marriage to him that made it all possible. When he stopped the car, he didn't cut the engine or help Mary get out or even help her with her luggage. As soon as Mary closed the back passenger door, he put the car in gear and left. Mary stood in the yard, worrying that her family was about to lose everything and that it was all her fault.

Inside the house, the old kitchen had been turned into a real dining room, the first bedroom had become the elder's office, and Martha and Ellie and the baby shared the new third bedroom off of the newly built kitchen.

"Hi, Mama," Mary said as she stood in the kitchen doorway, suitcase in hand.

Augusta looked up from the sink, where she worked cutting a chicken. She looked Mary up and down and then returned to her work. "Hmph," she grunted. "Put yo' bag in there in yo' sisters' room. Don't wake up the baby. What you do now?"

Mary sighed and walked around the kitchen table to the back bedroom. Her baby nephew, Ricky, slept on top of a tightly made bed. She lifted a corner of the small quilt covering him and looked at his chubby brown legs. She wanted to pinch them. She wanted to pick him up and hold and cuddle him, but that would probably wake him, and Mary was in enough trouble as it was.

Back out in the kitchen, her mother was still at the sink, rinsing and seasoning the chicken pieces. "Come sit down, girl," her mother said. "Tell me what you did this time."

Mary poured herself a glass of iced tea from the icebox and took a seat at the kitchen table. She didn't know where to begin. "Well, Mama, you gettin' another grandbaby." Mary sipped her tea.

Augusta paused and looked at her daughter. "How far gone are you?"

"Probably five months. I'm not sure."

"And since you all beat up, I'm guessin' you did wrong again."

Mary hung her head and didn't say anything.

Augusta turned back to the sink. "Well, it's probably too late to do anything easy—"

"I'm keeping it." Mary said. She hadn't been sure until that very second, but she wanted the baby. She knew this baby, the baby of her shameful behavior, was a blessing—no matter that he was conceived in sin... no matter that his mother was a whore... no matter that his existence would be the cause of her sisters losing out on a better life. This baby was a blessing.

"I see." Augusta said. "Well, you can stay here long as you want, but what you gon' tell yo' papa? *Elder Charles Johnson* is a important preacher now. This ain't gon' sit right with him, not one bit."

Mary thought for a minute. "I'm gon' tell him I'm havin' a baby," Mary said. "I still got a husband. Ain't nothin' wrong with a married woman havin' a baby. Will ain't gon' go 'round sayin' he been shamed. He too proud for that. My baby's daddy is gon' be my secret. Ain't nobody gon' know but me."

"Girl, yo' papa gon' see your face and know you did somethin' wrong—"

"And I ain't gon' lie. But I'm keepin' my baby, and if Papa want me to leave, I can go to Chicago with Ruthie—"

"Watch yo' tone, girl. You ain't gotta go nowhere, and you know it. I'm just sayin', that's all."

Mary hung her head again. She hadn't meant to snap at her mother. "I'm sorry," she said. She looked around the kitchen. "What you doin' with the chicken? Need some help?"

"I'm just gon' fry it. You can stir the beans on the stove. Whip up some cornbread right quick." Augusta shook her head. "I just don't know 'bout you, girl. I hope he was worth it."

Mary just sighed. How could she tell her mother it was she who had been shamed? It was she who had been seduced and abandoned... but maybe he was worth it, a little.

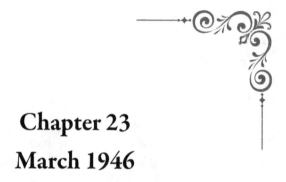

Chapter 23
March 1946

"**G**irl, quit frettin'!" Augusta said to her oldest daughter. "It just mean it's almost time. Baby dropped and ain't no room for 'im to move around. Be mighty funny if it's twins again. Probably too tight in there. Hahaha!"

Mary laughed a little and rubbed her belly. She did have pains in her back and a few cramps. Her mother was probably right. Nothing to be worried about... but she hadn't felt the baby move in two days, so Mary prayed. She prayed for forgiveness from God and her husband for her adultery. She prayed for forgiveness for shaming her family. She prayed for forgiveness for every imaginable sin. She turned her whole life into penance and prayer. She said grace over every meal, every drink, and every cigarette. She hummed gospel music and read only the Bible. It was in the Bible, in Genesis, where she found the name Judah. He was one of the children of Jacob, and the name meant "praise," and in spite of her sin or because of it, Mary would praise God, vowing to stay on God's good side no matter what.

Mary spent the last months of her pregnancy wondering and worrying about her unborn son. Would he have a short leg and stutter like his father? Would he look like him? Would Mary see her lost lover in her baby's smiles? Or would he look like somebody else? Mason Jr. had looked just like his grandfather Charles. Would baby Judah look like his brother? Would her baby boy be healthy and strong?

But despite her newfound devotion to God and her deep remorse for her sin, Mary's heart still ached. She hadn't been looking for love when she'd asked John Dixon how he felt, and each time he told her she was the finest woman he ever knew, she found love anyway. Of course, she knew she was doing wrong—committing adultery, shaming her husband—but eventually, it felt so right. In that one hour a week, John Dixon had felt like more husband to Mary than Will Bevers ever did.

Even though there was pain, Mary felt only relief when her labor actually started. She hadn't felt the baby move in days, and the light contractions were the first sign of her impending delivery. To bear her pains, she walked back and forth in the small space beside the bed she shared with her sister, Ellie. When she finally felt her water break, she took to the bed on a layer of towels over an oilcloth sheet to ride out the rest of her labor.

When she was in labor with Mason Jr. ten long years ago, Mary had thought she was dying. It was the worst *pain* she'd ever felt. She'd cried out to the God she hadn't really worshiped, begged for relief, and after hours that seemed like days, when she looked at her son's scrunched-up little face and when the wailing baby latched onto her breast, it seemed all memory of the agony left her. Then, when Rosie came a year later, the pain and labor were still bad, but Mary knew the outcome would be another precious little bundle, so the pain was bearable. When the time came for her third labor, sixteen months after Rosie, Mary felt she had childbirth well in hand, and she was up and caring for her twins shortly after Charles and Peter were born.

"Mama, leave me alone. I birthed four babies without cotton root and none of that junk. I know what's gon' happen."

"Well, I know wha's gon' happen too, and I birthed more than you!"

"But you never did two at one time, did you?" Mary and her mother continued their game of one-upmanship, their laughs and traded jabs occasionally punctuated by moans and groans from Mary. When Martha and Ellie arrived home from school, Martha insisted that since she'd given birth most recently, she obviously remembered much more than her mother and sister, and the Johnson women took turns sitting with Mary while she labored.

"Okay, Mary... it's gon' be all right." Ellie wiped her big sister's brow with a cool washcloth while Martha held Mary's hand and whimpered.

"Okay, baby," Augusta said from her place at the foot of the bed. "I see the head. Push!"

Mary closed her eyes, squeezed Martha's hand, and pushed until her strength gave out. Martha snatched her hand away and moved to the other side of the room.

"Come on now! His head is almost here! Ready, baby... push!"

Mary gripped the sides of the mattress and pushed again. In her mind, she imagined she felt every inch of her baby coming into the world. His head and shoulders, arms, legs, even feet and toes...

"It's a girl," Augusta said quietly.

Mary could hear tears in her mother's voice, and she laughed a little and collapsed back onto the pile of pillows behind her. "I ain't mad it's a girl," Mary said. "Hand me my baby." She tried to hold out her arms, reaching for her new daughter.

"Lemme get her cleaned up first." Augusta's voice cracked, and Martha and Ellie left the room.

"Why so quiet?" Mary looked up as her mother approached the head of the bed with her blanket-wrapped bundle. "Mama, why she not cryin'?"

Augusta placed the small bundle in her daughter's arms and backed away.

"Aw... she a sleepy li'l thing, ain't she?" Mary examined the tiny face with the pinched little mouth. The baby girl looked just like her sister Rosie had looked, with long lashes and thick curly hair. Mary adjusted the sheet covering her and pressed the baby to her breast. She ran a finger down her baby's cheek, gently opened her baby's mouth, and pressed her nipple to the baby's lips. "Mama, she not suckin'. I guess she not hungry yet."

"I'm sorry, baby." Augusta knelt beside Mary and reached for her hand. "Sometimes—" Her voice broke. "Sometimes—"

"Turn the heater up. It's chilly in here. She so cold..."

"Baby, I'm so sorry. Let me take her—" Augusta reached for her daughter's hand.

"No!" Mary snapped. She snatched away and held the baby tighter. "No! Don't touch her! Let us alone. She just tired from gettin' born." Tears burned behind Mary's eyes and nose. "I'mma let her sleep a while, then she'a be ready to eat..." Her tears spilled over and ran down her cheeks. "Turn up the heater and leave us alone. We gon' be just fine."

It may have been minutes or hours or even days later when Mary was awakened by her mother gently lifting the still baby from her arms. Mary opened her eyes and looked at her mother's tear-stained face. "Mama, don't cry." Mary reached out and touched the baby's light-blue blanket. "I'm all right." She scooted up in the bed and smoothed the blanket over her lap. "I'm not gon' cry no more ever again. I know this is God's will, and I know why."

"Baby, don't say that. Cain't nobody know God's mind—"

"Oh, I got a pretty good idea." Mary laughed a little and then blinked back tears again. "Her name is Dinah," Mary said. "It mean 'God will judge.'"

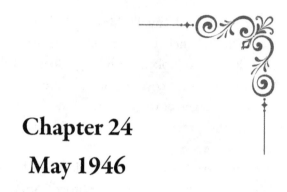

Chapter 24
May 1946

Mary sat in one of the chairs on her parents' front porch, enjoying coffee, a cigarette, and the bright spring day. After church all day on Sundays, she relished the calm quiet on Monday mornings. She felt like she was looking through new eyes; like after receiving God's judgment, the scales had fallen away, and she could see all the beauty in the world. The spring herbs and wildflowers were in bloom, and the daffodil blossoms swayed in the window boxes. The sights and sounds and smells of the country relaxed her. This place, her childhood home, was far from the cares of the city and free from the demons that had led her to sin.

But she'd done a lot of thinking and fasting and praying, and she understood everything now. She was actually amazed at her own hardheadedness. Every baby she had or almost had was gone. For her sin with Mason—fornicating, shaming the family—God had punished her real good, but she didn't learn her lesson. Then she lay with Mason's cousin while Mason was fresh in his grave. And then Slim and then John Dixon. And each time, the price of her sin was the life of a baby. But now—and Mary often laughed at herself, but she refused to cry—there would be no more sinning for Mary.

A fly buzzed around the rim of her coffee cup, and she shooed it away as her attention was drawn to the sound of a car out on the road. Mary watched the unfamiliar car turn onto their driveway. She stood up and shielded her eyes from the morning sun but couldn't quite make out the driver. It was likely a church member or somebody lost. She opened the screen door and called for her papa. He liked to be the one to greet anybody coming onto their land.

Elder Charles Johnson came out to the front porch, puffing his pipe, just as the shiny dark-green car came to a stop in front of the house. When William Bevers stepped out of the car, Mary's papa walked down the steps to the ground. Mary guessed that her husband was delivering her belongings and sat back down to watch the two men talk, her papa with his arms folded and Bevers with his hat in his hands. After a few minutes, Bevers pulled a piece of paper from an inside jacket pocket and handed it to Elder Johnson. Mary watched her papa and husband talk a moment longer before her papa shook Bevers's hand and then climbed the stairs back up to the porch. "You ain't gotta do nothin' you don't wanna do," Elder Johnson said to Mary, "but maybe you could hear 'im out." He went into the house, letting the screen door slam behind him.

Bevers came up a few steps and then stopped. "Mind if I sit with you for a while, *Miss Mary*?"

Mary shrugged. "Fine with me." She watched the old preacher climb the stairs and sit in the empty chair on the other side of the small table. "Want me to get you a drink?" She made no move to actually get up.

"Naw. But thank you." Bevers said. "I brung you some mail." He pulled a small stack of letters from his jacket pocket and passed them to Mary.

"Thank you," she said. "You came all the way out here to deliver some mail?"

"Um... yeah. And to see how you doin'."

"Oh." Mary looked down at the letters in her hands. "I'm fine. I see you got a new car."

"Yeah. Um... I'm sorry about the baby." Bevers said. "I know how much you want babies."

Mary looked over at her husband and said a quiet prayer of thanks. She had hoped that one day, she'd have the opportunity to apologize for her sin, and now God had sent her husband to her. He sat looking out into the yard, bouncing his hat in his hands.

"I told the church you had to go look after yo' family," he said. "Ain't nobody's business why you left."

"Oh," Mary said. "Thanks, I guess." She stared at the old man sitting across from her, fidgeting like a nervous schoolboy. His tan suit was neatly pressed as always—Mamie would make sure of that—his brown shoes polished to a brilliant shine. He was dressed in his Sunday best on a Monday. She looked at her watch. He was normally teaching a class or something at that time of morning. "Will, why you come out here?" Mary asked finally as she fought an internal battle with demons of uncertainty.

"Like I said... see how you doin'." He stood up and paced a few steps. "I know you probably bored out here in the country—"

"I ain't bored. I got plenty to do. I help with the chores. I cook and clean and read my Bible. Ain't got time to be bored."

It was Bevers's turn to say, "Oh."

"Well," he said, turning to face Mary. "I was thinkin' maybe you might wanna think about comin' back home... to Jackson."

Of all the things he could have said, that was the last thing she expected. She'd spent months praying for forgiveness, and now, it seemed her prayer was being answered. "Why?" she asked.

"Well, I know how you like city life, and... well... house don't seem right without a woman—"

"Mamie is a woman. She cookin' and cleanin' and ironin' yo' clothes—"

"Now, you know Mamie cain't cook. She back to cookin' like she was 'fore you came."

"Oh, so you want me to come replace the maid?"

"Dammit, Mary." Bevers sighed and sat back down. "Why you gotta make this hard?" He ran a hand through his gray-white hair and took a deep breath. "Listen. I been prayin' about it, and I been convicted in my spirit. The Lord put it on my heart that I was wrong. I wasn't mindin' my own house right, and a demon got in. That boy tricked you and... well..."

Mary hung her head. She had been tricked. John Dixon *was* a demon sent to tempt her to sin.

"The house is real quiet with you gone," Bevers said.

"You could turn on the radio."

"Yeah, I could. Um... I paid off yo' papa's tractor. I just gave him the paper."

"That's real nice of you." Mary smiled a little. "You didn't hafta do that. After what I did, I thought you was gon' take it back."

"What I'mma do with a tractor?" Bevers laughed and then sighed again and looked up at the sky. "Listen, Mary. I want you to come back home. I know I'm hard to live with, but I can do better. I won't beat you no more. You can take a couple'a classes at the college. I'a even take you out to the show sometimes."

Mary stared at the man occupying the seat across from her. Her tormentor. Her enemy. Her husband. "Will, how can you take me back after what I did?"

"Woman... I mean, *Mary*... you just under my skin, and I want you home."

SEATED AT THE KITCHEN table across from her mother, Mary sipped a cup of tea made with fresh sage leaves, honey, and lime.

"So, girl... you goin' back?" Augusta sipped her own sage tea and made a face. "This mess is nasty. I don't know how you drink it."

"I guess I'm just used to it." Mary took another sip and looked down at the pile of letters on the table. All were addressed from Chicago: two postcards and two letters were from Ruthie, and the fifth piece was an envelope with the initials *J.D.* over the return address. Staring at the envelope, she wanted to feel angry, but all she felt was resigned. She imagined it was a love letter... a letter of apology... a letter explaining why he left her. She turned the envelope over in her hands and looked at the back flap then again at the return address on the front. Maybe she should write and tell him about Dinah. Tell him of their beautiful baby girl that God took as punishment for her sin.

"So... you gon' read it?" her mother asked, pushing her teacup away.

"No, ma'am, I'm not," Mary said finally. She held the letter in her open palm, feeling its nonexistent weight, then she tore the sealed envelope in half and then in half again. "I ain't listenin' to no mo' demons."

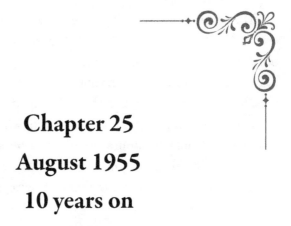

Chapter 25
August 1955
10 years on

Appropriate. That was the word for the day. Mary looked in the mirror and adjusted her hat and veil. She looked appropriate. The appropriate black dress with pearls at the collar. Appropriate black lace gloves. Appropriate black hose and shoes. She even had on an appropriate black slip and girdle.

Outside, the sky was appropriately gray, and the weather was cool for August. She climbed into the big black car with her parents and a sobbing Mamie. That old woman had worked for Will Bevers for thirty years and was inconsolable. The ride was short, just around the corner, really, but the fancy limousine was appropriate for the day. Mary sat staring out the window and tried to look appropriately aggrieved.

All draped in black and purple, Third Baptist Church was packed. More than packed, it was overflowing. Every space in the building was occupied by somebody there to pay last respects to Reverend Dr. William Bevers. Mary walked into the sanctuary at the head of a procession of family and local dignitaries. She let her knees wobble and leaned on her father's arm. She kept her head down and dabbed at her eyes with a dampened black lace-trimmed handkerchief. She carefully smeared her eye makeup to look appropriately tearful.

The service was long. It seemed like every student Bevers had ever taught had their two-minute say, and every church in the Central Mississippi Baptist Convention sent or presented a resolution. Mary sat there, not really trying to take it all in. She'd attended preacher funerals before, and they all seemed the same. Maybe two or three hours long, choirs all decked out in white, ushers and nurses ushering and nursing mourners; every so often, a wail or a shout would be heard from the congregation. But the service for the great William Bevers seemed to top them all. Every minister from every church spoke, and the music—it seemed a choir performed an A and B selection every twenty minutes. The president of the college spoke, and the head of the history department and all of the town clubs spoke. And then there was the eulogy... well over an hour of nice words and biblical admonitions and promises of resurrection in the last days delivered by none other than the superintendent himself.

After the fourth hour—or was it the fifth?—the service was nearing its end, and it was Mary's turn to perform. Typically, a preacher's widow approached the casket with church nurses by her side and screamed, wailed, and fainted. Mary had tried rehearsing her reactions, but every time she tried to scream or wail, she only coughed—or worse, laughed. She knew she was expected to cry, and she approached the casket with her handkerchief covering her mouth and nose. She looked down at her husband's body and tried to feel sad. She tried to feel all the feelings that widows were supposed to feel, but she felt nothing. She admitted to herself, he did look nice all laid out in his tan suit. He'd always preferred light colors. She'd let Mamie choose his outfit, and the grieving maid had chosen his best double-breasted suit, a subdued brown tie, and his best accessories. Mary shook her head. The old preacher was being buried with at least five hundred dollars in jewelry, including a gold watch he'd always said was for the son he never had.

Keeping her back to the assembled crowd, she covered her face with the handkerchief again and let her shoulders tremble. She hoped she looked like she was crying. She didn't dare try to make a sound, lest she fall into laughter. *Fall, that's it.* She swayed a little to the left and right, gripped the edge of the casket, and sank to the floor, drawing a gasp and more cries from the assembled mourners. It wasn't a full-blown falling out and carrying on, but Mary hoped her show of grief was sufficient.

She'd always thought she'd feel relief when death freed her from this marriage, but that Friday morning when his alarm clock buzzed and he didn't move to turn it off, Mary just felt annoyed. When she reached over him and turned the alarm off and he didn't move, somewhere deep in her mind, she knew he was dead, but she didn't feel like dealing with the whole rigmarole at seven o'clock in the morning, so she moved back to her side of the bed and slept for another hour. After her morning coffee and leftover sweet roll, Mary called for an ambulance. When the medic pronounced Will Bevers dead, Mary left the sobbing and wailing to Mamie and called the funeral home printed on the back of a church fan.

She secretly suspected the old preacher had died on purpose because their deal was complete. She'd stayed with him to get her papa a tractor and her sisters through college. The youngest sister, Ellie, had graduated college the past June and was planning her wedding to a nice young soldier named Bobby. The past ten years hadn't been bad. In fact, Mary would say that being on God's good side had made her life almost easy. Bevers had kept his promise not to beat her again, and she'd squashed her taste for the wild life and eventually drifted away from her friendship with Lena Ledell. She'd read her Bible cover to cover at least five times and had memorized her favorite psalms and proverbs. For the past ten years, Mary had finally been *the good wife.*

AFTER THE LONG FUNERAL, crowded burial, and overcrowded repast in the college dining hall, Mary decided she needed some time alone and chose to walk home from the college, something she hadn't done in years.

"Now, Miss Mary, the professor would have my hide if I let you walk home alone. Ain't safe for a lady to be out and about these days."

Mary almost laughed out loud as her old friend Joshua Floyd repeated the words he'd said the first time he walked her home so many years ago. Breaking all protocol, she gave the young man a tight hug and a kiss on the cheek. Even though he was one of Bevers's favorite students, Mr. Floyd had not been one of the many speakers at the service, so Mary was both surprised and genuinely happy to see him.

"So, I see you still wearin' your Sigma Alpha Omega Beta whatever pin," Mary said as they left the dining hall building.

"It's Phi Beta Sigma," Joshua said, laughing, "and yes, I am still wearing it. This is the exact pin I got when I first crossed over." He dusted the pin on his lapel.

Walking across the college campus, Mary couldn't help reaching out and touching a few of the trees. She recalled her wild days when she and Lena leaned against a tree and smiled at the college boys trying to flirt. She remembered hiding among the trees and bushes when her husband came out of the building unexpectedly as she was heading toward the library in the early days of her marriage.

"So, you was one of his favorite students. Why didn't you say nothin' at the service?" Mary shifted her black clutch purse to her left hand and took Joshua's hand to step over a puddle.

"Really, Mary? Hmph. I always thought he hated everybody. He was mean as hell."

"Ha, yeah, he was." Mary said. "But when your name came up, he always said, '...At least he ain't a idiot.' See, he liked you."

"Well," Joshua stuffed his hands in his pants pockets. "I useta think he was just a grumpy old professor, and I always tried to get on his good side, but that day I saw you at the bus station with yo' face all messed up... I was through with 'im."

"So why did you come all this way from Detroit?"

"You forget, this is my hometown. I still got people here, and I had to check on you. I'm honestly surprised you stayed with 'im this long."

Mary thought for a minute as they turned down a major street. "Honestly, I'm surprised too. I really didn't expect him to live this long."

"Really? You married a old man, waitin' for him to die?" Joshua sounded a little disappointed. "I never would'a took you for a gold digger, Mary. I mean, I didn't think you was in love with him or nothin' but—"

"Oh, you think I married him for money?" Mary swatted her friend's arm. "You saw how fine I was back then. I could'a married a lot better if I just wanted money." She sighed. "We had a under-standin'. I was a good wife to him, and my family got set up real nice. My papa is a bishop now. My sisters went to college. I never had to lift a finger 'cept to cook sometimes and be pretty."

"I see. So, what you gon' do now? You still young and fine, and I hear he left you well taken care of."

"I'mma keep doin' what I'm doin'," Mary said. "Mindin' myself and stayin' right with the Lord."

"But Mary, I remember yo' stories about life in Chicago and Harlem," Joshua said. "You know, in the navy, I got a chance to go to New York, and Harlem was just as jumpin' as you said it was. You the one got me interested in big-city life. Remember when I thought Jackson was somethin'?"

Mary laughed a little. "Yeah, you was so proud of this li'l old town with its two stoplights on Farish Street."

"Yeah, I was. But then you told me about the world outside of Jackson, bigger than the South. All that life out there, and yo' face would light up when you talked about it." Joshua shook his head. "I just knew you was gon' run off to Chicago one day."

"Wha's in Chicago for me now? It ain't nothin' but sinful ungodliness."

"Mary, don't you have a sister in Chicago? I bet you could find a whole life there too."

"Joshua Floyd, you sound like a demon, tryin' to tempt me back to sin and shame."

"Nah, I ain't no demon." He sighed. "I just don't want you to shrivel up an' die here."

Mary stopped at her front gate. She looked up the path to her front porch... the porch swing... the open front door. Somebody in the house, probably her sister Martha, had the music way up. She could see people milling about in the front room. Mamie was no doubt in the kitchen, showing off her painstakingly acquired cooking skills, and Mary's mother would be playing hostess, waiting for Mary to arrive. Going into the house meant she'd have to play the grieving widow and receive the guests that would stop by to deliver even more food. Being the widow of the legendary Reverend Dr. Bevers meant she would likely have to play the widow for the rest of her life.

"Joshua, to be honest, I don't wanna shrivel up an' die here, either." She took her friend's hand, ducked her head low, and looked around. "I'm not ready to go in yet. Let's walk some more."

"Okay, whatever you want, Mary." Joshua looked around, and they walked quickly back the way they came. "Now, you know you too old to be tryin' to sneak away from home." He laughed when they rounded a corner away from the house.

"I know. I'm bein' rude. I got folks wantin' to see me, and I'm out here hidin'." Mary and Joshua walked slowly toward downtown Jackson. "But honestly, what else I'mma do? I sinned twelve ways from Sunday, and the wrath of God been on my head since I was fifteen years old." She looked at the man walking beside her. "God punished me like Job, and I learned my lesson. My place is here, where God put me."

"But what if God wants you to be someplace else?"

"Then I'mma need a real big sign, all spelled out." Mary laughed.

"Big as that?" Joshua asked. He came to a halt in front of the bus station and pointed at a *Visit Chicago* poster advertising low bus fares to Chicago. "And look at that... The Chicago bus is waiting right here for you." He pointed at the Greyhound bus idling at the passenger loading area.

Mary swatted her friend's arm. "Get thee behind me, Satan." She laughed. "You ain't a demon. You the devil hisself tryin' to lead me back to hell and damnation."

Joshua laughed with her. "Well, you ain't gotta go back to hell and damnation, but seriously..." His tone sobered a bit. "I just want you to be happy. Even if you don't go back to Chicago or Harlem, I don't want you to turn into some old biddy, mindin' other folks' business and chasin' kids out the yard."

"Joshua, I promise I won't turn into that." She took her friend's hand. "Now, it's gettin' late. I guess I better show myself at home 'fore somebody come lookin' for me."

"Yeah, and folks see you out late with a fine young man like me." He dusted his lapels. "Who knows what they gon' think?"

They both laughed and traded jokes on the walk back to Mary's house. They hugged good-bye at the gate, and Mary didn't care who saw.

Inside the house, the visitors had all gone, and Mamie had gone home. Mary took off her hat and gloves and placed them in her bedroom. She found her mother in the kitchen, stuffing leftover food into the icebox. "Hi, Ma," Mary said. "Need some help?"

"Oh, so now you wanna help?" Augusta closed the icebox and faced Mary with her hand on her hip. "The least you could'a did was come home an see all these folks that came to see you. Yo' papa and Bobby out lookin' for you right now. Where you been?"

Mary pulled out a chair and sat down at the kitchen table. "Just walkin' around," she said. "Old friend came in for the funeral, and we just walked and talked." She accepted the glass of iced tea her mother poured.

"Y'all should'a came here. This house was packed with folks bringin' food and waitin' to pay respects to you." She motioned to the line of pound cakes on the counter. "Folks all wantin' to console you, and you out 'just walkin' around.' Girl, you so silly sometimes."

"I know, Mama." Mary hung her head and sipped her tea. "I would'a been here, but I just didn't feel like being the sad widow all day. I ain't got time to sit around—"

"Time? Girl, you got nothin' but time. You got all the time in the world now. What you in a hurry to do?"

"Nothin', I guess." Mary sighed. "I don't feel like thinkin' about it right now."

THE NEXT MORNING, SUNDAY, Mary woke up the same way she'd been waking up for the past week and a half. The alarm went off, she waited for Bevers to turn it off, then she remembered that he was dead and that it was up to her to silence the alarm. She said a prayer, thanking God for allowing her, to wake up and then got out of bed to start her day. She typically put on the coffee and then made a breakfast of grits, bacon or ham, eggs, and biscuits—except for Mondays, when she made sweet rolls instead of biscuits. This Sunday morning, however, she found her mother in the kitchen, fully dressed, having already made breakfast.

"I thought you was gon' sleep forever," Augusta said when Mary entered the kitchen. "Yo' papa's out on the porch. How you feelin' this morning?"

"I'm fine." Mary poured herself a cup of coffee and fixed herself a plate. She marveled, as always, at how her mother's scrambled eggs were always perfectly light and fluffy and perfectly seasoned with salt and specks of black pepper. She felt her mother watching her as she buttered her biscuit and took her plate to the dining room. Her mother followed her and leaned against the doorway.

"Baby, I been knowing you thirty-five years, and you ain't fine."

Mary said grace and dug into her plate. Everything was probably as delicious as her mother's cooking usually was, but Mary didn't really taste anything. As a matter of fact, she didn't really feel anything... just numb. "Yes, I am," Mary said around a mouthful of grits and eggs. She looked around the table for the morning paper, but of course it wasn't there. Bringing the paper in was her husband's job. She didn't sigh. She just looked straight ahead and kept eating.

Augusta brought her cup of coffee and took the empty seat at the head of the table. "Me and yo' papa goin' home after church."

"Okay."

"Maybe I should stay a while and see after you, though."

Mary stared at her mother for a minute before she realized what seemed off. Her mother was sitting where Bevers usually sat. "If you want to," Mary said, digging into her plate once more.

"I never been a widow," Augusta said slowly, "so I don't know how you feelin', but I can tell you however bad you feelin' is gon' pass."

"I know," Mary said. She kept eating. She couldn't tell her mother how she felt because she honestly felt nothing. Not grief, not sadness, not fear, not hope... nothing. Maybe God was testing her. "Mama, God ever tested you?"

"Ha!" Her mother laughed. "I birthed five babies and raised four. God tested me every day." She laughed some more. "You was the biggest test of all!" Augusta sipped her coffee.

"No, I mean a real test. Like when God puts somethin' in front of you to see what you do?"

"Baby, God don't do that. Anything God put in front of you is for you to do somethin' with. If God put it there, you use it."

"But what if it's bad—"

"Ain't gon' be bad... if it's from God." Augusta put down her coffee cup. "Why we talkin' 'bout this?"

"No reason." Mary got up from the table. "I guess I gotta get ready for church."

Mary chose a sleeveless black dress with white trim. For a hat, she picked a sunny straw boater with black ribbon and left off the veil. To keep things appropriate, she slipped on a black cardigan with pearl buttons. In church, for the first time since she moved to Jackson, she didn't have to sit in the front pew. She sat with her family in the third row, and after service, she received more hugs and condolences and assurances from church members. She turned down invitations to dinner and promised to visit and have guests over soon. Back at home, Mamie had prepared roast chicken and dressing, and Mary whipped up a peach cobbler like she had so many years before on her first Sunday in Jackson. After dinner and cleaning up, Mary sent Mamie home for the day and said good-bye to her parents.

"Now you watch yo'self, girl," her papa said. "You holla if you need anything. I'll be back here in two weeks to visit the church." He hugged his daughter and headed to his car.

"So, how you feelin' now?" Augusta asked. She flicked invisible dust from Mary's shoulders.

"Honestly, Mama," Mary said, "I wish people would stop askin' me that. I'm not feelin' a thing. I'm not sad or mad or happy or nothin'. I'm just feelin' tired of folks tryin' to make me feel better when I'm feelin' just fine."

"Well, excuse me. Hmph." Augusta hugged her daughter. "I know you a strong, grown woman and all, but you ain't that tough. And folks just offerin' kindness. Don't you go bein' all ungrateful."

"I'm not ungrateful, Mama." Mary hugged her mother again. "I promise I'm not. I'll be fine in time."

"I know you will, baby." Augusta headed down the stairs toward the car. "I'll be back here with your papa in two weeks. You take care now."

"I will!" Mary waved as her parents' car pulled off. She looked at her watch. It was almost time to leave for the church again, and though she usually changed clothes for the second church service, she didn't feel like going, let alone like changing clothes. Mary went back into her empty house.

The morning paper was on the dining room table. Her papa must have brought it in. She stood in the doorway of her husband's office. It smelled like pipe tobacco. Staring into the somewhat cluttered room—the only room Mamie wasn't allowed to clean—Mary tried to picture Bevers at the desk and conjure feelings of sadness or loss or something... but Mary felt nothing. Mary could picture her late husband in each room of the house but felt nothing more than curiosity at her lack of feelings.

She took a slow walk to the church. It was still a bit early, so she kept walking to the corner store to buy a Coca-Cola. She turned the bottle up and took a long swallow... then looked around quickly. She wanted to wipe her mouth with the back of her hand, but she'd already behaved badly enough by drinking from the bottle in public.

After walking another block or two, Mary looked at her watch and realized she'd be walking into church late even if she turned back immediately, so she kept walking.

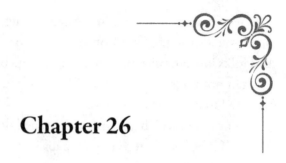

Chapter 26

Standing at the vending machine, Mary put in a nickel, pulled the knob, and retrieved a box of Milk Duds from the tray. At the next machine, she bought a Coca-Cola, opened it, and took a long, unladylike swallow, then wiped her mouth with the back of her gloved hand. She was surprised at how hungry and thirsty she was. She opened the box of candy, said grace, and poured a few of the chocolate-covered caramels into her mouth, again, very unladylike. The big clock on the wall said it was almost midnight. She looked around the colored waiting room in the Memphis bus station, surprised again that she was there.

ON HER WALK TO CHURCH that afternoon, after stopping for a beverage, Mary had taken a seat on a bench at a bus stop. She drew a few stares, and a couple of people had paused to let her know the buses didn't run on Sunday. Mary sat enjoying her drink, and since she was missing church, she opened her Bible—the only book she allowed herself to read—to Psalms. Her place was marked by an old letter from Ruthie. Mary had read the letter probably ten times over the past few years, but she unfolded the yellowing paper and read it again.

Dear Mary,

I can't believe Martha is having another baby. That girl is crazy. I don't know how or why she does it. I got a new place. It's real nice, away from the riff raff. I look out my front room window and see a park. It's real pretty. I decided this is my last year teaching. These little kids are too bad and I don't want to teach at a high school. I think I will go to cooking school and be a chef. They make good money, even more than teachers. I will start at Washburne school in the summer and see how I like it. I been here a long time and you still don't come visit. Even Mama and Papa come to visit me but you don't. I know you all holy now and you think I don't do nothing but sin, but you will be surprised, I think. My church is not too big, but I go most Sundays and I pay my tithes. I wonder if you are happy. I read your letters over and over and I think you are not really happy. You should come visit me. I promise I won't take you to any place sinful. We will go to church and to the museum and the big library. There are parks and the zoo and you can see all the beautiful things that god makes. See Mary, it's not all sin here. I guess the old man will let you visit over his dead body but he so old he will be dead soon enough. Hahaha. I know, that's not funny. Anyway Mary, try to come visit ok. I always have a place for you.

Love Ruthie

Mary read the letter again. She had other letters from her younger sister, but this one had served as a bookmark for the past two or three years. It wasn't particularly notable except for the cartoon drawing of two stick people next to a church. The people were labeled Ruthie and Mary, and the Ruthie person had two big circles for breasts. Mary giggled and then pinched herself for laughing at the unholy image. She'd still need a sign from God to get her to visit Chicago.

After she had finished her drink, she resumed her walk as storm clouds gathered overhead. She was near the bus station when the sky opened up and sent down sheets of rain. Grateful for her hat, Mary picked up her pace and ran to the colored waiting area under the eaves. The first thing that caught her eye was the Visit Chicago poster. She laughed a little. She'd just read a letter from Ruthie and now the poster. Mary took a seat on a damp bench to wait out the storm. As more people crowded under the eaves to get out of the rain, Mary watched a security guard waving a baton, wading through the crowd, evicting the loiterers.

As grumbling people stepped back out into the rain, the surly guard stopped in front of Mary. "You got a ticket, gal?"

"Not yet," Mary said. "I just got here."

The guard rubbed the baton against her knee. "Where ya headed, gal?"

Mary wasn't looking forward to stepping back out into the rain. "Chicago," she said. She looked up at the Chicago bus pulling up to the passenger pick-up area.

"Where's yo' bags?" he rubbed her knee again.

She stood up, removing her knees as a target. "It's a short visit." Mary looked around the waiting area. A couple of people stood in line at the ticket window, while others lined up to board the bus. A lightning flash and loud thunderclap made her jump. She had told a lie, and God was warning her.

"Well, git over there and get yo' ticket. Cain't sit here without a ticket!" The guard folded his arms and looked at Mary like he was daring her, so Mary went over to the ticket line. When it was her turn at the window, she looked around. The guard was still watching. Mary had more than enough money for the bus ticket, and she hung back, waiting for the short line of passengers to board the bus. After a minute, she stepped out of line and prepared to brave the storm and walk home, but more lightning and thunder made her think better of it.

"You gettin' on the bus, or do I hafta take you in for loiterin' and disorderly conduct?" The smiling guard stood beside Mary, rubbing the baton against his open palm. "Ain't no rain in the jailhouse."

"All aboard!" the bus driver called, stepping off of the bus.

As the guard stood laughing, Mary handed the driver her ticket. She ignored the guard's comment about an unplanned trip and found a window seat near the middle of the bus. The last bus Mary had been on was a tour bus full of musicians, and this bus smelled exactly the same. It had come up from New Orleans, and the driver announced Memphis, Chicago, and all stops in between. Mary didn't really have a problem taking the unplanned trip, especially since God warned her by shaking the skies every time she thought about getting off the bus. As the bus pulled out of the station, she ignored the guard's laughing and pointing. She wondered if he could even understand that God had just used him to get Mary on the bus to Chicago.

THE MEMPHIS STOP WAS a twenty-minute layover, and Mary took the time to use the restroom and stock up on snacks for the road. She bought more Milk Duds and another Coca-Cola. Back on the bus, she'd left her hat holding her place in the window seat on the nearly full bus. The aisle seat beside her was now occupied by a woman holding a basket on her lap, occasionally yelling at the three fidgety children seated in the row in front of them.

"I'm sorry, y'all. They gon' be sleep in a minute. Watch." The woman with the basket apologized to everybody within earshot. Sure enough, the small children did fall asleep almost immediately. Mary suspected they had been given cough syrup.

It was too dark on the bus to read her Bible, so Mary sat staring out the window, watching the stars on the horizon. Though she recognized the constellations, she wouldn't name them because they were not of God. An hour into the ride, her seatmate tapped her and handed her a foil-wrapped packet. "You hungry?" the woman asked. "Here, it's chicken."

Mary thought about the Milk Duds in her purse, thanked the woman, and accepted the gift. When she opened the packet and was greeted by the smell of a spicy fried chicken leg wrapped in Wonder Bread, she said grace and realized how hungry she actually was, but she tried to eat like a proper first lady. Then she remembered that she was no longer the first lady and took a whole bite of the chicken, bread and all.

Her appetite sated, Mary settled back in her seat and dozed off, dreaming of her late husband. It wasn't a particularly significant dream, but in the dream, he was strong and healthy. Over the last few years of their marriage, though his mind remained sharp, arthritis had begun taking its toll, and Mary often had to help him with simple tasks. But in this dream, they were seated at the breakfast table, and he read the newspaper out loud.

Mary woke up slowly as the sun was rising. She stretched as best she could and watched the highway and checked the bus schedule—three hours to Chicago. She was hungry again. Though she longed for another chicken sandwich, her seatmate was still fast asleep, so she opened the box of Milk Duds, said grace, and inelegantly poured some into her mouth. She quickly regretted it as the hard chocolate-covered caramels formed a solid sticky ball in her mouth that she couldn't chew, and she had nowhere to spit it out. She said a prayer for forgiveness for her gluttony and managed as best she could.

Stepping off the bus at the fancy Chicago Greyhound station, Mary was at first surprised then unnerved at the people. She hadn't seen so many in one place since her days in New York. She clutched her purse tightly and moved through the crowd. There were no separate facilities for colored and white people, so she stopped in the closest restroom to freshen up then stepped out into Chicago's afternoon sun.

The first thing Mary did was find a pay telephone. She dropped in a dime and asked the operator for a number for Ruth Johnson. Of course, there were too many Ruth Johnsons to try them all, and Mary hung up the phone. Outside, she was again grateful for her hat, this time as a shield from the burning afternoon sun. Thanks to her seatmate's generosity, she wasn't hungry, so she found the taxi stand and hailed a cab.

Climbing into the cab, Mary tried to suppress a cough. Even though all the windows were open, the musty mix of summer sweat, worn leather, and a putrid cigar nearly made her gag.

The red-faced driver twisted in the front seat, turning to face Mary. "Where to?" he asked around the cigar he held in the corner of his mouth. He cleared his throat a couple of times, and ash from the cigar fell onto the already dirty floor. "Sorry, did I getcha?" He took the cigar out of his mouth and wiped his mouth with the back of his hand.

"Naw, I'm okay," Mary said. She read him the address off of the envelope and settled back as the driver pulled out into the downtown Chicago traffic.

"Don't mind if I smoke, do ya?" the driver asked. "Tell you what, I'll blow it out the window. That way, you get to breathe fresh air. Ahahahaha!" He laughed at his own joke until he coughed. True to his word, he held the cigar and blew smoke out of the window... and the smoke and ash blew right back in through the open back window. Mary just shook her head and scooted closer to the passenger door.

"So, where ya from? What brings you to our fair hellhole?" He laughed again. "Nah, just kiddin'. I love this city. The life, the people, the skyscrapers—ya could find anything ya want in Chicago!" He coughed again. "So where ya say ya from?"

She'd thought about saying Jackson, but would that be a lie? She was really from Flora, but most people outside of Madison County had never heard of Flora. "I'm from Mississippi," Mary said.

"Yeah, I could tell... the accent an' all." Mary caught the driver's eye in the rearview mirror. His friendly eyes crinkled at the corners. "Ya gonna like it here. Ya been to Chicago before?"

"Yes, but it's been a while." Mary looked at the scenery passing by as the driver weaved in and out of traffic. "I don't recognize nothing no more."

Mary rode in silence, while the driver slammed on the brakes, yelled at pedestrians and other drivers, and described the landmarks. That year she spent in Chicago, twenty years ago, she hadn't ventured off the West Side except that one time to go downtown to a big parade. She had never visited the South Side, and as the taxi inched along in traffic on South Parkway, she took in the sights and sounds of the Bronzeville neighborhood. She watched children running down the sidewalks, ducking and dodging well-dressed men and women, street vendors pushing carts and ringing bells, and a window washer cleaning the windows of a grocery store.

Turning onto 47th Street, the traffic slowed to nearly a crawl, and cars and buses and pedestrians converged at crowded intersections, while a lone traffic cop tried to keep everything moving. "Okay, the building is right up there." The driver stopped the meter. "I figure better I let you out here than keep the meter runnin' while we sit here waitin' to go twenty feet."

"Thank you, sir," Mary said, reaching into her purse. She paid the fare and tipped him a whole dollar. "Keep the change."

"Wow, thanks, lady! Next time you need a ride, call this number." He handed her a matchbook with Checker Cab printed on the front. "Call that number and tell 'em you want Rodney. That's me. I'll come get you. I usually run up north, but for a nice lady like you, I'll come to the South Side. Got it?"

"Got it!" Mary couldn't help smiling at the friendly driver. She dropped the matchbook in her purse and climbed out of the cab. Looking again at the envelope, she started up the street. After a minute, she found the address over a door near the end of the block between a dry cleaner and a beauty parlor. She pushed open the heavy wood and glass door and stepped into the tiny foyer. Looking at all the mailboxes, Mary had a flash of panic. What if this wasn't Ruthie's address anymore?

On the panel of mailboxes, there were two Johnsons. She pressed the button labeled RJohnson 3B. There was no answering buzz. She pressed again and again and still no answer. Mary stood in the foyer, which smelled of lemon cleaner. At least the building super was conscientious. She pressed the bell marked 0A with a star, hoping against hope that would be the right bell. She leaned in to the speaking tube over the mailbox and was rewarded for her efforts by a gruff voice asking what was wrong now. She imagined the super in gray overalls with a cigar clenched in his teeth.

"Hello!" Mary shouted into the tube. "I'm lookin' for Ruth Johnson! She live in this building?"

"You don't hafta yell," the voice said. "Who's askin?"

"I'm Mary Bevers. I'm her sister."

"Oh yeah? She never said she got a sister."

"She got three sisters." Mary didn't know why she was still talking to the man. This was obviously the right address. "I'm the oldest," she said.

"Gimme a minute," the voice said. "I'm coming up."

A minute later, the left side door opened, and a tall, thin man came up from the basement. He had a cigar clenched in his teeth but was wearing blue denim overalls. He wiped a hand on his thigh and offered it to Mary. "Hi, Miss Mary. I'm Mr. Chauncey, the building super." He jingled a large ring of keys.

Mary shook the man's hand but didn't look at it. As rough as the hand was, she imagined it was grimy, but then she remembered that she'd not changed clothes or washed up since yesterday morning and probably looked a mess, and she said a quick prayer for forgiveness for being uppity. "Hello, Mr. Chauncey. Do you know what time my sister gets home?"

The man looked at his watch. "I don't be in people's business like that. She a nice girl, though. Always say good morning and whatnot. I guess she ain't expecting you, huh?"

"Naw, I'm surprisin' her. She been wantin' me to visit for years, so I'm here." Mary held her arms out to her sides but caught a whiff of herself and quickly lowered her arms.

"Well, she up in 3B." He chewed his cigar a little. "Since she ain't expectin' you, I cain't let you in her place, but you can wait up there in the hall." He cleared his throat and wiped the tip of his tongue on the back of his hand. "There's a few places up and down the block if you hungry. Harold's got the best chicken in town."

"Well, I'mma go to that store I saw and get me a Coca-Cola," Mary said, "then I guess I'll come back and wait by her door, if that's okay."

"Don't make me no nevermind," Chauncey said. He pointed at the doorbell panel. "Just ring me three times, and I'll buzz you in, and you can gon' on up there. I hope she don't keep you waitin' too long. Gets real warm in these hallways."

Mary thanked the man and started out down the block to the corner store.

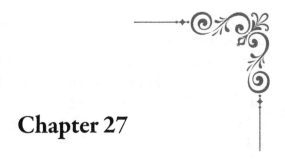

Chapter 27

"Well, I'll be damn!"

Mary opened her eyes and smiled up at her surprised sister.

"You scared the hell outta me! I thought another bum got in." Ruthie shifted from one foot to the other. "Now get up! I gotta get in and pee!"

"Oh... sorry," Mary said from her seated position leaning against Ruthie's front door. She scooted over and ducked while Ruthie unlocked the door and stepped over her. "Nice to see you too, little sister," Mary mumbled.

Ruthie's apartment was not at all the small shabby place that Mary had imagined. While her sister was occupied, Mary wandered from room to room. Besides the living room, dining room, and kitchen, there were two bedrooms, but the smaller one had been turned into a dressing room with racks of clothes and a lighted vanity with all kinds of makeup.

"Maaaaary!"

Mary spun around to see her sister standing in the dressing room doorway, grinning. "Girl, what are you doing here?" Ruthie asked.

"Well, now you just scared the hell outta me, so we even. Gimme a hug, girl!" Crushed in her younger sister's embrace, Mary felt stirrings of emotion for the first time in almost two weeks. "I was in the neighborhood and decided to stop by." Mary laughed.

Seated at Ruthie's kitchen table, freshly showered and changed into something of Ruthie's, Mary stirred her tea made with rubbed sage from a can. It was extra bitter, nothing like fresh sage, but Mary sipped it anyway. The dinner of Harold's fried chicken was truly the best fried chicken Mary ever tasted.

"So, you just got on the bus," Ruthie said. "With no bags, no food, no nothin'?"

"Well, it was that or go to jail for loiterin'." Mary sipped her tea again, made a face, and reached for the sugar. Ruthie didn't keep honey.

"Don't make no damn sense." Ruthie fussed as she poured herself another glass of red Kool-Aid. "So the mean ole white man made you get on the bus. Why you didn't just go home? Why was you scared of the rain?" She reached for another piece of chicken.

"I wasn't scared of the rain, but I wasn't tryin' to get struck by lightnin'," Mary said. "The Lord wanted me on that bus, and the man just gave me a push. Every time I thought about goin' out in the rain, the Lord sent lightnin', so I knew I had to come."

Ruthie shook her head. "Girl, you crazy."

"So, you still being a glamor girl?" Mary looked around the well-appointed kitchen. The flowered curtains looked familiar, but she couldn't remember why. Shiny white appliances and Formica countertops. "It must pay a lot. You got all this fancy stuff and all them fancy clothes. 'Cept them magazines you send, you don't have hardly no clothes on. I couldn't show Will or Papa."

Ruthie laughed. "Ain't no shame havin' arms and legs. That's all that was showin'."

"Yo' titties was almost out too. That bathin' suit was sinful." Mary sipped her tea again.

"Ha! Church ladies show more than that every Saturday night and sometimes on Sundays if it's a special occasion."

"An God is gon' get 'em too."

"So, big sister..." Ruthie stood up from the table and stretched. "...how long you stayin'?" She reached up on top of the refrigerator and pulled down a bottle of brown liquor. She poured some into her glass of Kool-Aid and offered the bottle to Mary.

"Girl, I quit liquor a long time ago," Mary said. "An you ain't got no business—"

"Aww, hush!" Ruthie laughed. "First miracle was at a party, and Jesus brought the good liquor, so ha!"

"Well," Mary mumbled. "He might'a brought it, but it don't say he drunk it." She stood up from the table and looked around. "Don't make no sense not to have food in yo' icebox. An' that pantry is a shame. No beans, no grits? What *do* you cook?"

"Girl, I cook all day. I ain't tryin' to cook at home too." Ruthie walked over and hugged Mary. "But you can cook all you want, all day every day, and I'a eat everything you cook as long as you here."

Mary hugged her sister back. "While you at work tomorrow, I'mma go down to that store and get you some real groceries. Hmph."

STRETCHED OUT ON RUTHIE'S flowered couch, Mary awoke, surprised that it was after nine a.m. Back home, she was usually up before seven. She only chided herself a little, though, because she hadn't really slept on the bus the night before. In the kitchen, she found a note from Ruthie, five dollars, and the keys to the doors. The note said there was a folded shopping cart in the front hall closet and to use the money for groceries and whatnot.

After having her coffee and rummaging through her sister's dressing room for suitable clothes, Mary made a grocery list and set out on her mission. Back home, Mamie had handled all the grocery shopping, and over the years, Mary had grown accustomed to not worrying about such things. She found herself looking forward to her shopping trip.

Outside, Mary was greeted by other people out for late-morning walks. She passed the corner store where she'd bought a Coca-Cola the day before, and she paid a nickel for a newspaper from a man by a little green-painted shack on a street corner. The High-Low grocery store was a three block walk down 47th Street, and Mary had never seen a store with such a selection. After picking out a few personals, Mary made her way through the aisles, picking out the items on her list, marveling at the many brands of breakfast cereal. She grabbed canned goods, dry goods, milk, eggs, and cream for her coffee. At the butcher counter, she picked enough meat for a few days.

At first, Mary ignored the two young children—a boy and a girl, likely siblings—carrying a loaf of Wonder Bread and a can of Pet milk. The little fat boy couldn't have been more than eight or nine. His baggy brown shorts rode up between his thighs, and his ashy knees rubbed together. They lingered in the bread aisle near the shelf with Hostess snack cakes, and Mary saw the boy stuff a package of Twinkies into the front of his shirt. She followed the children to the produce section, where the little girl picked a small bunch of grapes and dropped them into one of the pockets of her pinafore.

"Hey! What you got there?" Mary grabbed the little girl's arm. The little boy dropped the bread and canned milk and took off running. "Hey, git back here!" she called after the boy, but he rounded a corner and disappeared down an aisle.

"Nothin'," the little girl said. She looked so terrified, Mary almost felt sorry for her.

"Girl, Bible say don't steal!" Mary shook the child by her arm. "God gon' send you straight to hell for them grapes!"

"Hey, lady! What's the big idea yellin' at the kids?" A teenaged boy wearing a stained white apron and pushing a broom approached Mary. "What'd they do to you?"

"They thievin' li'l heathens!" Mary said. "Somebody need to take a strap to 'em!"

"So she picked a few grapes. So what? That's no reason to cause a ruckus!" The boy pulled the little girl away from Mary just as the trio was approached by the manager.

"Andy, get back to work! Quit botherin' the customers."

"Aw, Mr. Jim." Andy let go of the little girl and pointed at Mary. "She started it. Picking on this kid—" The little girl took off running in the direction the boy ran. "Hey!"

The three of them looked after the little girl weaving her way through the produce section and vanishing down an aisle. Andy bent over and picked up the can of milk and the loaf of bread. "I'll go put these back," he grumbled as he walked away.

"Sorry about all the fuss, ma'am," the manager said to Mary. "Been trying to get those kids all summer. Andy is just soft. What'd they get this time?"

Mary looked at the grapes. "Hmph. The boy got a Twinkie, and the girl got some grapes. Thievin' li'l heathens. Where they mama at?" Mary moved along the counter, looking through the selection of fruit and picking enough cherries to fill a small brown paper bag. "Kids these days got no home trainin'."

"Well, I bet you scared 'em plenty. They won't be back for a while," the manager said. "You know, if somebody like you worked here, I bet a lot of these little hoodlums would do their stealin' someplace else."

"YOU GOT A WHAT?"

"I said I got a job." Mary stood at the stove, turning fried pork chops in hot grease. "Set the table so we can eat."

Ruthie folded her arms and leaned against the kitchen doorway. "So you just gon' up and leave everything in Mississippi without talkin' to nobody? What about Mamie and the house and—"

"Girl, quit fussin'." Mary laughed as she placed the hot pork chops on a plate lined with brown paper. "I ain't leavin' nothin for too long." She set the plate on the kitchen table and turned back to the stove for the mashed potatoes, green peas, and cornbread. "I gotta get back to my garden. This can stuff is a mess."

"So what you gon' do, then?" Ruthie laid out silverware and plain white plates that were so heavy, Mary suspected they were probably stolen from the restaurant where Ruthie worked.

"Well..." Mary poured the Kool-Aid and took a seat. "I'mma work at the store for a few hours every day, and in a couple'a weeks, I'mma quit. Ain't neva' had a job before. I figure I'a have somethin' to do while you at work... might be fun."

"You in my seat," Ruthie said. "Let's change."

"What difference do it make?" Mary sipped her drink and made a face. "Too much sugar."

"I like to sit facing the door with my back to the icebox. So I can see if somebody come in."

"Girl, you silly." Mary stabbed a pork chop with her fork and lifted it over to her plate. "You got two locks on that door. What if they come through the back door?"

"Mary, just get outta my seat, okay?" Ruthie picked up her cup and empty plate and moved to stand by the icebox and waited while Mary took her time getting up. "Thank you," Ruthie huffed, setting her plate down and taking her seat back. "I just like sitting at the head of the table."

"Ruthie, the table is round. Ain't no 'head of the table.'" Mary snickered and bit into her pork chop.

AFTER WORKING AT THE High-Low grocery store for three days, Mary couldn't understand how any woman would want to spend months, let alone years there, but some of the cashiers had, indeed, been sitting behind the cash registers for years. Every day, Mary said a quick prayer of thanks that she had the choice to leave. She had never really thought about working. Throughout her life, her papa then Mason then Bevers had taken care of her, so she'd never had to worry about money, but listening to the other women who worked at the High-Low grocery, Mary was amazed at the struggles of these women. One was a bored widow like Mary, but the others were poor women who had to work to survive.

Mary's cash register was always the one facing the aisle with the bread and snacks. Kids— and adults—stole other things, but part of her job was to deter kids from stuffing snack cakes down their shirts. After a week, it seemed the local kids started keeping out of the store.

"So, Mary..." A cashier named Ladora sucked a deep drag on a cigarette. She offered her pack to Mary with a book of matches. "I think you crazy. I ain't never been so bored that I wanna come to work."

Mary declined the pack and sat down in one of the orange plastic chairs in the grocery store's breakroom. The room was slightly decorated with faded beige streamers from somebody's long-past celebration. There were signs taped to a wall about cleaning up and a copy of that week's work schedule. "Ain't nothin' wrong with me," Mary said. "My house is clean, ain't got no kids, church only open on Sunday. What I'm supposed to do, sit around and listen to the radio all day 'til it's time to cook dinner? Tha's how folks get caught up in sin. The idle mind is the devil's workshop."

"If you say so," Ladora said. "I just think folks can find better things to do than help make somebody else's money." She dropped her cigarette pack into her smock pocket and stood up to leave the breakroom. "Party time's over. See ya' later."

As Ladora left the room, Mary looked at the clock. She still had fifteen minutes on her break, and she'd forgotten to bring her Bible to read, so she bent down and picked up Ladora's dropped matchbook and read it. "Get a High School Education at Home for Only $6 a Month," the large bold print on the American School matchbook cover practically shouted at Mary. She read the message and felt what she often called a stirring in her spirit, a call, an inspiration to do something.

"NOW, MARY," RUTHIE said to the back of Mary's sweat-covered shirt. She spoke loudly to be heard over the drone of the box fan in the kitchen window. "I think it's a real good idea you goin' back to school, but don't you think you should close up things back home first? What about the house and all yo' stuff?"

"Ruthie, quit fussin' all the time. The house belong to the college, and all that stuff was from Will's last wife." Mary wiped her brow and laughed a little. "Oh, I guess I'm his last wife now. Haha. Anyway, I'm not leavin nothin'. I'm goin' to the American School. I send them six dollars every month, and they send me all the schoolbooks, and I study at home and get my diploma." Mary stood in front of the fan, where she was enveloped by the billowing blasts of hot moist air of Chicago's late summer. "So I *gotta* go back home cuz I think I'mma go to the college when I finish high school."

"Really, Mary?" Ruthie peeled off her sweat-soaked chef's coat and stood in the kitchen doorway in her brassiere, balling up the coat and wiping sweat from her chest and underarms. "I thought you said married women didn't need college. Quit blockin' the fan."

"Well, I ain't married no more, am I?" Mary turned and faced her sister. "Girl, put on some clothes! Folks can see straight in here through that fan!"

"Hmph. Mary, when you ain't here, I be all the way naked. I'm in my own house, and I ain't gotta wear clothes if I don't want to."

"That's why every pervert and Peepin' Tom in Chicago probably be right outside that window, and you just drivin' 'em all to sin."

"Dammit, Mary, it's hot!" Ruthie loosened the drawstring in her work pants and soon stood in the kitchen in nothing but her brassiere and underpants. "I'm not finna sit around here and die from heat stroke."

"Lord Jesus, forgive my sister," Mary prayed, rolling her eyes at Ruthie, "even though she know exactly what she doin'."

"And Lord," Ruthie said, "forgive *my* sister for turnin' on the oven and makin' meatloaf in August!"

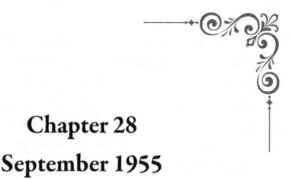

Chapter 28
September 1955

"Ruthie, it's plenty churches in our neighborhood, two right on the block." Mary took a seat beside her sister on the bus. "Why we gotta take a bus 'cross town to go to church and on a Saturday?"

"We not goin' 'cross town." Ruthie yawned. "And it's not my church we goin' to."

"Good," Mary fussed. "Cuz that place is so dry and dead and boring and—"

"And ain't nobody making you go to my church. I'm sorry we don't whoop and holla enough for you. Sorry my church likes to read and study the *Word* instead of watchin' the preacher hoppin' around."

"Hmph." Mary sat back in the seat and adjusted her hat. "You ain't wearin' a hat. Yo' arms all out. Whose church gon' let you in like that?"

Ruthie sighed. "Mary, we goin' to a funeral, and it's probably gon' be really crowded and really hot."

"Oh. Whose funeral?" Mary fidgeted in her seat and adjusted her hat. "And why you ain't tell me? I would'a wore something different."

"I thought you might not wanna come, and I don't wanna go by myself," Ruthie said. "A friend of mine lost her son."

"Oh. Was he sick? How'd he die? Was he one of these ol' street hoodlums? Seem like tha's all young boys do these days is cut up and act a fool. Always causin' some kinda mess—"

"Dammit, Mary, would you just *shut up*? He was lynched!" Ruthie snapped, not bothering to keep her voice down. "My friend's fourteen-year-old son was lynched." Ruthie wiped a tear, smearing her makeup. "If you take yo' head outta that damn Bible sometime, you might see what's goin' on in the world."

Mary's hand went to her chest, and she fingered the pearl necklace she wore. "In Chicago? When?"

"Naw, in Mississippi. Last week."

"Was he with one of them groups always stirrin' up stuff? You know, the Bible say..." Mary opened her purse, reaching for her Bible. She watched as Ruthie rolled her eyes and then got up and moved to a different seat.

The sisters got off the 47th Street bus at State Street and rushed across the street to catch the State Street bus. The driver let them off at 43rd because of the stand-still traffic. They managed to walk two blocks before reaching the crowd waiting to enter the church a block away.

"Ruthie." Mary laid a hand on her sister's arm. "This crowd ain't movin' that much. Let's walk up some."

"Don't matter," Ruthie said. "Seem like everybody tryin' to get to the same place."

As the crowd moved slowly forward, Mary watched the people. There were people carrying flowers and Bibles. A few people looked angry. There were even people talking and laughing. It didn't seem at all like a funeral procession. It felt more like a bunch of people heading to a revival meeting.

After about an hour, the temperature started rising, and Mary's feet ached. Ruthie was still not talking, so Mary listened to the crowd. She picked up bits and pieces of conversations. It seemed this lynched boy was somebody real important, and he had whistled at a white woman. In Mississippi. Everybody knew Negroes couldn't do that. A colored man could only tip his hat and step out the way of white women. Anything else was a death wish. Obviously, that boy brought it on hisself, but Mary didn't say that out loud. It seemed Chicago folks didn't know the rules.

By the second hour, Mary had shed her jacket and was fanning herself with an old church program she'd found in her purse. The crowd narrowed down to two lines, and they filed into the church. Up a couple of steps to the burgundy-carpeted narthex and then into the sanctuary. The first thing Mary noticed was the smell. She looked around. Did nobody else notice that terrible smell of death?

As they drew closer to the front, Mary heard screams and cries... sobs and shouts for Jesus. Nearing the casket, she noticed a woman sitting in the front pew, staring straight ahead, and guessed that must be Ruthie's friend, the boy's mother. Suddenly, she wanted to look anywhere but that casket. She tried to step out of line, but the crowd moved her forward. She looked to her left, but in her peripheral vision, she saw something so impossible, she had to look.

"Demon." That was Mary's thought. The swollen, disfigured creature dressed up to look human. *Demon.* A horrible, bloated monster. Gross. Disfigured. Mutilated. Nothing resembling a face. And if it was a real person, what had he done to attract the wrath of God like this? Then again, maybe it wasn't the boy's sin. Mary knew God often took children to punish parents. Maybe it was his mother's or father's sin.

When Mary felt the bile rising in her throat, she finally looked away. She saw her sister standing, fists clenched, jaw set, tears streaking her face. She took Ruthie's arm and led her away from the horror. She felt sorry for her sister and for the mothers here whose sins had been visited on their children. They obviously didn't understand that this was God's will.

Chapter 29
November 1955

DEAR MISS MARY

I PACKED ALL OF YOUR STUFF UP LIKE YOU SAID. YOUR PAPA CAME AND GOT IT. IM GOING TO MISS YOU. I DONT KNOW WHAT I WILL DO FOR WORK NOW BUT I PRAY THAT THE LORD WILL KEEP YOU SAFE UP THERE IN CHICAGO.

LOVE MAMIE.

Mary read the telegram twice, and then she read it again. She felt she'd made a good decision. Ruthie had been mostly right in her letter way back then. Her whole life wasn't just sin. And though Ruthie's church was boring, Mary had easily found one to her liking only a block past her job. She wished she could find a mailing address for her old friend Joshua Floyd. He would be real proud of her, deciding to stay with Ruthie in Chicago.

On her walk to work every day at the High-Low grocery store, Mary looked down the tree-lined side streets. She'd forgotten how beautiful God painted the big-city trees in the fall. The November air was nippy, but she dressed warmly enough. She often admitted that she missed the warmth and her garden, and she really missed fresh sage leaves, so she started drinking more coffee and even found she had a desire for cigarettes again.

But unlike Ruthie and these other big-city girls, she would never walk down the street smoking. "How you just gon' be out in public like that? It's just wrong. It ain't ladylike at all."

"Mary, when you know me to be ladylike?" Ruthie laughed and then flicked her cigarette away as the bus pulled up. The sisters were taking their weekly trip to the fancy library downtown. "I dress like a cook, and I wear pants everywhere but church. Cain't nobody tell I'm a woman."

"Believe me, Ruthie," Mary said. "*Everybody* can tell you a woman."

On the bus, Mary headed toward the back, but Ruthie grabbed her arm and took a seat in the front. "Why you always go all the way to the back? You ain't in Mississippi. You in Chicago now."

Mary looked around the uncrowded bus. "Well, what if a lotta people get on?" she said. "Then it's more room and easier to—"

"Let *them* go to the back, then," Ruthie huffed. "I ain't been at the back of no bus since I left the South, and I'm not about to give up my seat—"

"Why you always gotta be so willful, Ruthie? Why you cain't just let things be like they gon' be? Why you gotta fight against everything?"

"Mary, you used to fight against everything, and I mean *everything*. Mama and Papa got you with that switch so much, I'm surprised you can sit down today. Everything was a fight with you. You didn't like something, you just went yo' own way—"

"Yeah, I did," Mary admitted. "And I paid a mighty price for my rebellious ways."

Ruthie pulled out a cigarette, lit it, and took a long, slow drag. Mary rolled her eyes in disgust.

"Mary, you ain't pay no price for rebellion. That ol' man beat you cuz you let him. I wish a mutha—"

"You know what, Ruthie." Mary looked at her younger sister sitting there... no hat, no gloves, no makeup, wearing a man's peacoat and pants, and smoking. "I think you confused. You did all that modelin' stuff, tryin' to show off all yo' business, and now you tryin' to hide. You need to just find a good, godly man. You a real pretty girl... make somebody a real good wife if you just quit bein' so willful."

"You finished?" Ruthie blew a long stream of smoke at Mary.

Mary turned away from her sister. Growing up, Mary might have been willful, but after many years and hard lessons, she'd learned her purpose and her place. And though she seriously doubted he ever would, Mary vowed that if God ever sent her another husband, she'd be the best, most perfect wife. And if she was ever blessed with another child, she'd raise that child pure and holy and in perfect fear of the Lord.

Inside the library, Mary found a nook with an empty table. She spread out her schoolbooks and sat down in a hard wooden chair while Ruthie wandered off. The American School had sent Mary her first set of books. Studying wasn't hard, and Mary actually enjoyed the math lessons. History and literature, though... Mary saw no use for such subjects. What godly woman cared about such things? She found all the history and literature she needed in her Bible. As she worked her way through a page of math problems, she again wondered if finishing school would serve a purpose.

All her sisters had finished high school and graduated college. Ruthie had been first, and she was a smart, beautiful woman who might make somebody a good wife if she wasn't so headstrong and willful. She was always so busy she claimed not to have time for men. Mary wondered if Ruthie might live to regret so much education. Martha, the next sister, had five children and was on her third husband, and she, too, had finished college. But her house and kids were dirty. What kind of woman let that happen just so she could go to college? But the baby sister, Ellie, seemed to be all right. She was happy teaching and kept a good house and took care of her husband, like a proper godly woman should.

Mary knew she didn't want to work at the High-Low forever, and finishing high school meant she could probably get a better job. But college... did she really want to do that? Could she go to the teachers' college like Ruthie did? But what if God really did send her a new husband? All of this education stuff would be for nothing.

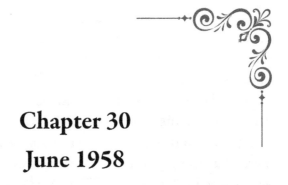

Chapter 30
June 1958

Mary tried to stay calm, but the music Ruthie listened to was sinful, heathen blasphemy... and she was playing it on Sunday morning while not getting ready for church. And that church she went to—when she went? All a bunch of heathens too. No hats, no gloves, and the preacher didn't wear a robe. Just blasphemous!

Mary tossed her smoldering cigarette in the toilet and looked in the mirror. She pinched her cheeks and smeared Vaseline on her lips. Adjusting her hat, she smiled at herself but then frowned. Smiling at yourself in the mirror was vain and prideful. Something that Ruthie might be, but Mary was definitely not.

Mary had decided not to attend Sunday school at Lakeshore Christian Fellowship Church that morning. Instead, she slept in, watered her window-box herb garden, and took her time getting ready for church. At least that was the plan until Ruthie woke up blasting that heathen noise. Then Mary hurried up and stepped outside a full thirty minutes before she'd planned. The late-spring Sunday morning was warm but not too hot. The last of the pink mulberry blossoms floated on the breezes, and the neighborhood was just waking up at ten a.m. Gospel music from WVON poured from open windows. Little boys in their Sunday clothes sat on front stoops playing rock teacher. Little girls played hopscotch because they couldn't jump rope in Sunday dresses.

That day, Mary sat in church, fanning herself and listening to Reverend Riley Porter preach about the sins of Israel and how God punished the Israelites—or, rather, how God allowed the world to punish the Israelites. As she did with every sermon, she took the words to heart and vowed to continue her sin-free life, carefully avoiding the terrible and swift wrath of God. Back at home after church, Mary was annoyed to see that Ruthie had not only skipped church but had also left messes everywhere. Her breakfast dishes were still on the kitchen table. The music was still blasting, and she had been smoking something that definitely wasn't a cigarette.

"Ruth Johnson, it's Sunday!" Mary slammed the door behind her and stomped into the kitchen, where her sister sat still in her night clothes. "You ain't been to church, and you layin' up smokin' reefa like some kinda heathen!"

"I may be a heathen," Ruthie said, getting up from her seat at the messy kitchen table, "but I'm a thirty-year-old grown heathen, and I can skip church and smoke whenever I want to... and I'm not layin' up. I'm sitting up." Then she laughed and laughed.

Mary stomped into the living room and put down her purse. She opened all the windows and hoped the slight breeze was enough to blow out the smell of smoke. Though it had been nearly fifteen years since she last indulged, Mary remembered the smell of reefa and prayed against the demons of temptation. Not that she was even remotely tempted, but she prayed and waved her paper fan around the room anyway.

Back in the kitchen, Mary found her sister washing dishes and dancing to the worldly music. She moved past Ruthie and went to the icebox to take out the dinner she had prepared the evening before. Sunday dinner was Mary's specialty, and though she wouldn't dare call it pride, she always felt good about her cooking skills.

Apparently, so did Ruthie.

Everything had been picked over. There were no ham hocks left in the greens. The braised oxtails were mostly bones, and the bread-pudding dessert was all but gone. The spoon was still in the pan!

"Ruthie, you greedy heffa!" Mary slammed down the nearly empty pan. "You couldn't wait for dinner, and then you almost eat it all."

"I was hungry last night and this morning," Ruthie said, still dancing. "Your stuff is good."

"I don't care how good it is! You was supposed to wait for dinnertime. Plenty other stuff to eat in the pantry. Now what we gon' have for dinner?"

"We gon' have whatever else you decide to cook."

"I'm not cooking nothin' else!" Mary snapped. "I do all the cookin' and cleanin', and I even do yo' laundry." She set the pots on the stove and opened the oven to light it. "Don't know who she thinks I am, but I am *not* the maid." She pulled a small mixing bowl from the cabinet. Flecks of cornbread batter had dried in the bottom. Mary slammed the glass bowl on the counter. "Cain't even wash the dishes right," she mumbled.

"Mary, you know what?" Ruthie turned to face her fussing sister. "I'm sick of you criticizing everything I do—"

"Then maybe she should stop bein' a heathen and do something right for a change," Mary continued to mumble under her breath as she slid the bread pudding into the oven and began stirring the pots on the stove.

"And I'm damn tired of you talkin' like I cain't hear you!"

"Well, you act like you cain't hear me all the time. Everything I say go in one ear and out the other. You might as well be deaf." Mary turned to face her sister. "Ruthie, you a hard girl to live with and—"

"Dammit, Mary, I'm not a girl! I'm a grown woman, and if you can't live with that, maybe you should live someplace else!"

Both sisters paused and stared at each other. Then Ruthie turned back to the sink, and Mary turned back to the stove.

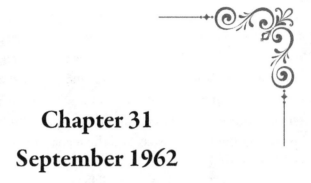

Chapter 31
September 1962

Mary's feelings had been hurt the day of the argument, but in the days afterward, she knew Ruthie was right. It wasn't like she wanted to keep treating her sister like a child. She just knew better and knew more about life, and if Ruthie couldn't respect that, then maybe they shouldn't live together.

Finding an apartment had been relatively easy. She'd looked in the want ads and found a nice two-bedroom first-floor unit in the same building as Ruthie. The sisters loved still being close, but Mary relished being in her own space for the first time in her life. She took the largest bedroom for herself. It had a connecting door to the bathroom. She wasn't sure what to do with the second bedroom, but she was certainly not going to make it a dressing room like Ruthie had. In the end, she put a bed in there and made it a guest room.

Life at the High-Low grocery store went on as usual. Mary sometimes laughed at herself because seven years ago, she couldn't imagine how anybody could spend years as a cashier. Yet every morning at 8:55 a.m., she punched her time card and greeted whoever she passed on her way to her checkout lane. The store wasn't often very busy at that time of morning, so Mary used the downtime to help the stock boys by straightening the snack aisle.

The first afternoon the Jays potato-chip delivery driver greeted her, Mary spoke back and continued arranging the Hostess snack cakes while he stacked tins of potato chips on the other side of the aisle. The snack-cake section was a mess, and Mary was quite aggravated when she said a prayer and began humming the tune to "Pass Me Not, O Gentle Savior." When she got to the chorus, she was joined in her humming by the sound of a smooth baritone quietly singing the words. By the end of the song, a couple of shoppers had paused in the aisle to listen, and the manager stood tapping his foot with his arms folded... but he had a slight smile too.

The next Tuesday, the Jays delivery driver arrived and handed Mary a crumpled, grease-stained brown paper bag. Though offended, Mary bit her tongue and pointed him toward the door to the back room. "It's a garbage can back there. Ain't my job to get the trash."

"Naw," the man said. "It's donuts. Sorry the bag so messy. They real fresh. I had some extra. Thought maybe you or somebody here might want 'em."

"Oh... well..." Mary accepted the bag, holding it by two fingers. "I'll put 'em in the breakroom. Somebody eat 'em." She turned and headed toward the back of the store.

"You welcome!" the man called after her.

Mary just waved and kept walking.

The following week and each week after that, the Jays delivery driver brought more donuts. Soon, the cashiers looked forward to Tuesdays and the special treats. They also teased Mary about having an admirer.

"Y'all just silly," Mary said one Tuesday morning as Ladora and a cashier named Eva fussed over Mary's hair and tried to get her to put on lipstick. "He been bringin' potato chips here for years. I don't know why y'all think he suddenly lookin' at me."

"Who knows why men do anything?" Eva misted Mary's hair with perfume. "Maybe he just got single... wife died... divorced... who knows?"

"Or he just got brave." Ladora took out a cigarette and offered the pack to Mary. "Maybe that li'l singin' y'all did lit his fire."

Mary took a cigarette and tapped it on the breakroom table before lighting it. "Naw, I got no time for men." She took a long, slow drag just as the store's overhead music came on. The store would be opening in five minutes. "I don't even know his name." She blew the smoke out and took one last puff before squashing out the cigarette and heading out to open her checkout lane.

Mary stayed at her register on this Tuesday, but she could look down the aisle and watch the Jays driver wheel in his hand truck piled high with boxes of potato chips. He wasn't especially handsome. His slightly graying hair was cut short, with sideburns connecting to a neatly trimmed beard. His short-sleeved work shirt showed off huge arm muscles and stretched tight over his obviously well-fed belly. The giant of a man could easily see and place chips on the top shelves. When he finished his work and looked up at Mary, she blushed and quickly averted her eyes but not before seeing him smile and head in her direction.

When the big man stepped into Mary's checkout line, she flipped off the light switch and hung up her Closed sign then chided herself for being nervous. There was really no need for nerves. She'd be polite, and if he said something wrong, she knew plenty of scriptures to rebuke him. Mary forced herself to focus on her job, giving each remaining customer in her line her full attention. She imagined the other cashiers giggling as her line dwindled down to just him. She had to look up at the tall man. Not only was he tall—he was wide. She knew the other cashiers were staring, but she couldn't see around him to scowl at them.

"Hi, I'm Paul." He offered his hand, but Mary didn't shake it. It wasn't proper, and besides, his giant hand might have crushed her small one.

"It's nice to meet you, Paul." Mary grabbed a rag from under the counter and began wiping the conveyor belt. "What can I do for you?"

"Well, they say a closed mouth don't get fed, so here goes..." He cleared his throat. "What time you get outta here? Lemme buy you some ice cream."

"She get off at three!" Ladora shouted from the next lane over.

Mary wanted to say something about the store selling all the ice cream she could want. She wanted to say something sassy and send the man on his way. But what came out was "Okay."

Paul smiled. "Good. I'll be back here at three." He started walking away and then turned back. "Your name is Mary, right?"

Mary glanced down at her nametag and then nodded.

"I'll see you this afternoon, Miss Mary."

As Paul headed back to the store's loading dock, Mary wondered what possessed her to agree to an outing. But it was only ice cream, and it wasn't like it was a real date. And besides, she was forty-two—too old to be dating anyway—and he had to be fifty if he was a day. They were probably just goin' to the Tastee Freeze or something. She'd eat her ice cream and then go home... but... *He smells so good, and he has a nice smile... and look like he got all his teeth too.*

HER TUESDAY OUTING with Paul led to another outing the following Tuesday, again a walk to the Tastee Freeze for ice cream. The third Tuesday brought rain, so they drove to the White Castle hamburger stand on 79th Street and sat in the car, enjoying an early dinner, listening to music, and watching the storm.

Mary sat in Paul's car, as far to the right as she could... as was proper. The light-gray leather was cracked and worn in places, and it smelled of cigars and the man's aftershave. She tried not to enjoy the worldly music. Jackie Wilson, the Platters, and pretty much every song Herb Kent played on the radio were all so good, it had to be a sin. But when a Sam Cooke song came on, lightning flashed and thunder crashed, and Mary reached over and turned the radio off.

"What you turn it off for?" Paul reached for the knob but was blocked by Mary's hand. "That's one of my favorite songs," he said.

"Didn't you just see God shakin' everything up?" Mary lowered her voice to almost a whisper. "That man used to sing for the Lord, but he got caught up in the world, and God don't like it."

"Are you serious?" Paul looked at Mary, and she blushed a little, but she set her jaw and kept her hand in front of the radio.

"Yeah, I'm serious. Bible say don't consort with demons. You'a have the wrath of God come down on yo' head." Mary knew she was right, and she took a sip of her drink, ending the discussion.

"Okaay," Paul said. He reached into the sack between them and pulled out a hamburger. "So, is it all right to listen to his old music, with that gospel group?"

Mary reached for another hamburger, but Paul passed her the one in his hand. "Yeah," she said. "Gospel music is always good."

"But that Jackie Wilson music wasn't gospel. Why is that okay?"

"Wasn't no lightning. God didn't get mad. I guess he never turnt on God." Mary took a small bite and quickly chewed and swallowed. "I guess Lord knows he don't know no better, but that Sam Cooke knows he doin' wrong. God will not be mocked."

"I see," Paul said. He stroked his beard and looked over at Mary. "I forgot to tell you, you look real nice today. I like them earrings."

Mary took a long drink, chided herself for blushing like a schoolgirl, and desperately wished for a cigarette.

"So, Miss Mary, what church you go to?"

"I go to Lakeshore Christian Fellowship up the street from my job. Pastor David Taylor is the head pastor. He a real good preacher, but I like Reverend Porter better."

"Big church?"

"It's a pretty good size. Few hundred people. Gon' outgrow that buildin' soon."

"Well, maybe I visit one Sunday." Paul reached out and turned on the radio. "You okay if I smoke, right?" He opened the ashtray and pulled out a half-smoked cigar. He pressed the lighter and rolled down his window just a crack.

When the cigarette lighter popped out, Mary watched him light the cigar, cupping his hand around the glowing coil like he was guarding a real flame. He inhaled deeply, laid his head back against the seat, and exhaled slowly. The sweet smoky smell of the burning cigar reminded Mary of a cross between her papa's pipe and Slim's cigars. *Slim.* Mary hadn't thought of him in years. Paul was big like Slim was... probably bigger. But Paul was cleaner, probably owned a couple of suits. Yeah, he listened to worldly music, but he didn't seem an outright sinner like Slim was. Sitting there, listening to music and the rain, Mary pinched herself and said a silent prayer to drive out thoughts of her old life.

"OOOH, MARY! YOU KEEPIN' secrets! How you just gon' get a man and not tell yo' own sister!" Ruthie sat in Mary's kitchen, stirring a tall glass of iced tea. While Ruthie's kitchen was on the side of the building that got the most morning sun, Mary's kitchen often glowed golden from beautiful sunsets. She'd chosen plain white curtains and accessories, and though Ruthie pretended not to notice, Mary had *borrowed* some of Ruthie's white dish towels, which Ruthie had *borrowed* from the restaurant where she worked.

"I don't have a man." Mary stood at the stove, stirring a small pot of chicken and noodles. "We just friends. We go out for White Castle and ice cream on Tuesdays. We sit in the car an' talk. Tha's all."

"Like teenagers?" Ruthie sipped her tea. "Y'all ain't been out on a real date?"

"Naw," Mary said. "It ain't like that."

"Well, it's like somethin, cuz you wearin' perfume."

"Girl, hush." Mary giggled and scooped creamy chicken and noodles onto two plates and set them on the table. "I don't need a man. I just like talkin' to him."

"Girl, ain't nothing wrong with a woman havin' a somebody. Don't yo' Bible say it's not good to be alone?" Ruthie dug into her dinner. "What's his name?"

"Paul."

"Paul what?"

"I don't know. I told you we ain't like that. I'm not all up in his business, and he ain't in mine."

"Hmph. He ain't told you his last name, huh? I bet he married or something... but you probably didn't even ask... *'cuz y'all ain't like that.'"*

"MARY, YOU KNOW MY NAME. You know where I work. You know what books I read..."

"Naw, Paul. I might know a lotta stuff, but you never told me yo' last name."

"Well, if I didn't, I'm sorry." Paul reached across the seat and shook Mary's hand. "Hello, Miss Mary. I'm Paul Bishop the Third, and I'm very pleased to meet you."

"I'm pleased to meet you, too, Paul Bishop the Third. I'm Mary Bevers." Mary giggled and then caught herself. She did sound like a teenager.

"So now that we been formally introduced, you gon' let me take you out for real? All this White Castle and ice cream ain't good for a man." He patted his belly. "How 'bout we go for a nice steak dinner somewhere... maybe go to the show or something?"

"Paul Bishop, I believe you tryin' to court me."

Paul took Mary's hand again. "Miss Mary, that's exactly what I'm trying to do."

Mary looked down into the cup of ice cream melting in her hand. She didn't know what she felt. There was a pressure in her chest and knots in her stomach. She pulled her hand from Paul's. She hadn't been courted in twenty years. Her mind flashed back to the men she'd known. Besides Mason and Bevers, no man had ever courted her or made her feel special. And she didn't know how Paul made her feel or what could make the man interested in her. She'd never been a proper girlfriend. She'd only ever been a wife or a mistress. Did she even deserve the courtship of a decent man like Paul?

She felt him shift in his seat. "Well," he said, "ain't you gon' say somethin'?"

"I don't know." Mary felt embarrassed, but she didn't blush. Maybe she wasn't embarrassed. She was confused. He did know the gospel music she liked, and he knew the Bible, and he looked her in the eye when he spoke to her. Bevers had told her a demon couldn't look a saint in the eye. Had God sent Paul to her for a reason? "I don't understand why you wanna court *me*. I ain't got nothin' a man want."

"Woman, hush." Paul laughed a little then got serious. "I wanna court you cuz you got everything *this* man wants." He leaned in and kissed her on the forehead. "I like you, Mary, and Lord willin', I think we could have a real good thing together." He sat back in his seat and patted her hand. "So, we courtin' or what?"

"Yeah, Paul. I guess we are." Mary sighed. She could think of no good reason to say "no."

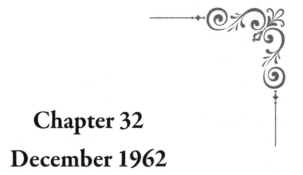

Chapter 32
December 1962

The H&H restaurant was decked out for the holidays. The chandeliers were hung with ornaments and tinsel, and the waitresses wore sparkly red and green party hats. As she and Paul took their seats, Mary tried not to notice people staring.

"You know you the finest woman in the world tonight, don't you?" Paul reached across the small table and laid his hand on Mary's. "Don't get me wrong. You fine all day every day, but folks in this room still looking at you. I bet they tryin' to figure out who you are."

Mary tried not to blush, but she couldn't help it. In Ruthie's little black dress with her shoulders dusted with sparkly powder, she knew she looked beautiful and felt like a movie star. She pinched herself for being vain and prideful. The couple enjoyed a shrimp-cocktail appetizer, and Mary had a small New York strip steak. Paul ordered the porterhouse, and Mary sat mesmerized, watching the big man eat. For dessert, they ordered the peach cobbler, and Paul ordered a bottle of Cold Duck champagne.

"I don't know why you got a whole bottle," Mary fussed. "I'm not drinkin' none."

"Well, you don't hafta drink none," Paul said as the waitress returned to their table with the bottle of sparkling pink wine and two glasses. "That's just more for me." The waitress poured the wine and set the bottle on the table.

"No, you not gonna sit here and drink the whole bottle. How you gon' drive straight?"

Paul laughed. "Woman, you see how big I am. I need three bottles 'fore I feel anything." He lifted his glass. "Since you ain't gon' toast *with* me, I'll toast *to* you. Here's to the finest woman in the world. *Who can find a virtuous woman? Her price is far above rubies.*" Paul spoke a little too loudly, and someone at a nearby table said "Amen." And Mary wished she could hide. Paul turned up his glass and drained it then poured another. "Woman, you don't know what you missin.'"

Mary sat turning red and covered in goose bumps as Paul made toast after toast, reciting nearly the whole thirty-first chapter of Proverbs, with people at the nearby tables raising their glasses and clapping. As he poured the last of the bottle, he tapped his half-full glass against Mary's untouched one. "C'mon, Mary, just one little toast. It's time to celebrate and drink to life and all that stuff." He held up a finger and ordered another bottle.

Mary looked across the table at the man smiling at her. He was handsome... no, not exactly handsome. His nose was a little too wide, but his eyes were bright, and his lips looked... Mary shook her head, clearing the demons of lust. She loved kissing him, he always made her laugh, and when they were apart, the thought of him made her smile. What if God actually *had* sent him—what if he was gonna be her husband?

"Paul, I got a question for you. Serious for a minute." Mary fingered the stem on her champagne glass and looked up at him.

"Okay." Paul poured himself another glass but pushed it away slightly. "What's on yo' mind?"

Mary stared down into her own glass, watching the bubbles rise to the top. "I know we courtin' and all..." She took a deep breath. "...but what for? What you wanna do?"

Paul leaned back in his chair and reached for his glass. "Oh, you got a *real* serious question, huh?" He took a sip and set the glass back on the table then leaned forward and placed his hand over Mary's. "Well, since we bein' serious now, I think you know I'm real serious about you. Ain't got no other women. I think we real good together, and one day, you gon' be my wife."

Mary's breath caught in her throat. She knew—or at least suspected—that Paul wanted a wife... but to hear him say so out loud? Mary didn't know how she felt. She fingered the stem on her glass again and took a sip. What harm could a few sips do?

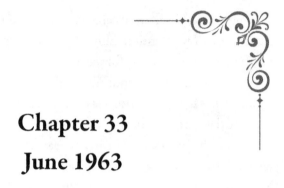

Chapter 33
June 1963

Riverview Park was not Mary's favorite place to go on a date. It was always packed full of teenagers and families with young kids. And the food... nothing but fried salt. And then there were the rides. Aside from the Tunnel of Love and a few other mild rides, Mary would never say she had fun there. But, of course, Paul loved everything that shook you up or bounced you around or did pretty much anything that could probably hurt you. She imagined her children—who'd all be grown-up by now—running around, cutting up, and having fun, and it made her a little sad. But every couple of weeks, she and Paul ventured to the amusement park and avoided the African Dip, which was insulting, the Hades and the Funhouse—demonic—and the Freak Show, which Mary was sure housed real live demons. Sometimes they took Ruthie and one of her friends, but mostly, it was just the two of them, walking around, laughing, talking, and holding hands.

"So, Mary, I got somethin' serious I need to run by you." The couple took seats at a picnic table near the corn dog stand.

"Okay, Paul." Mary took a sip of her drink and braced herself only a little. She'd come to understand that Paul's "serious" ideas were rarely that serious.

"I been thinkin'." Paul sighed a little and bit into his third corn dog. "It's time for me to look into buying a house."

"Oh, really? What for?" Mary fidgeted in her seat. A pebble from the gravel under her feet had gotten into her sandal, and she tried to dislodge it without bending over and removing her shoe.

"Well, I figure you might wanna marry me one day, and I'm gettin too old to be tryin' to carry you up to my third-floor place over the threshold."

"I see." The pebble now gone, Mary turned her attention back to her Coca-Cola and french fries. "Paul, I promise you, *if* I marry you, you ain't *carryin'* me up to nobody's third floor."

"You want a backyard, right? Maybe I'll build a brick barbecue. You could plant you a garden. I wouldn't get nothin' too big. Two bedrooms, nice big kitchen, maybe a bar in the basement. You could decorate the whole house however you want."

Mary looked at Paul then back down into her drink. "I see you thought about this a whole lot, huh?"

"Yup. A whole lot." He reached for his drink. "So, yeah, umm... I quit haulin' potato chips. You ain't gon' see me at the store no more. But I'll still see you much as I can." He took a long drink, emptying the cup, slurping the last bits of Coca-Cola. "I signed on with Phillips Truckin'. Gonna drive a big rig all across the country."

"All across the country?" Mary said a little more loudly than she intended. "That means you gon' stay gone?"

"Naw, not all the time. I'll be gone for six weeks, then off for a week—"

"I see." Mary wanted to reach into her purse for a cigarette. She knew all about truckers... a woman in every town, bringin' home diseases and crabs... if they came home at all...

Paul reached across the table and took Mary's hand. "This is a good move for me. I'll make real good money. Won't hafta pay no rent cuz I'll live in the truck most of the time. I can save up a lot real fast. I get to see the country and—"

"But Paul, six weeks is a long time—"

"I promise I'll send you postcards from everywhere... bring you good stuff too. I'a even send you money so you can—"

"Naw, I don't want yo' money." Mary tried not to snap at him, but he sounded like a teenager talking about his dreams, not like a fifty-year-old man. Didn't he know how much danger was out there... and the demons of temptation that could get at him? She finally gave in and lit a cigarette. Here he was, sitting there practically dumping her and trying to act like it was a good thing.

"Well, what you think?" Paul asked.

Mary took a long drag on her cigarette. The man's mind was obviously made up. He was leaving. Mary felt pressure behind her eyes, but she didn't cry. She'd lost people before. But losing Paul... Mary shook her head. It wouldn't be a big deal. It wasn't like she sinned with him or anything... aside from a few kisses....

She blew the smoke out slowly. "I think this is a real good thing for you, Paul. I hope it works out."

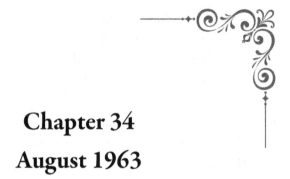

Chapter 34
August 1963

Dear Mary,

I signed on to take a load up thru Canada to Alaska. Now I know I promised to see you soon, but this load pays big money. It might take 3 or 4 months on account of I got to wait for a load coming back this way. Not much coming back this way from way up there, but the pay is worth it—

Mary stopped reading the letter and tore it in half. Paul wasn't coming back. She couldn't say she was surprised. He'd said he'd be away for six weeks, then it turned to seven, then eight. She knew she was right not to get her hopes up. Paul was just a man. This must be part of God's plan.

On a whim, she applied for a city job. File clerk. The ad didn't say where, but Mary took the bus downtown and sat for the city-worker test. It was simple, just basic math and alphabetizing, a little reading, nothing that gave Mary any trouble at all. In fact, she finished before everybody else in the room.

A month later, she got a call for an interview at the police station at 89th and Commercial. She took the 87th Street bus to Commercial Avenue then walked the two blocks to 89th Street. The police station was a big old brick building that Mary thought looked like something from a TV show. It smelled like the college library building but with smoke. The officer at the desk smoked a cigar and didn't look up from his newspaper.

"Yeah?"

"Hello. I'm Mary Bevers. I have a interview—"

"Upstairs, to the right. 204."

"Thank you." Mary turned to head up the stairs. She paused. "And *you* have a good day."

"Yeah, likewise."

On her way up the stairs, Mary said a quick prayer for the rude officer and found her way to room 204, which happened to be to the left not the right. The interview was fast. She answered all Mrs. Milton's questions and promised that she wasn't going to have a baby or even get married any time soon. Being a twice-widowed single woman making it on her own appeared to impress Mrs. Milton. Since Mary didn't drive, she'd rely on the bus system, so she had guaranteed transportation. Three weeks later, Mary got a letter from Paul, which she didn't read, and a letter from the city offering her the police-department position, paying more than twice what she made at the High-Low grocery store.

On her last day working at the grocery, the manager and employees threw her a going-away party, complete with a good-luck cake, flowers, streamers, and a paper crown. She got hugs and pats on the back from her regular customers, and even some of the kids who used to shoplift in the snack aisle said they were sad to see her go.

"Honestly, Mary." Ladora stood beside Mary at the checkout counter while Mary rang up a customer. "I think you gon' hate workin' for the city, especially the police. You gon' see so much mess, you gon' come runnin' right back here."

"Hmph, thanks. Good luck to you too." Mary huffed. Ladora had been her best friend at work for nearly ten years, and Mary understood that the woman was not happy to see her leave.

"Naw, don't get all funny actin'. I don't mean nothin' by it," Ladora said quickly. "I just think it's gon' be harder than you think it is. You walkin' outta here all happy and stuff... I just don't want you to get yo' hopes up, that's all."

"You know what, Ladora?" Mary turned and was surprised to see tears in her friend's eyes. "Yeah, I'm gon' miss you too." The women hugged. "I'mma be back in here every Saturday for groceries. It's gon' be like I never left."

"So, what Paul got to say about your new job?" Ladora went back over to her register as customers started to line up.

"Nothin'." Mary found the price stamped on a box of corn flakes and entered it into the cash register. "It ain't none of his business." She turned her attention to her customer and continued ringing up merchandise on her last shift as a High-Low cashier.

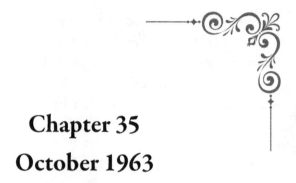

Chapter 35
October 1963

Changing jobs was one thing, but Mary didn't stop there. She opened a charge account at Paddor's clothing store and changed her wardrobe then her hair, and then, when her church moved to a big fancy building in the South Shore neighborhood, she decided it was time to move to an apartment closer to her church and her job. She didn't leave a forwarding address.

"So, you just changed yo' whole world, huh?" Late on a Saturday morning, Ruthie stood in Mary's new living room, which was stacked with cardboard boxes. Mary worked on unpacking her knickknacks and framed photos. This first-floor apartment on 75th Street wasn't much bigger than her place on 47th Street, but it was walking distance from the newly integrated Rainbow Beach and maybe six blocks from her church. It had tall windows and gleaming hardwood floors. The freshly cleaned and painted rooms smelled of lemon polish and pine cleaner.

"Yup." Mary stepped out of the way as movers placed her new couch in front of the dark-wood-trimmed windows. "I got a big-city office job now. It's time to make some changes."

"Girl, I remember when all you wanted was big-city night life. Now listen to you... talkin' 'bout a big-city *job*." Ruthie laughed at Mary and went back to unpacking the kitchen.

As the movers deposited more furniture, Mary walked through her new place and paused in each room to say a prayer for protection from demons and sin, dabbing a bit of oil on each windowsill. When she was done, she let herself take a deep breath and thanked God for his blessings. She was living a life free from sin, and God had blessed her with the desires of her heart. She laughed at herself a little. There had been a time when all she wanted was fun and high living but not now. She had suffered God's punishment and learned the error of her ways, and now, here she was, blessed beyond measure.

"Okay, Mary." Ruthie caught up with Mary in the second bedroom of the two-bedroom apartment. "Here." She handed Mary a glass of iced tea. "The kitchen is finished, and we gon' toast to your new life." She touched her glass to Mary's and then took a long drink.

Mary took a swallow then glared at her sister. "Get thee behind me, Satan! I rebuke you!" She snapped, "You put liquor in this!"

"Of course I did." Ruthie tapped her glass to Mary's again. "That's how you make a toast." She took another swallow. "A little bit won't hurt you."

Mary left the room, walked straight to the kitchen, and emptied her glass into the sink. "Ruthie, I'm sick of you tryin' to get me to sin. You act just like the devil dancin' around the rocks." She shook her finger at Ruthie. "Well, just like Jesus, I ain't gon' do it! I been pure and holy for more than fifteen years, and not you and nobody else gon' make me do wrong."

"Well, Miss Pure and Holy, I guess you just too good for the rest of the world, cuz I don't know nobody pure and holy as you. 'Cept I think you a little prideful about all yo' pureness. And you ain't that holy." Ruthie took a swallow of her tea. "You don't give everything to the poor, and you don't visit the sick and shut-in. I mean, who are you really helpin' with all your holiness? What good is yo' holiness doin'?"

"Well, the Bible say—"

"I know the Bible too," Ruthie snapped. "And it say, 'All your righteousness is like filthy rags,'" she quoted.

Mary massaged her temples and said a silent prayer for patience. "Ruthie, is it time for you to go home yet?"

Chapter 36

Every weekday, Mary sat at the high counter in the police station's records room. Her work was the usual sorting incoming files and fulfilling record requests. If anybody asked her, she'd never admit she was bored, but... she was bored. She missed the hustle and bustle of the grocery store and the nonstop chatter of her friends. Though she hadn't actively participated in the sinful gossip fests, she did miss the stories. Mary made the trek to 47th Street every weekend, mostly to see Ruthie but also to stop by the High-Low grocery store. She'd usually find a few things on sale that she could use and didn't mind hauling home on the bus. Whenever she visited the store, her old manager let her sit in the breakroom for an hour and chit-chat with whoever happened to be taking a break. When a new manager came along though, Mary's visits to the store ended, and her friendships faded.

It was in her second week at the police station that she met Officer Reives. The young man was probably in his late twenties and kept his hat on inside. He wasn't much taller than Mary, but he puffed out his chest and walked around like he had to duck under doorways. Mary didn't really like the cocky young man.

"Well, damn! So, you the new girl, huh?"

Startled, Mary closed the file she shouldn't have been reading and went over to the front counter. "Yeah, what can I do for you?" She handed him a file requisition form.

"You can start by giving me your phone number," the young man said. "They told me the new girl was fine, but they didn't say you was a full-grown woman. You look like somethin' I might want." He smiled, showing a mouth full of perfectly straight teeth.

Mary looked down at his name badge. "Is it a file or somethin' I can get for you, Officer Reives?"

"Oh, you one of them *serious-about-ya-job* kinda women, huh? You just like ol' Milton, huh?"

"Did you come in here for a reason, Officer?" A lifetime ago, she might have found his attention flattering, but now, Mary tried not to grind her teeth and cut her eyes at the man. He was getting on her nerves.

"Oh, yeah." He took the req form and filled in the blanks, copying from his notepad. "Can I come get this in a hour?"

Mary looked down at the form. He had nice handwriting. "Gimme two hours," Mary said. "Got some ahead of you."

"Okay, Miss..." He looked down at the nameplate on the counter. "Miss Mary Bevers. I'll see you in *one* hour."

Mary shook her head and sighed at the man leaving the room. She hoped he was the last one. It seemed like every Negro man in the building felt a need to stop by and flirt with her, and after Paul, she had no interest in men, especially not policemen. If truckers were bad, cops were the worst. And it wasn't gossip she was listening to. She overheard so much scandalous talk from the cops themselves, she was starting to think Ladora had been right. She took the form and went to the correct cabinet and pulled the file. It took her all of five minutes, but Mrs. Milton, her trainer, had told her to allow two hours for every request. Mary hadn't committed the sin of lying because she was just following orders, and she wouldn't release the file until two hours had passed.

An hour later, Officer Reives returned with a greasy brown paper bag that smelled of barbecue. "I brought you somethin'." He placed the bag on the counter on top of Mary's clean notepad. "I figure if it's takin' you two hours to pull files, you too busy to get lunch. I got you some rib tips."

Mary looked down at the bag then at the officer. "I... uh... Th... thank you," she said. She wasn't sure what else to say. "That's real nice of you. How much do I owe you?"

"You don't owe me nothin'... if you let me sit in here and have lunch with you." He smiled again.

Mary looked up at the big clock on the wall and then back at the flirtatious officer. He was surely young enough to be her son, and it was still thirty minutes until her lunchtime... but those rib tips smelled like they'd be a lot better than her leftover chicken from last night's dinner... or was it the night before last? "Okay, fine," Mary said. "I break for lunch at twelve."

"Mary, I'm Melvin." He held out his hand and Mary shook it. "I'll see you at twelve, then."

An hour later, Mary sat laughing with Melvin as he shared stories of his early years with the department. Some of the stories were harrowing or sad, but many of them were just plain funny. He also told of the time he got pulled over in another precinct and was almost beaten up until his sergeant showed up and rescued him. He talked about what it was like being one of the first Negro cops in the precinct and all the Jackie Robinson and janitor jokes he'd endured before he'd proven himself.

"So why you not out there policin'?" Mary asked. The rib tips were delicious, and she wanted to lick her fingers, but instead, she used a napkin that only managed to stick to the sauce on her hands. "How you got time to spend all day in here?"

"Hmph. They got me on desk duty 'cause I got hurt chasin' a mugger. I caught 'im, but I forgot I'm not a kid anymore. Cain't bounce back like I could in high school. I'm goin' back out next week, though."

Mary looked up at the clock. "Melvin, I need to go get my hands clean so I can get back to work." She stepped out into the hallway and rinsed her hands in the drinking fountain. "Thank you for lunch." She held out her chilled hand and wasn't surprised that he kissed the back of it.

"I would'a licked 'em clean for you." He winked at her.

Mary bristled. "Oh, well. I thought you was nice, but I guess you just like all the rest of these—"

"C'mon, Mary. You know I was just playin'. I know you a lady an' all."

"I'm a good Christian woman, and I don't mess around like that—"

"I'm sorry, Mary," Melvin said. "For real. That was stupid of me. I'll be nice from now on."

"Hmph." Mary walked over to her desk and grabbed the file he'd requested. "Here's your file. Good-bye." She handed him the file and then turned her back. As entertaining as the young officer was, Mary was not about to let him think such behavior, even as a joke, was acceptable.

As winter winds blew into Chicago, true to his word, Melvin remained respectful and brought Mary lunch each day that he was in the office and then at least once a week after he went back out. He reminded her of her friend Joshua Floyd, a little prideful and full of himself, but seemed to have a good heart. After a month of lunches, Melvin started asking Mary on dates, and each time, she declined.

"Boy, I'm way too old for you. You need to be findin' girls your own age," Mary said as they sat in the file room, sharing Harold's chicken wings.

"Woman, you think I don't know you older than me? I don't want some young girl." He reached out with a napkin and dabbed at the mild-sauce spot on Mary's chin. "I need a real grown woman, and you exactly what I want."

Mary shook her head. Paul had said something similar. "Listen," she said. "It's cute that you like me and all, but I cain't go with you. It ain't right. You gotta find somebody yo' own age and make a life and have babies and all that. I cain't do nothin' for you."

"So you really just gon' turn down what might be the best man of your life?"

Again, Mary shook her head. "Jesus is the best man of my life. I don't need nobody else."

ON AN ESPECIALLY FREEZING December night, a police car pulled up beside the bus stop where Mary waited. The lights flashed and a bullhorn came on. "Mary Bevers, it's too cold for you to be on the bus!" The three other people at the bus stop looked around, and Mary covered her face with her gloved hands.

"Jesus, I rebuke this silly man!" Mary said a little too loudly. The other people stepped away from her.

"Don't make me come get you, Mary!"

Mary shook her head and looked down the street. There was no bus in sight.

"I got handcuffs!"

"Girl, it's cold as hell out here," one of the other women at the bus stop said. "Just go with 'im, or I will." Then, as if through divine intervention, Chicago's legendary Hawk winds practically lifted Mary's skirt and blew her toward the curb. She sighed and walked over to the car.

"So, you gon' let me take you home, or do I hafta call for back-up?" Melvin smirked at her, and Mary admitted to herself that the light-skinned man was nice to look at. She made a mental note to pinch herself later because she was wearing gloves at that moment.

"If I ride with you, you gon' leave me alone?" Mary asked.

"Nope. Long as it's this cold, I'mma see you home." He got out of the car and opened the back driver's side door. "Hop in."

Mary hesitated. "Why I gotta ride in the back like a criminal?"

"It's the rules." Melvin said. "Too much paperwork for you to ride in the front." He flashed her a smile and nodded toward the back seat. "Get in."

Mary hesitated for another moment, and the wind picked up again. She sighed and got in the car, and when Melvin closed the door behind her, she realized there was no handle on the inside. She wouldn't be able to let herself out. She took off her gloves and pinched herself for liking the man and pinched herself again for probably making a bad decision. The ten-minute ride to Mary's apartment building was uneventful. Melvin talked about the neighborhood and pointed out places where he'd made arrests or had exciting adventures. When he parked the car and let Mary out, she was grateful that he only said goodnight.

As the winter grew colder, Mary lost her hesitation and accepted more rides. Each time, she pinched herself because she wasn't sure if she was leading him on by riding with him. On the fourth or fifth ride, she invited him into her apartment to fill his thermos bottle with leftover chicken and noodles.

"Now, Mary, how you expect me to leave you alone when you feed a man like this?" Melvin sat at Mary's kitchen table, shoveling the warmed leftovers into his mouth. "This is better than my mama makes."

"Don't you hafta get back out in a few minutes?" She placed his filled thermos on the table. "Folks gon' see your car parked out front and wonder."

"Yeah, you right. I cain't hang out here too long." He stood up and wiped his mouth with the back of his hand. "But I gotta get somethin' before I go." And before Mary could think, he pulled her into a kiss. She pressed her hands against his chest and tried to push him away, but he pulled her closer.

Mary tried to say "*stop*," but he held the back of her head and pressed harder.

"You don't really want me to stop, and you know it," he whispered.

Mary struggled in his embrace, and when his probing tongue pushed into her mouth, she clamped her teeth down on it.

"Ow, ow, ow!" he said as best he could while having his tongue bitten. "Okay, I'll stop." He let go of her and took a step back.

"Satan, I rebuke you!" Mary shouted. "Now get outta my house, you demon!"

Melvin picked up his thermos and keys from the kitchen table. "You gon' be sorry you wasn't nice to me when you freezin' yo' ass off out there."

"You just get outta my house and don't talk to me no more!" Mary followed him to the door and slammed and locked it behind him. She immediately rinsed her mouth with rubbing alcohol and stuck herself with a safety pin for obviously leading him to think that kiss was okay.

That kiss.

It wasn't that bad.

Tasted like chicken and noodles.

She stuck herself one more time for good measure.

Mary saw no more of Officer Melvin Reives at work, and as winter wore on, she wasn't sorry for biting him, but she definitely missed his rides. Other men asked her out, and she was always careful to be absolutely clear that the answer was "*no*."

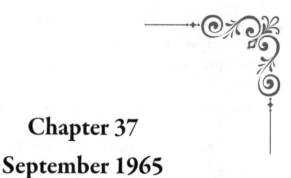

Chapter 37

September 1965

Mary sat fanning herself in the eighth row on the right side. The September afternoon wasn't really warm or anything, but fanning herself helped her stay awake. Reverend Taylor was good but kinda dry sometimes. The message today was about Jesus charging the disciples to spread the gospel and promising damnation to non-believers. Mary had heard sermons on that story all her life, and she used to wonder if people who never heard the gospel were still going to hell. But that was back when she used to be a sinner. She didn't question God now.

After the sermon, the "doors of the church" were opened, and any guest who didn't have a church home was invited to join Lakeshore Christian Fellowship. The choir always saved the best song of the day for the invitation. Usually, two or three people came to the altar, sometimes couples, sometimes whole families. Mary watched a woman with tears streaming down her face approach the front. Her dress was much too tight. A man in a baggy suit and probably run-over shoes came up next. The congregation clapped each time. Reverend Taylor held his hand out and asked if there was another soul seeking a home with the Lord. That meant it was almost time for offering, so Mary dug out her offering envelope and pinched herself for not having a pencil to sign it. More clapping drew her attention to the front of the church, and Mary's jaw dropped, and her eyes went wide as a third person went to stand with the other two new people. *Paul.* Mary's hand went to her pearl necklace... then her chest... then her hat. *Why did I wear this today? I have so many nicer hats.*

After service, during coffee hour, while Mary waited in the social hall for Paul and the other guests to come out of the special meeting with the pastor, she was again approached by Mother Nanetta Robinson about joining the hospitality committee. "All you gotta do is turn on the coffee pot at offering time so it's ready when service is over. That ain't so hard, now, is it?"

Mary watched the door to the pastor's study. "It's not hard at all, ma'am," Mary said to the older woman. "But I like to put my tithes and offerin' in the plate—"

"Now you know God don't care where you put it as long as he get it." Mother Robinson laid a hand on Mary's arm. "So, I got you down for next Sunday, and if you could bring a couple cakes, that would be real good. You from down south. I bet you make a real good pound cake."

Mary looked at the long table, covered in white cloth and bowed in the middle from the weight of the desserts. Pound cakes—dry. Coffee cakes—dry, too, but with raisins. Somebody tried to make a butter cake. It was moist and salty. The only thing good was the cookies, and that was because they came from the store. The women at Lakeshore Church who liked to bake couldn't do it very well, and Mary knew she'd be permanently in that position if she got on the hospitality committee. "I don't know if I can—"

"Nonsense." The old woman leaned on her cane as Paul approached them. "Ain't nothin' to it. You'll see. You'll like hospitality." She lowered her voice to a pretend whisper. "And I know there's men here who love a woman that can cook." Mother Robinson walked away before Mary could think of a response.

"If you cookin', I guess I picked a good time to join. You can still cook, right?" Paul laughed.

Mary wanted to roll her eyes, but that was rude and a sin, and besides, she couldn't help smiling. "I still cook a little." Mary tried not to sound prideful. "Don't tell me you joined my church just to get me to cook for you."

"Well, Mary." Paul's tone got a little serious. "I joined *our* church cuz I think it's a good church. Pastor is real smart, music is good, teachin' is sound... yeah... a real good church. And if you and yo' cookin' comes with it, well, that's just a bonus."

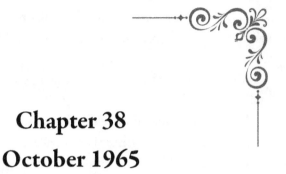

Chapter 38
October 1965

"Ruthie, this is too tight! I look like —"

"Dorothy Dandridge. You look like you just came outta *Ebony* magazine." Ruthie adjusted the neckline on the gold brocade dress that Mary wore. "Not showing a lotta skin but still lookin' fine as wine." She dusted Mary's shoulders with sparkly powder.

The fitted dress accentuated her curves, and looking in the full-length mirror, Mary imagined she did look like Dorothy Dandridge. "Ruthie, I don't know... It is pretty, but I'm not tryin' to stir up demons of pride and vanity. And we just goin' out to eat and—"

"Mary, you goin' to Robert's Show Lounge. That's the best club on the south side. You gotta go in looking like a million bucks, and in this dress, you look like five million."

Mary studied her reflection some more then pulled at the neckline and reached around back for the zipper. "Naw, Ruthie, I cain't wear this. Unzip me."

"Nope," Ruthie said with a laugh. "Only person unzippin' that dress tonight is Paul! Ahahaha!"

"Doggone it, Ruthie!" Mary turned and stretched every which way but couldn't feel the tiny zipper pull. "If I hafta cut this dress off, I will!"

"Girl, hush and cover your face." Ruthie held up a can of hair-spray and started spraying before Mary could protest. "I wish you would let me do your makeup."

"No! Now, that's where I draw the line. You ain't paintin' my face up like—"

"...Like you used to do yourself." Ruthie grabbed a rouge compact and tried to dab at her sister's cheek. "I was there, remember? Now, be still. It's just a little. It won't hardly show."

Mary covered her face with her hands. "If it won't show, then I don't need it."

"Fine, then." Ruthie put down the makeup. "But a little lipstick wouldn't hurt."

"I'm fine with Vaseline," Mary said. "And no mascara either. I'm not puttin' nothin on my face. Period."

At exactly seven-fifteen, the doorbell rang, and Ruthie ran to the buzzer to let Paul in. "He's heeere!" she sang. She opened the door with a flourish, and Mary crushed out her cigarette and pulled on her black wool coat.

"Well, hello, Paul. Welcome to Mary's home," Ruthie said. "I honestly thought you was gone for good. Damn, you still big!"

"Haha. Hey, Ruthie!" Paul shook Ruthie's hand and pulled her into a hug. "It's good to see you too."

"Can I take your coat? You hungry? Can I get you somethin' to drink?" Ruthie stepped back so Paul could enter the apartment then closed the door behind him.

Mary cleared her throat. "Ruthie, stop. You know we goin' out."

"Mary, I'm tryin' to be polite. You know... like you supposed to do when you have company." Ruthie huffed. "And besides, you cain't go yet. You gotta change coats. I told you I brought you my fur wrap. You ain't wearing no old-lady coat over that dress."

Mary pulled her coat more tightly around her. "What's wrong with my coat? It's freezing outside, and this is the warmest coat I got."

"Paul, talk to her. I'll be right back." Ruthie shook a finger at her sister and left the room.

"I'm sorry about Ruthie," Mary apologized. "She don't got no manners. I don't know where she gets it from. Mama used to—"

"Your hair looks real nice," Paul interrupted Mary's brewing tirade. He stepped closer to her. "You smell good too."

Mary reached up to lightly pat her hair but quickly moved her hand back down. Primping was vain. She looked up at Paul and couldn't help smiling. He looked good, too, freshly shaved in his black overcoat over a gray double-breasted suit. The suit was well cut and was obviously tailored just for his massive frame. Mary thought he looked like a big fancy movie star or something. And his cologne reminded her of cherry tobacco smoke and sweet whiskey... and she loved the smells of cherry tobacco smoke and sweet whiskey.

"Here ya go." Ruthie rushed back into the living room, holding out her fancy mink wrap.

"Girl, I'mma freeze to death in just that li'l thing." Mary pulled her coat tight again.

"Yo' car got heat, right, Paul?" Ruthie slapped her sister's hands and began peeling off Mary's coat. "Girl, quit bein' so silly. Take off this ugly ole thing."

Mary didn't think herself silly at all, and she was getting tired of her little sister's bossiness, but she let Ruthie take the coat anyway. "Okay, fine. I guess you ain't gon' be happy 'til I freeze to death."

"Well, then you'a be beautiful in your casket. Now put this on."

"Eh-hem." Paul cleared his throat, seeming to startle the bickering women. He tapped his watch. "We got a table at eight o'clock. It's not too cold. How bout I carry your other coat, and if you start freezin', you put it on?"

Mary scowled back and forth between Ruthie and Paul. The whole discussion was ridiculous, really. It was just a dinner date, and it wasn't like she'd have the coat on inside the club. Mary snatched

the wrap from Ruthie and headed out the door, not saying goodbye
and not waiting for Paul.

The Roberts Show Lounge was packed, and the house band was
performing when Mary and Paul arrived. The club was on par with
the Crystal Palace in Jackson, Mississippi, but still not as elegant as
the DeLisa or the Savoy. They were led through the maze of tightly
packed tables draped in white cloths to a table with a couple already
seated. The man stood and introduced himself as Harold, shaking
Paul's hand. The woman remained seated and didn't speak, and Mary
would've sworn she'd rolled her eyes. Paul ordered a whiskey, and
Mary ordered a Coca-Cola.

Up on the stage, the MC brought out Nipsey Russell to warm
up the crowd. The comedian wowed the audience with his jokes and
signature poetry. Paul and Harold roared with laughter, and Mary
couldn't help laughing too. She liked Nipsey Russell. Even his most
risqué jokes were mild compared to some other comedians'. The other woman at the table, who never introduced herself, sat with her
arms folded and never cracked a smile. Mary decided not to try to
make friends.

After the comedian came the headliner for the night... Mr. Ex-
citement, Jackie Wilson! The crowd went wild. Even Mary was on
her feet, and she pinched herself several times, but she couldn't tear
her eyes or ears away from the gorgeous man with the gyrating hips.

"So, I guess you havin' fun, huh?" Paul asked her when the singer
switched to a soft, slow ballad.

"Yeah, I am." Mary laughed a little. Her eyes were closed, and she
swayed to the music. "This is so nice." And it was nice. Mary sat in
a night club, looking like a movie star and feeling twenty-five years
younger. The only things missing were a cigarette and a whiskey. She
opened her eyes and looked around the room. Nearly every woman
at every table held a drink and a cigarette. She never felt smoking was
a sin, just that doing it in public wasn't proper. But... it was a spe-

cial occasion, and it wasn't like she would be walking down the street blowing smoke or anything. Reaching into her purse, she pulled out her fancy beaded cigarette case and had a flash of a memory... the time at the Crystal Palace when her husband had snatched the case from her. Her hand shook a little when she pulled out the unfiltered cigarette, and she was startled when Paul held out his lighter and lit it for her. She took a long, deep drag, drifted on the music, and ached for a whiskey, but she would not give in to the demon of alcohol.

After the show, Mary let Paul lead her to the dance floor. Given his size, she was amazed at how light he was on his feet. They dipped and swayed and twisted and bopped, and when the music changed to something slow, Mary found herself relaxing in his arms. Moving to the music, she allowed herself to indulge in nostalgia for a few minutes. She'd slow danced with Mason, Slim, and John Dixon, and she was familiar with the feel of a man's loving embrace, but Paul was different. He held her carefully, like he was scared he might crush her or something. Grateful that Ruthie had insisted she wear high heels, Mary still had to reach up to get her arms around Paul's neck. She leaned against him, and he pulled her a little closer.

Over the past two years, she really had missed him. He felt so good again—his warmth, his strength, his scent. She looked up at him and then laid her head against his chest. She wished he would kiss her, but that might be a sin in public, and she didn't have the benefit of enough alcohol to excuse such behavior. On the ride home, Mary sat close to Paul, and he held her hand. Maybe when he walked her to the door, he'd try for a goodnight kiss.

"YOU HUNGRY?" MARY ASKED as she unlocked her apartment door. "Wanna come in for a minute? I got some good stew I could heat up."

"Naw, I'm not hungry, but if I could use your bathroom, that would be good."

Mary opened the door, stepped inside, and groaned. "Lord have mercy, that girl."

"What's the matter?" Paul reached over Mary's head and pushed the door open.

"Oh, nothing, Ruthie just left a mess." The living room lamps were on but draped with red scarves. A slow Jackie Wilson tune had been left playing on the record player, and on the coffee table sat a bottle of Cold Duck, two champagne glasses, and a giant slice of cake with two forks.

"I see. She ain't shy about nothin." Paul laughed.

"Well, she need to get her some business and quit mindin' mine." Mary pointed Paul to the bathroom and went to the lamps and removed the scarves, flooding the living room with light.

"Damn, it's bright in here." Paul came back into the room. "But that cake look kinda good." He pointed and took a step toward the coffee table.

"Oh... w... well," Mary stuttered. "Yeah, Ruthie makes cakes better than mine. You want it?"

"Only if you wanna have it with me."

"Okay, gimme your coat. I'll put on some coffee." Mary laid Paul's coat over the back of an armchair and placed his hat on the seat. She didn't bother putting anything in the closet—he wouldn't be staying that long. In the kitchen, Mary fussed under her breath. Ruthie needed to mind her own business and get herself a man and quit messin' around in Mary's life—

"You okay in there?" Paul called from the living room.

"Yeah, here I come. You can turn off that music if you want."

"Naw, I like it." Paul stood up when Mary entered the room carrying two cups of instant coffee. He'd taken off his jacket and laid it over his coat on the chair. "Let me help you with that."

Seated side by side on the couch, Mary and Paul talked and laughed and shared the cake and sipped the coffee until it was lukewarm. Pushing away the coffee cups, Paul picked up the champagne bottle. "You know, it'a be a shame to waste this. Look like Ruthie went through a lot of trouble. Let's open it." Before Mary could think of a reason not to, he opened the bottle and poured champagne into the two glasses. "Here's to us and a new beginning." He tapped his glass against Mary's and then tossed back its contents. "Ah, that's good stuff."

The record ended, and as the mechanical tone arm repositioned itself, Paul stood up and took Mary's hand. "Gimme one dance, and then I'mma head out."

Mary didn't say anything. She just stood up and stepped into the man's open arms. They swayed to Jackie Wilson's golden tones singing about being loved, and Mary again found herself looking up at him, thinking about that kiss. All he had to do was just do it. He'd done it before. Before he left, they'd kissed all the time. Didn't he know that when a woman looked up at you, you were supposed to kiss her? And then, as the song neared the end, as if he was reading her mind, he leaned down and pressed his mouth to hers. It wasn't a soft and gentle kiss. It was a firm, hard, hungry kiss, and Mary decided the taste of coffee, pound cake, and champagne was her new favorite flavor. And the kiss lasted long past the end of the song, and when the song restarted, they took a breath and kissed some more.

"Mary, we gotta stop. Ain't tryin' to start nothin' we ain't gon' finish." Paul pulled away and loosened his tie. "It's kinda warm in here, huh."

Mary stepped back and patted her hair. She started to pinch herself but changed her mind. It was only a kiss, and nothing in the Bible said a kiss was a sin. But kissing that man was so good, it had to be. She tried not to smile, but she had goose bumps.

"Well, let me get on outta here." Paul slipped on his jacket and picked up his coat. "How 'bout I come by and fix you breakfast tomorrow?"

"Okay, that'll be real nice." Mary followed him to the door. "I had a real good time tonight. That Nipsey Russel is a fool." She laughed.

"Yeah." He pulled her into his arms and kissed her again. "I had a good time too. Now, let me get outta here fo' I forget to leave."

Mary kissed him one more time and then opened the door. When she closed the door behind him, she froze. *Dammit, Ruthie!* She snatched the door open. Paul was still standing there, poised to knock. "Uh... I left my hat on the chair," he said.

"Oh... um... I need your help." Mary looked up at him and then looked away. "See, Ruthie helped me get dressed, and I cain't reach the zipper and... um..." Mary blushed.

"Heh heh..." Paul laughed nervously. "Uh, Mary... You want me to help you outta yo' clothes, you gon' get us both in trouble."

"Paul, we ain't teenagers." She stepped back and let him in. "We got sense."

"Yeah, we do." Paul pushed the door closed behind him and pulled Mary into his arms again. He reached around behind her, unhooked a tiny hook, and carefully pulled the zipper down her back.

Mary looked up into his eyes and moved her arms around his neck. Just one more kiss.

Chapter 39

"It was a accident," Mary said. "I didn't mean to. It just hap-pened."

"Accident, my ass!" Ruthie laughed at her older sister. "Girl, it took you twenty minutes to get that girdle on. How the hell you *accidentally* take it off?"

"I hafta break up with him." Mary sat at her kitchen table, smok-ing a cigarette and sipping bitter sage tea. "Whenever I'm with him, the demons get at me real easy."

"Well, that's mighty mannish of you." Ruthie laughed at her sis-ter again. "You wine and dine with him, then you dump him after you get some. Yeah, you actin' just like a man."

"Ruthie, this ain't funny. I could get God all riled up at me, or what if I die in sin and wind up goin' straight to hell?"

Ruthie sipped her coffee. "Mary, we both went to the same Sun-day school, so we both heard the same things. If you repent, God forgives you, blah blah blah... You know the rest. God ain't gon' do nothin' to you. You ain't goin' to hell."

Mary glared at her sister then stared straight ahead again. "You don't know that. Whenever I sinned, God got me real good. That's why all my babies died. That's why I ain't sinned in fifteen years."

"Mary, that's crazy talk." Ruthie got up and poured herself more coffee. "I know what happened to you was bad, but God ain't mean like that—"

"Yeah, he is. You just don't know it yet. All the sin you do, maybe the devil is protectin' you, but God don't let me get away with nothin.'"

Ruthie sat back down. "So, how did you burn your hand?"

"With the iron, like I said. It ain't so bad. Hurt like the devil, but it'll be okay. I told you God don't let me get away with sin."

"So you think God punished you for sleepin' with Paul by burnin' your hand?"

"Yeah," Mary sighed. "And for backslidin'... skippin' church and goin' out drinkin' and listenin' to worldly music and stuff. That man makes me wanna sin all over the place." Mary sighed again. "And that's why I know God is gon' get me, 'cause I cain't repent 'cause I really don't wanna stop sinnin'..." Mary's hand shook as she lit another cigarette. "So I gotta break up with 'im."

"You know you sound crazy, right?" Ruthie got up and went to the oven and checked on the pot roast. She stabbed at it with a fork then closed the oven and turned to face Mary. "Mary, you in love, and God don't punish you for bein' in love. God wants you to be in love and get married and have babies and all that. Y'all both single, and it's what you both want. I don't see the problem. Why you cain't just enjoy yo' life?"

Mary stared down into her teacup then took a long drag on her cigarette. Ruthie wouldn't understand... couldn't understand. She had never felt the judgment and wrath of God like Mary had. Last night, she had been overwhelmed by demons... demons of alcohol and worldly music... demons of gluttony and dancing and lust. And when she had woken up the next day to see Paul propped up on an elbow, staring down at her, she had let demons of lust get to her again, and they skipped church and made love some more. It wasn't against her will. It wasn't against her wishes. It was the deepest desire of her heart, so it had to be a demon possessing her to make her give herself to this man... to fornicate... to sin.

So while Paul cooked breakfast, Mary washed the taste of alcohol and sin from her mouth, plugged in the iron, and held it against the back of her hand until her skin blistered. The burn, she hoped, would be enough punishment to rid herself of the demons and ward off God's wrath.

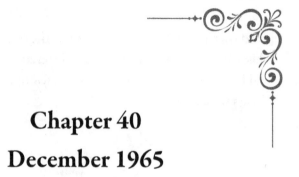

Chapter 40

December 1965

Mary knew women who went through *the change* in their mid-forties, so when her monthly didn't come in October, she praised and thanked the Lord and hoped that she was done with the whole mess. In November, she chalked the light-headedness and cramps up to the change. Her mother had often told her how bad she felt during that time. Then came Thanksgiving, and every smell in Ruthie's kitchen made her retch, and Mary lay down and wanted to die.

She had fitful, demon-filled nightmares where Will Bevers called her a whore and beat her and tore Dinah from her arms; where she knelt over Slim's body covered in blood, holding an infant gasping for breath; where she rocked her cold, lifeless babies while Mason sobbed. And each time she awoke, her pillow was wet with tears.

"Mary! Wake up!"

Mary opened her eyes to see Ruthie's and Paul's anxious faces staring down at her. She looked over at her alarm clock. It was after three o'clock, but daylight shone through the space between the curtains, so she knew it was afternoon. She pulled the covers up over her head. "Leave me alone, and I'm putting a chain on that door tomorrow," she said.

"Well, too late now." Ruthie pulled the covers back. "Damn, you stink. Get up and take a shower. Me and Paul brought some dinner. I'll go heat it up."

Mary reached for the covers again, but Ruthie held them tight. "No, thank you. I'm not hungry." Mary grunted, trying to pull the covers up. "Leave the food in the kitchen. I'll eat later."

"Paul, get her up." Ruthie snatched the covers out of Mary's hands. "She probably been in this bed since last week." She left the room, dragging the covers behind her.

Mary felt the bed sink as Paul sat on the side. He smelled like fresh air and cigars and Old Spice.

"Mary, wha's the matter with you?" Paul shifted his weight, and the bed groaned. "I been callin' and callin', and Ruthie said you left her place Wednesday and ain't nobody seen nor heard from you. An' you wasn't in church today, and I been real worried."

Mary lay under her flowered sheet, angry at Ruthie for taking her blanket. The room wasn't cold, but she felt exposed without it. "Paul, I'm fine. I just been a little tired and didn't feel like gettin' up."

"Woman, it's Sunday. Sound like you been in this bed since Wednesday."

"Hmph... I guess I have," she said. "But I'm fine." Just then, the smell of Ruthie heating leftovers reached her, and her stomach roiled. "Paul, I gotta get by you to the bathroom." She scrambled around him and practically ran to the bathroom. Her stomach quickly emptied itself of saltines and ginger ale and then spasmed until her ribs ached. She rinsed her mouth with Listerine and splashed her face with cold water.

"You okay in there?" Paul called.

She looked in the mirror. Her eyes were puffy and bloodshot. Her skin was gray. She was not okay. "Yeah, I'm fine." Mary splashed her face again. "I'mma wash up right quick. Gimme a few minutes."

She knew Ruthie had been worried enough to use her emergency key, but why did she hafta bring Paul?

When she came out of the bathroom, she could feel him staring at her. "I heard you throwin' up," he said. "Stomach bug?"

"I guess." Mary pulled on a robe and sat on the bed beside him. "I'm just not feelin' too well."

"Do we need to get you to a doctor? If you been throwin' up for days, somethin' is real wrong." He stood up and took her hand. "C'mon. Let's get you some coffee and try somethin' to eat."

In the kitchen, the scents of coffee and leftovers set Mary's stomach to churning. Ruthie sat at the table, reading a copy of *Jet* magazine. "I hope you hungry. I brung a little of everything and some dessert too," she said. "You ran out so fast last week, I thought you was mad about somethin'. What's wrong with you? Why you look like death?"

"Cuz I'm dyin', Ruthie." Mary laughed a little then reached for her cigarettes on the table.

"Mary, that ain't even funny," Ruthie snapped. "Don't joke about stuff like that."

"You better not be dying." Paul opened cabinets until he found cups. "Took me two years to get you back. You ain't leavin' me now." He laughed a little. "Sit down, Mary. I'll get ya coffee."

Mary sat down and took slow, deep breaths. "No coffee. It's some ginger ale in the ice box. I cain't keep nothin' down hardly."

Paul looked back at Mary then at Ruthie, worry showing on his face. "Okay, but you gon' try to eat a little somethin'."

Mary nodded. "I'll eat in the dining room. It's too hot in here." She got up and left the room. The dining room was almost as hot as the kitchen, and she reached over the radiator to open the window. A blast of cold November air seemed to drive the heat from her bones. She tried to bend over to get her face closer to the open window, but the burning-hot radiator was in the way. She thought about placing a fan in the window, but that would be crazy in November.

"Mary, what's wrong with you?" Paul set her plate on the table. "It ain't hot in here."

"The fresh air helps my stomach." She went to the table, took a deep breath, and sat down in front of a plate piled high with chicken and dressing and greens and baked macaroni and sweet potatoes and... She jumped up from her seat and ran to the bathroom, where she gagged and dry heaved until she could hardly breathe. This *was* punishment. She couldn't eat or drink, couldn't keep anything down, couldn't sleep for the nightmares. She would slowly waste away and go mad and die, all because she'd sinned.

She cleaned her face again and walked into the kitchen to face Ruthie and Paul whispering and exchanging worried looks. "Y'all gotta go," she said. "I'mma eat somethin' a little later, but I'm too sick right now, and I gotta get up early for work."

"Nope." Ruthie stood up. "I'm not leavin' you like this. I'mma help you get dressed, and Paul is gon' drive us to the emergency room—"

Mary groaned. "I don't need a doctor. I'll be fine if I get some rest—"

"Woman, you been restin' for a week," Paul said. "Why you won't let us take care of you? What's goin' on with you?"

"Mary, are you pregnant?" Ruthie asked suddenly.

Mary looked from Paul to Ruthie and back again... then the tears came. "I'm forty-five years old. I can't be pregnant." She began to cry deep, choking sobs, so heavy she could barely speak. Paul crossed the kitchen and pulled her into his arms in a hug that nearly crushed her. She laid her head against his chest, and he held her.

MARY SAT IN THE KITCHEN with Ruthie and Paul. She sipped ginger ale and smoked a cigarette. The back door was open slightly, the smells of cooking were dissipating, and her stomach seemed to have settled.

"Y'all don't understand. God don't let me have babies." Mary's hand trembled as she smoked. "He gon' punish me by taking this baby like he took all my other ones."

Ruthie shook her head. "Mary, you cain't know that—"

"I do know that." Mary didn't snap at her sister. She just stared into her glass of ginger ale as she spoke. "I do know that 'cause every time I sinned, God took a baby from me." She looked over at Paul leaning against the kitchen counter. "I sinned again, and now..." She took a short puff of her cigarette and looked at the back of her hand. The burn hadn't been enough.

"Listen, Mary." Paul unfolded his arms. "What's done is done. We gon' get you to a doctor... get you somethin' for your stomach so you can eat. Then we gon' get married. We can get the papers next week."

"Paul, you don't wanna marry me. Then God is gon' get you too."

"Mary, my God ain't like that." Paul sipped his coffee. "If you really are havin' a baby, it's a blessing, and we gon' have a good life."

"But Paul, God took two husbands and seven babies from me." Mary was surprised she didn't feel like crying again. She'd been crying and throwing up for days, but now, talking about her pregnancy out loud, it felt like a terrible weight had been lifted.

A week later, seated in the waiting room at the Presbyterian-St. Luke's Hospital clinic, Mary looked at the other pregnant women and decided she looked not like a mother but like a soon-to-be grandmother. Mason Jr. would've been almost thirty and would surely have had a family by now... and Rosie and Charles and Peter, all grown up and old enough to be parents. Even Dinah would have been almost twenty. Mary sighed and wished for a cigarette.

Though she wasn't married yet, she signed the forms as *Mrs. Mary Bishop*... another lie... another sin. The doctor was surprised at Mary's age and even more surprised at her pregnancy. She got a prescription for stomach medicine and instructions to take vitamins and to rest as much as she could.

"MAMA, I'M SCARED FOR real." Mary sat on the wooden telephone bench in her living room, holding the phone with her shoulder and trying to light a cigarette with trembling hands. "I think God is just gon' kill me this time."

"Now, Mary," her mother said, "you of all people know babies ain't punishment—"

"Dead babies are." Mary lit her cigarette. "God took all my babies. Why he gon' send me another one, conceived in sin, 'cept to punish me by takin' it away?"

"Mary, God ain't like that," her mother said. "You was raised in the church, and you ain't never read in the Bible where God punished somebody with a baby. A baby is a blessing. What the daddy say? Do you love him?"

"He out on the road. Ain't seen him in a couple of weeks."

"Oh?"

"It's okay. I need to stay away from him anyway. Demons get in me when I'm with him." Mary blew out smoke in a thin stream. "Make me wanna drink and listen to worldly music and miss church and—"

"Doggone it, Mary, you in love!" Her mother laughed. "You mournin' when you should be celebratin'. Is he a good man?"

The thought of Paul made her smile a little. He was a good man... a real good man. "Yeah, Ma. He is. We gettin' married over Christmas. If we come to Flora, you think Papa would marry us?"

"Baby, I'm sure he would. 'Course he gon' wanna talk to y'all first, but yeah, he would."

Mary inhaled deeply and blew out smoke through her nose. Was she really ready to be a wife again?

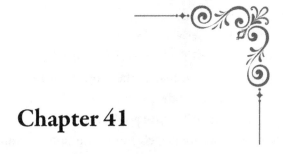

Chapter 41

The road trip to Flora, Mississippi, was uneventful. Ruthie sat up front with Paul, and Mary sat in the back, where she could lie down when she needed to. They arrived just before sunup on Tuesday, December 21, and were met on the porch by Reverend Johnson.

"Good morning, sir!" Paul called as he got out of the car and opened the back door to help Mary out.

"Hey, Papa!" Mary said as she practically ran up the stairs.

"Guess she really gotta go, huh?" Reverend Johnson shook hands with Paul as Mary ran by.

After everybody freshened up, Ruthie and her mother got to work preparing enough breakfast for ten people. Mary's morning sickness had calmed down, and she ate her mother's biscuits with gusto.

"Miss Augusta," Paul said between bites, "this is the best breakfast I had in a long time. I see why yo' girls such good cooks."

"Why, thank you, Paul. It's nice to be appreciated," Augusta said.

After breakfast, the men went out to the front porch to smoke, and the women cleaned up the kitchen. "I like Paul." Augusta sat sipping her coffee while her daughters did the work. "He big, though. Same size as Bobby, but yo' papa is nice and slim, so I don't know where you and Ellie pick these giants from."

"They just like 'em big." Ruthie giggled. "If you know what I mean. Ahahaha!"

"Girl, hush!" Augusta laughed. "That ain't none of yo' business."

Mary stood washing dishes while her mother and sister laughed and talked, occasionally commenting or pinching herself or saying a silent prayer. "Y'all a mess." She rinsed a pan and passed it to Ruthie to dry. "Can we change the subject, please?"

"Okay, let's talk about the wedding!" Ruthie said. "Is it gon' be at the church? What you gon' wear?"

"Oh no... definitely not in the church. God'll strike and burn the whole buildin' down and everybody in it." She saw Ruthie roll her eyes, but she didn't say anything. "I figure we could do it here in the front room. No company... just us." Mary finished washing the last of the silverware and emptied the dishpan into the sink.

"Well, if you do it on Christmas Day, it's gon' be company here," Augusta said. "You know how we do. And we gon' be too busy Christmas Eve, what with church and all the cookin'."

"Hell, let's do it tomorrow." Ruthie wiped off the counters and grabbed the broom. "Ain't nobody got plans tomorrow. What you gon' wear?"

"Okay, yeah." Augusta held out her coffee cup to Mary, and Mary refilled it. "Tomorrow is a good idea. I can cook up a nice wedding dinner. Ruthie, you make a cake tonight. I'll make you a grocery list. Get Paul to take you to the Piggly Wiggly. I can call everybody to-day—"

"Whoa... hold up." Mary sat down at the table with her cup of sage tea. "This ain't gon' be no big thing. Just me and Paul and y'all. That's it."

"Mary, you not gettin' married in my house without all yo' sisters here, and you know they come with kids." Augusta sipped her coffee and grimaced. She pushed the cup away. "It's not gon' be too big, and if they don't wanna come, they won't, but you gon' invite 'em all."

Mary sighed. "Yes, ma'am. But can we save the big dinner for Christmas Day? Just have somethin' small?"

"It's gon' be small." Ruthie put on a fresh pot of coffee. "I'm only makin' one cake. Ain't gon' have a bride and groom on it or nothin'. So, you never said what you gon' wear."

"I brought your black dress and a hat with a veil," Mary said. "I'm not wearin' a regular wedding dress."

"Oh no, you not wearin' funeral clothes to your weddin'," Ruthie snapped. "Mama, when you call Martha, tell her to bring something pretty."

"I certainly will," Augusta said. "This is gon' be a celebration, and we ain't gon' look like we mournin'."

Mary shook her head. "But, Mama—"

"No! Now, I'm sick of you blasphemin'! God is not gon' get you for gettin' married and being happy! Yes, you s'posed to fear God, but you s'posed to thank him, and worship and praise him too! So we gon' call Martha and get you something to wear, and we gon' have a nice weddin' tomorrow, and that's the end of this discussion. Understand?"

"Yes, ma'am," Mary mumbled, rolling her eyes at a smirking Ruthie.

"YOUR PAPA JUST WENT in," Paul said when Mary came out to the porch. "I think he don't hate me."

"So, what y'all talk about?" Mary took a seat in the chair across from Paul.

"Well, we talked about a li'l everything but mainly talked about yo' mama."

"Mama? What for?"

"I think he was tryin' to teach me something. See, I ain't no young buck, so he cain't give me no basic newlywed talkin'-to. He told me what all he did to keep yo' mama happy now days in they old age. He say he love her like the day they got married, and she still treat him like that day too."

"Naw, I don't believe that." Mary pulled out her cigarettes. "He always grumpy, and she be real disrespectful sometimes. I cain't believe they was like that when they was young."

"Haha. They was probably worse." Paul said. "I know I wasn't as mellow as I am now back when I was married to my ex-wife. But now, I got some sense. Ain't gon' argue and demand my way all the time. I'mma listen a lot more. Talk it out instead of stompin' off and sulkin'."

"I guess you right." Mary inhaled deeply and blew smoke out slowly. "I was too feisty with my first husband. I was a fast teenager with a foul mouth, and I never did him wrong, but I might as well have—I cussed him so bad all the time." She took a long drag. "And when I married the old preacher, it was a *arrangement*, and I admit I shamed him every chance I got." She took another puff. "But Will was good to me when I did right. He taught me fear of the Lord... how to be *the good wife*."

Mary and Paul sat looking at each other for a long time. "Paul, can I ask you a serious question?"

"Of course. You can ask me anything. What's up?"

"Why you wanna marry me? If it's 'cause of the baby, you don't hafta. I got plenty money, and I can take care of myself and the baby just fine. I'm not some young girl that—"

"You can stop now," Paul said firmly enough to get Mary's attention. "I told you you was gon' be my wife a long time ago. I admit, we acted like young kids and got caught up"—he laughed a little—"but you who I want. I wanna marry you 'cause you the best woman I ever met. You a good Christian woman, you can cook, you smart, and you fine as hell. You make me wanna be the best man I can be."

"But, Paul—"

"You know, I think God is givin' us both a second chance. My son is almost grown, and I didn't always do right by him, but I'mma do better this time. We love each other, and I know neither one of us planned on havin' no mo' babies, but here we are."

"But Paul, all my babies died. God punished me by takin' all my babies." Mary kept her head down and blinked back tears. She was growing tired of trying to explain to Paul, Ruthie, and her mother how God treated her. They couldn't... or wouldn't... understand. And now Paul was walking into this marriage and worse because of a baby, and she was letting him. "I don't want God to punish you too," she whispered. She heard Paul's chair creak as he stood up. She lifted her head and watched him get down on one knee.

"Listen, Mary." He reached out and lifted her chin and looked into her eyes. "I don't believe in that punishment stuff, but even if it's true, I'm marryin' you 'cause I love you. I'm marryin' you for better or for worse, so no matter what comes, we gon' deal with it together. Understand?"

Mary nodded and wiped the tear that escaped down her cheek.

"Well, while I'm down here, I may as well do this right," Paul said. "Ain't got a ring or nothin', but Mary Johnson Bevers, will you marry me?"

"But, Paul—"

"Woman, I drove all the way down here to marry you. This just a formality. We gettin' married. Now say *yes* so I can get up. My knee and my back is killin' me."

"Yes, Paul, I'll marry you." She took his face in her hands and kissed him. "Now, how you gon' get up from there?" She laughed.

"Just watch me." Paul twisted and turned and grunted a few times but managed to get back to his feet. "Now that that's settled, when is the big day? Christmas Eve? Christmas Day?"

"Nah, too much goin' on those two days. Mama and Ruthie are plannin' everything for tomorrow."

"Damn, that was fast." Paul laughed. "Wait! Now hold up. You let me almost break my back gettin' down there, and you already got the weddin' planned?"

"Not me. It's Mama and Ruthie. Mama is probably on the phone now, callin' Martha and Ellie. And Ruthie is plannin' the food. They actin' like this ain't my third time. They wanted a big show at the church and stuff, but I put my foot down."

"Hmm... it was you and yo' foot against Mama and Ruthie, huh? And you told them, huh?"

"I sho' did."

"Now, why do I think they would tell me a whole different story?" Paul grabbed Mary's hand and pulled her to her feet. "C'mere, woman." He pulled her into his arms and pressed his lips to hers.

Mary wrapped her arms around him. "Who you gon' believe, them or yo' wife?"

The screen door slammed, and the couple separated.

"Break it up, y'all. Weddin' ain't 'til tomorrow," Ruthie said. "Mary, you gotta go help Mama get the food started. Paul, you gotta take me to the Piggly Wiggly for a few things." She headed down the stairs to Paul's car. "Martha is on her way over with some dresses!"

"Yeah, you put yo' foot down, huh?" Paul kissed Mary on the forehead and headed down the stairs. "I'mma just follow directions... and not get in nobody's way."

Mary waved at Paul and Ruthie as the car pulled out of the yard, and then she went inside to help with the food, hoping against hope that her mother and sisters wouldn't go overboard.

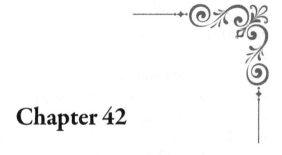

Chapter 42

On December 22, 1965, Mary awoke before sunrise. The electric bedside clock showed 5:13. Since her papa had given up running a working farm, her parents never rose before six. She crept out of bed in the back bedroom, careful not to wake Ruthie. In the kitchen, she turned on the lights and put on coffee. Her mother always prepared the coffee pot the night before, so all she had to do was turn on the stove. Mary made a mental note to start doing that when she got back home.

Home. Where would she and Paul call home? She imagined they would live in her apartment until he saved up enough to buy a house. Would he be on the road as much? Would he take another load to Alaska and be gone for months? Would he be there when the baby came? And where would she have the baby? She'd never had a baby at a hospital—well, except that once. And why did she need to go to the doctor anyway? She never went to the doctor any other time. The doctor had said her pregnancy was high risk because of her age. Granted, Mary didn't know many women who had babies at her age, but still.

While the coffee was brewing, Mary moved as quietly as she could starting breakfast. First, she whipped up a small batch of biscuits and set the water to boiling for grits. She hoped Paul would like her biscuits. While the dough was resting and the water was heating, she fried some sausage patties and made some gravy. Did Paul like his gravy thick or thin? Then, at just the right time, she put the grits in the pot, the biscuits in the oven, and scrambled the eggs. When her mother padded into the kitchen at six o'clock, breakfast was almost ready.

"I be forgettin' you y'all grown now," Augusta said. "You cook as fast and good as I do." She poured herself a cup of coffee and stirred the gravy on the stove. "Everything smells good." She took a seat at the table.

"Well, Ma, I had the best teacher." Mary poured herself a cup of coffee and wished for a cigarette, but she was never comfortable smoking in front of her mother. "I just couldn't sleep, so I got up and cooked breakfast. You ready to eat?"

"Since I didn't hafta cook, 'course I'm ready."

Mary fixed two plates and took a seat across the table from her mother.

"Oh, so y'all started the party without me, I see," Ruthie said from the bedroom doorway.

"Good mornin', baby," Augusta said to Ruthie. "C'mon and join us before the men get up. We just sat down."

Ruthie laughed as the floor in the dining room creaked. "Too late. They up."

Reverend Johnson came through the kitchen doorway, followed by Paul. "Can you believe they started without us, Paul?" Reverend Johnson said.

"Well, I hear they got a big day planned." Paul poured coffee into the two cups remaining on the counter and passed one to the reverend. "So, what's the plan, ladies?"

"Well," Ruthie said, "y'all gon' go to Ellie's in Jackson and hang out with Bobby and do man stuff. Be back by two o'clock. And we," she pointed at her mother and sister, "gon' stay here and get everything ready for a wedding."

"So y'all eat up and stay outta the way," Augusta said. "Unless y'all wanna learn some woman hoodoo." She wiggled her fingers at the men and laughed.

"See how they do me, Paul? A man cain't have this nice breakfast without gettin' kicked outta his own house." Reverend Johnson took his seat at the head of the table while Mary got up and fixed his and Paul's plates. Ruthie shook her head but said nothing.

BY EIGHT O'CLOCK, THE men had gone, and the wedding preparations began in earnest. Ellie and her daughter Jillian arrived from Jackson with flowers and streamers and paper wedding bells and all the decorations anyone could imagine.

"We made some Jell-O molds last night." Ellie set a cardboard box on the kitchen table. "They're in the car, and I got some Jordan almonds and some butter mints. We tied them up in these cute little bundles for wedding favors." She held up a handful of light-blue bundles. "I bought ten yards of tulle yesterday and started making them. I made about fifty. Do you think we need more? I brought my fancy punch bowl set for the frappé. And got all the paper cups and plates we'll need. Martha said Mary was wearing light blue, so I got enough baby-blue tulle to make a veil."

Mary, Ruthie, and Augusta stood listening to the youngest Johnson sister detail the wedding preparations she'd made. They exchanged worried looks and nudged each other, but they let Ellie keep on talking. Finally, Ruthie interrupted her. "Ellie, it's only gon' be maybe ten or fifteen people."

"Oh no, it's gonna be much more than that." Ellie pulled packages of paper goods from the box. "I called the aunties, and they all said they're coming, and you know if the aunties are coming, the cousins are coming, and—"

"Ellie, you know they all comin' Christmas Day, too, right?" Mary had her head in her hands. *Why did Ellie always hafta go over-board?* "We only made enough food for maybe twelve people. It's supposed to be a small wedding."

"Well, nobody ever heard of a small wedding—"

"Dammit, Ellie! Martha have a small weddin' every year!" Ruthie threw her hands up. "How the hell we gon' cook for fifty people right now?"

"Ma, tell her to stop cussin'!" Ellie turned to her sister. "Well, Ruthie, you're the chef. I'm sure you can do it. I'm just the decorating committee. I got more stuff in the car. Y'all come on and help."

As the women carried boxes in from Ellie's car, Mary wondered what Paul would think. She had told him they had planned a small, quiet wedding, and here Ellie had gone and invited the *whole* family.

Chapter 43

While Ellie, Mary, and Augusta finished the decorations—turning the front room into a wedding chapel and the dining room into a reception hall—Ruthie went into the kitchen and got to work. The menu was... eclectic. Besides the wedding cake and classic soul food that had been prepared the night before, Ruthie whipped up enough spaghetti for an army. With garlic bread, a nice green salad, and a lot of cussing, the meal was ready when family and friends began arriving at one thirty, and Martha whisked Mary away to their parents' bedroom to get her ready.

"I brought three more dresses." Martha had laid the three dresses out on the bed. "I always get married in light blue. It represents the sky and infinite possibilities." She ran her hand over a short dress with layers of tulle. "I really like this one for you. You have real nice legs."

"Yeah, that is pretty." Mary actually thought it looked more like a nightie than a dress. "But I don't want a short dress. I like this one." She picked up a floor-length sky-blue chiffon gown with a high waist and held it against herself. "Yeah," she said to her reflection in the full-length mirror. "This is the one."

"Oh, Mary, you'll be simply glorious... You'll look just like Mother Nature. And it's so loose and flowy, you won't hafta wear a girdle."

At two o'clock, just as Mary was *fastening her girdle*, a banging came at the door. "They're here! They're here, and Uncle Paul is a giant, just like Daddy! Let me in!"

Martha unlatched the door, and in bounced six-year-old Jillian, looking like a big ball of taffeta in her yellow flower-girl dress. "They're here, and Daddy and Uncle Paul and Grand-da have on suits, and it looks like a little man and two giants!" She held up three fingers.

Then Ellie pushed her way into the room, carrying two bouquets of carnations. "Mary, why aren't you dressed? There's a house full of hungry people, and the music is about to start. I'm gonna hafta be your bridesmaid because Ruthie still has on her chef uniform, and there's no time for her to change... but it's not like she likes wearing dresses anyway."

As the opening swells of Jackie Wilson's "To Be Loved" started playing out in the front room, Mary looked from Martha, who was extolling the virtues of the light-blue dress, to the nonstop chattering Ellie and Jillian, and she wanted to scream at everybody to just shut up... and of course, she was nauseated and hungry at the same time too. "Let's get this over with."

She held her arms up, and Martha and Ellie helped to get the dress over her head, careful not to smear the little makeup she wore. Ellie quickly restyled Mary's hair and added a flowered comb with a veil attached. Just as the song ended and restarted, Mary stood up, smoothed the dress down, and looked in the full-length mirror. She did look like Mother Nature, and she felt beautiful. She pinched herself twice for feeling very, *very* vain.

"Ready, Mary?" Martha grabbed the doorknob.

Mary nodded. "Yup."

Martha left the room first, then Ellie, holding a small bouquet, and then came Jillian, sprinkling flower petals. Finally, Mary made her way from the bedroom to stand beside Paul by the front-room windows. They stood silently until the song ended then clasped hands.

"Dearly beloved," Reverend Johnson began, "we are gathered here today to join these two people in holy matrimony..."

Mary tried to concentrate on her papa's words and to feel reverence for the occasion, but all she could feel was wonder. She had never had a romantic, loving wedding. Yes, she had loved Mason deeply, but their wedding had been quick and fraught with drama. Her wedding to Bevers had been merely a formality, sealing a contract. But this time, as she held Paul's hands and looked up into his eyes—*did he have tears in his eyes?*

"Mary!" Ellie whispered. "Say something!"

"Oh... I do... yeah... I do," Mary stuttered and laughed a little. Paul had looked a little scared, but he laughed too. Her papa went on with the ceremony, and Mary was careful to pay attention and get the rest of her lines right. The exchange of rings drew a few more laughs when Bobby fumbled and almost dropped the bride's ring, but when Paul and Mary were pronounced man and wife, there were tears and cheers, and only one cousin mentioned that Mary's wedding dress was the same one Martha got married in two weddings ago.

After everybody ate, the couple decided to forego the bridal dance and get right to the cake cutting. Ruthie had pulled off a miracle that morning, creating a two-tiered cake and decorating it with fresh flowers and baby's breath. It was so pretty that Mary didn't want to cut it, but Paul eagerly wrapped his hand around Mary's and the knife handle and made the first cut. They shared the slice, with no cake smashing or anything.

For the bouquet toss, Mary stood on the porch while all her single aunts and cousins stood out in the yard. Ruthie, her only single sister, refused to participate. There was a bit of chaos when Mary's cousins Pam and Tammy both caught the bouquet, but in the end, they agreed to a retoss, and Aunt Laura was the winner. It was almost sunset when the last guests left, promising to come back for the huge feast on Christmas Day.

It was late when the newlyweds finally retired to the back bedroom and Paul helped Mary out of her girdle. "I don't know why y'all wear these ugly things." He pulled her into his arms and reached behind her. His thick fingers deftly released the tiny hooks.

"If I don't wear it, I be jigglin' and floppin' all over the place." She stood on tiptoe and slid her arms around his neck. "You wouldn't like that at all."

"Woman, I like you any way you come. You ain't gotta squeeze yourself in this thing for me." He peeled the garment from her chest and down over her hips. "Matter of fact, I don't want you to wear one. It cain't be good for you, and you gon' squish the baby."

Mary stepped out of the girdle and kicked it away. "But it gives me a perfect hourglass figure—"

"Nope." Paul ran his hands down her sides. "I like you just like this... the way God made you." He kissed her forehead. "If you like being all *squoze* up, that's fine with me... but just so you know, I think you perfect without it."

Mary looked up at her husband. "You know, you the best man I ever met. I feel really blessed to be married to you, and I know if this baby survive, you gon' be the best daddy in the world."

Paul pulled her arms away from around his neck and started unbuttoning his shirt. "Baby gon' be just fine. You watch. Whatever you think God is gon' do ain't gon' happen. It's gon' be a pretty li'l girl. She gon' be glorious. An if something do happen, we gon' still be fine. Like I said, we gon' deal with it together."

He pulled off his shirt and finished undressing. "Now c'mere and gimme a goodnight kiss," he yawned. "We goin' sightseein' tomorrow... do some Christmas shoppin' in Jackson." He kissed his wife and climbed into bed, pulling the quilts back so Mary could get in on the other side.

Mary turned out the light and slid under the covers. "Um, Paul..." she whispered into the darkness.

"Hmm?"

"It's our wedding night. Don't you wanna... you know..."

"Honestly, woman," He snaked an arm over her belly and pulled her close. "I definitely don't wanna... you know... in yo' mama and daddy's house. I don't care if it is our weddin' night. But come Sunday night when we get back to Chicago, I'mma get at you real good. You better believe it."

Mary smiled and scooted closer. She said a prayer of thanksgiving and for protection, and she prayed that she would be *the good wife* Paul deserved.

Chapter 44

July 1966

Chicago, Illinois

"**M**ary and Paul sittin' in a tree... K-I-S-S-I-N-G!"
         "Y'all so silly, soundin' like li'l kids." Mary laughed at
her sisters singing one of their favorite childhood taunts.

"Yeah," Ruthie said. "They doin' a lot more than kissing. Ahahaha!"

The four Johnson sisters gathered in the kitchen of Mary and
Paul's apartment. They laughed loud and talked even louder to be
heard over the drone of two window fans. Mary stood at the sink,
washing mustard and turnip greens, while Ruthie stood at the stove,
stirring her famous homemade barbecue sauce. Outside in the backyard, Ellie's and Martha's children waged a war with wet sponges, and
the men—Paul, Bobby, and Martha's husband, Reggie—smoked cigars, drank beer, and manned the grills.

The sisters and their families were all together in Chicago, celebrating the Fourth of July and all the big changes in their lives: Ellie's
master's degree, Martha's newest husband, Ruthie leaving the restaurant business and joining Root Photography, Paul buying his own
truck, and Mary and Paul's new baby girl.

"I still cain't believe y'all did that to that baby," Ruthie added
a little more brown sugar to the sauce pot. "She gon' get her butt
kicked every day. Kids be mean as hell."

"I think she's gon' be just fine." Ellie placed the baby bottle on the table then held the baby against her shoulder, patting her back for a burp. "Other little girls are gonna be jealous their mamas didn't pick such a pretty name for them."

"I think *Glory* is a perfect name for a glorious little girl who'll grow up into a glorious ray of light." Martha raised her glass of iced tea. "May she be as smart and strong and talented and beautiful as she is loved."

"And may she have wisdom and intellect and understand that all education is important." Ellie rocked from side to side, rubbing the baby's thick, dark hair.

"And Lord, let her learn," Ruthie put down her spoon and lifted her glass, "that she don't ever hafta put up with no bullshit from men." Ruthie looked around the kitchen as if daring her sisters to say something.

"And may she be humble and obedient." Mary said. "And not give in to demons of vanity and pride. And may she stay pure and holy and free from sin—"

"Okay, Mary, you talkin' crazy again." Ruthie put down her glass and picked up the sauce spoon and sampled it with a finger. "That's a baby, and she gon' be a Johnson woman. Ain't gon' be nothin' humble, obedient, pure, or holy about her. She gon' be normal in spite of her name. And I'mma see that she don't grow up crazy like you."

The toasts were interrupted by a knock at the screen door. "They wanna know is that sauce ready," the young man at the door said.

"Come in, darling." Martha stood up from the table and went to greet her husband. "Reggie, you know you don't hafta knock." The nervous young man came into the kitchen at Martha's behest. He nodded at all the sisters and stood waiting patiently while Ruthie poured sauce into a smaller pot and handed it to him along with a barbecue mop.

"You be careful, now," Ruthie said. "Don't trip."

"I got it, ma'am." Reggie took the items and headed back out the door.

"Hmph." Ruthie grunted. "Martha, I don't care what you say. That *boy* is not twenty-five. I bet you yo' son Ricky is older than him... callin' me 'ma'am.'"

"Ruthie, I think you're just jealous that in the waning of my youth, the young men still seek me out." Martha waved off her sister.

"Ha! They don't *seek you out*. They keep trippin' over you cuz you hang out at the high school," Ruthie said.

"That was one time, and me and his mother came to an understanding." Martha huffed, but then she smiled. "But y'all know he was fine, fine, fine."

"Yeah, girl!" The sisters all laughed.

"Okay," Ruthie said, "I think *Glory* could be a cute name for a girl, but why not something normal like Gloria? It means the same thing, just in Latin."

"Cuz every time somebody say her name," Mary said, "they gon' be praisin' the Lord in *English*." She wiped her hands on her apron and went and picked up the squirming baby from Ellie's lap. "This baby is a miracle and a gift from God, and the world is gon' know it."

"If you keep her in church, she just gon' be confused when folks start shoutin' and they sayin' her whole name."

"She'll learn," Mary said. "And she'll understand how much of a blessing she is. I'll be right back. I'm gonna change her and put her down for a nap."

Mary took the baby to the cradle beside her and Paul's bed. "*Glory Hallelujah Bishop*, it don't matter what they say. I'mma make sure you stay humble and obedient and pure and holy," Mary whispered to the bundle in her arms. "God ain't gon' never hafta punish you like he punished me." She took off the baby's wet diaper and wiped and oiled and powdered her little bottom. "Ain't no demons gon' ever get at you. I'll give you back to God 'fore I let the devil have you." Mary kissed little Glory's forehead and laid her down to sleep.

———— ❧ ————

THE END

Afterword
Mary's Recipes

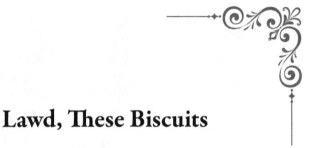

Lawd, These Biscuits

About 2 cups of self-rising flour and a pinch of salt and sugar. Cut in about 4 tablespoons cold butter or lard. Add enough cold buttermilk so the dough doesn't stick to the bowl. Knead the dough a few minutes but not too much. Roll it out to half-inch thickness and cut into circles with a glass. DO NOT twist the glass. Put parchment paper on the baking pan and place biscuits touching a little. Bake at 450 degrees for about 10 minutes until golden.

Cornbread Dressing
Fritters

M ake a small batch of cornbread dressing mix using your favorite ingredients. When it's time to add the broth, add a little extra so it's thick like good grits. Heat a half inch of oil in an iron skillet. Drop by big spoonfuls into the hot grease. Fry on both sides 'til nicely brown. Drain on a paper towel or brown paper.

Mary's Peach Cobbler

Mix equal parts sugar, self-rising flour, and milk, like maybe a half cup each. Add another splash of milk so the batter is a little thin. Add a dash of nutmeg. Melt a few hunks of butter, about half a stick, in a medium iron skillet (make sure it's kinda deep). Pour in the batter... do not stir. Drain a regular can of peaches and cut 'em up a little. Mix in some sugar and another dash of nutmeg. Spoon peaches and sugar syrup on top of batter... do not stir or anything. Bake in the middle of the oven at 375 to 400 degrees until nice and dark golden brown. If the skillet is too small, it might bubble over, and if the skillet is too big or too low in the oven, the batter won't rise over top of the peaches, so be careful and plan ahead. You might hafta try a few times to get it perfect.

Good Crowder Peas

Take 8 slices raw bacon—'bout a half pound—and cut 'em up real little. Fry the bacon bits in a good-sized pot 'til they're brown and crisp. Chop up a small onion and a small green bell pepper and add them to the pot with the hot bacon and grease. Stir it all up and fry on low for a couple of minutes, then add some chopped-up garlic (as much as you like but not too much). Add in a pound of frozen or fresh crowder peas and enough water to cover the peas by about an inch. Drop in a little thyme and a couple of bay leaves and some season salt as you like. Let it boil, then cover, and simmer for about 40 minutes until the peas are tender. Add a little parsley for color. Make a pan of cornbread to go with the peas...maybe fry some pork chops too.

Green Beans and White Potatoes

Take a good ham bone or a few big smoked ham hocks (or some sorta smoked turkey) and put them in a pot. Cover and boil for a couple of hours until the meat falls off the bone. Add some chopped onion and a little garlic, maybe green pepper if you want. Add some black pepper and salt and stuff as you like. While the meat is boiling, pick the ends off a pound or two of fresh green beans (or buy frozen ones if that's what you fancy). Before you add the beans, the broth should taste like a rich soup—like you could just have it all by itself. If it's watery, boil uncovered for a while 'til it tastes better. After you add the beans, peel a few good-sized potatoes and chop 'em up kinda big. (if you decide not to peel 'em, wash 'em real good). When the beans are just tender, add the potatoes and keep cooking 'til the potatoes are cooked through—but not too long cuz you don't want 'em mushy. Serve with your favorite meat dish (chicken, pork roast, whatever).

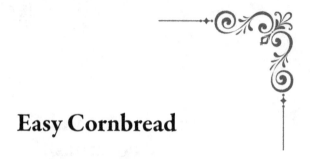

Easy Cornbread

P ut some butter or bacon grease (about 3 to 4 tablespoons) in an iron skillet or a square pan and put it in the oven on 400 degrees. While the pan is heating, mix 1 cup self-rising flour, 1 cup cornmeal (I like yellow), a half teaspoon salt, and 2 or 3 tablespoons sugar. Add 1 egg and about a cup of milk (or buttermilk), enough to make a thick batter. Stir it up real good, then take the pan out of the oven and pour the hot butter or grease into the batter and mix it some more. Pour the batter into the hot pan and bake at 400 degrees for 20 minutes or so. Check it with a toothpick or knife. Brush it with melted butter when it's done.

Old-Fashioned Sweet Rolls

S cald a cup of milk and water ('bout a half cup each). Add 4 tablespoons of cold butter and stir 'til the temp is 120 degrees. Mix
1 pack of quick-rise yeast, 1 tsp salt, 4 or 5 tablespoons sugar, and a
dash of cinnamon into a cup of flour. Add the liquids and mix to a
thick batter. Add a teaspoon of vanilla and 1 egg plus 2 yolks. Mix in
another cup of flour to make a sticky dough, then add more flour to
make a soft not-sticky dough (about another cup). Knead for 10
minutes, then roll it out to a big rectangle. Spread with a lot of soft
butter, a lot of brown sugar, and a whole lot of cinnamon. Roll it up
from the long side, wrap it in plastic wrap, and put it in the icebox
overnight. In the morning, cut the dough into 12 rolls and put in a
buttered pan with high sides. Let rise for a couple hours 'til really big.
Bake at 350 degrees for about 25 to 35 minutes. If they brown too
fast, cover with foil and turn the oven down to 325 degrees. Spread
with cream cheese icing or sprinkle with powdered sugar.

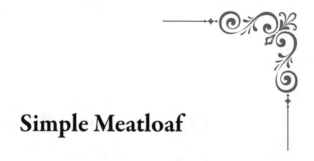

Simple Meatloaf

To make a simple meatloaf, take about a pound of ground beef, maybe a little more. Mix in a beaten egg, a small chopped onion, maybe a half a chopped-up green pepper, and three or four torn-up slices of old bread—tear 'em up real small. Add some seasoning as you like it and a few splashes of milk and mix it up real good but not too mushy. Shape it like a loaf in a greased pan and pour some barbecue sauce or ketchup over it. Put it in a 350-degree oven for about an hour. Maybe make some mashed potatoes and corn and peas and carrots. Probably shouldn't try this recipe in August unless you have working AC.

Braised Oxtails

First off, oxtails are actually beef, not ox. In a big ovenproof pot, brown some oxtails in hot oil (I like bacon grease). Take out the browned meat and add chopped onions, garlic, and green peppers to the hot pot. Cook for a bit and add a can of diced tomatoes, juice and all. Add a cup of broth (I like beef) and your other seasoning (salt, pepper, red pepper, bay leaves, etc.) and maybe some carrots and celery. Bring to a boil and add the browned meat. Cover the pot and put it in a very low oven (275 degrees) for about 3 hours or until the meat is tender. You might hafta add some more broth from time to time as it cooks out. Serve over rice or something like that.

Mary's Pound Cake

Preheat oven to 325 degrees. Grease and flour a large tube pan. Take a pound salted butter, smush it up till it's soft. Mix in a pound of sugar real good. Add 9 or 10 room-temperature eggs ('bout a pound) one at a time. Mix well. Add a pound of sifted cake flour a little at a time. Add a tablespoon vanilla. Mix until the batter is smooth but not too long. It's really thick. Flour the pan again and shake off the excess then add the batter. Spread it around so it's even. Drop the pan on the table a few times to clear air bubbles. Bake for 45 minutes and then check with a toothpick. If it's not done, bake for 15 more minutes and check again. Keep doing it until it's done.

While it's cooling, make a butter sugar glaze—1 stick butter, 1 cup sugar, 6 tablespoons water, 1 tablespoon vanilla. Heat until butter melts and sugar dissolves. Let it boil for about 2 minutes. Put the cake on a plate and poke holes in top with a skewer. Spoon hot glaze over cake and brush glaze on the sides. Use all the glaze. After it cools, sift some powdered sugar over top.

Fancy Party Frappe

Dust and wash out your best punch bowl. Put in a half-gallon container of sherbet ice cream (I like orange, but any flavor works). Break it up some. Pour in one to two 2-liter bottles of cold Canada Dry ginger ale. The ice cream will float and look foamy. Stir it a bit to mix and spoon it into cups with a little foam on top and serve. For a more adult version, trade one big ginger ale for one or two bottles of champagne or Asti spumante.

Acknowledgments

This was a tough book to write. Having met Mary in *Glory Bishop*, I found myself wondering what in her life could've made her the person she was. I didn't start out to write a bitterly tragic story. Honestly, I didn't. I just told the story as it came to me. This story happened to come to me at the same time Kindle Vella was launching on Amazon, and it seemed like a good opportunity to share the story as it was developing. Family and friends and writing colleagues were my anchors through the whole process. They got to listen to my angst as I wrote myself into tiny little corners and mile-deep plot holes. They laughed as I talked out loud to myself, and they cheered with me when I resolved dilemmas. My sisters even took me out to celebrate writing *The End*. I wish I could thank everybody individually, but here are a few:

My "sisters," cousins, and friends: Angela, Cheryl, Jennifer, Rae, Miranda, Jilon, Nicole, Della, and Simone, whose beta reading, critiques, editing, and genuine love and support helped me make sense of Mary's life and get the story told.

The awesome, incredible women of Revel, The Woolfer, and especially the ladies in the Writer's Room.

Red Adept Publishing, especially Lynn, the editors, and the proofreaders for their faith, time, and infinite patience.

Carol DaLuga and Geraldine Cunningham, my sixth- and seventh-grade teachers, respectively—the only teachers who actually let me exercise my imagination and write whatever I wanted.

The creative writing department at UW Madison for guidance and encouragement, especially Christine, Kristin, Laurie, Chris, Kathy, and Laura.

The great writers and instructors at The Novel-In-Progress Bookcamp & Writing Retreat.

And last but not least: Jovanda, Joseph, Jeremy, Marcus, and James. The lights of my life and my reasons for living. Thank you for your patience with me. I love you.

About the Author

Growing up, Deborah L. King always wanted to be an author. She published her first short story when she was seven years old. When she's not writing, she can be found enjoying cooking, photography, and watching cartoons and *Star Trek*.

Born and raised in Chicago, Deborah has managed to achieve all her childhood dreams and still lives in the area with her husband and two youngest children. According to her daughter, she has "literally aced her life"!

Read more at deborahlking.com.

About the Publisher

Dear Reader,

We hope you enjoyed this book. Please consider leaving a review on your favorite book site.

Visit https://RedAdeptPublishing.com to see our entire catalogue.

Check out our app for short stories, articles, and interviews. You'll also be notified of future releases and special sales.

Printed in the USA
CPSIA information can be obtained
at www.ICGtesting.com
LVHW090724070724
784824LV00007B/126